J. A. BOULET

I0653163

THE
WARS
BETWEEN
US

Copyright © 2021 J. A. Boulet

Published by J. A. Boulet

Book cover design: J. A. Boulet

ISBN: 978-1-7772112-7-1

The front cover contains an original photograph of the last remaining corvette warship, HMCS Sackville. The ship is currently on display in Halifax, Nova Scotia as part of the Canadian Maritime Heritage District. HMCS Sackville is a National Historic Site and was designated Canada's Naval Memorial in 1985. The ship is lovingly maintained to this day by the Canadian Naval Memorial Trust. The photograph of the ship was taken by Douglas Struthers and appears on the cover with his permission.

This book is dedicated to all the Canadian Navy personnel who served during the Battle of the Atlantic. God bless their souls.

NOTE TO READER

This book is a work of historical fiction. I have attempted to be accurate with most historical events although some details may have been used solely to propel the story. This is a fictional saga of bravery, addiction and unwavering love. It should be read as such.

J. A. Boulet June 1, 2021

PART ONE

THE GREAT DEPRESSION

1935

CHAPTER 1

The fields were dry, so dry in fact, that swirls of dirt and sand kicked up in the winds making it difficult to see. The terrible drought had devastated most of the fields and ruined many farming families. Zack was upset that everyone was struggling, even the people who still had family and properties. Many people were becoming destitute. His half-sister, Annabella, and her farming family were hit hard. They were barely surviving, but they somehow managed to grow their own vegetables for food, using the chickens for eggs and fish for dinner. Gimli was still enduring throughout the Depression, with the fishing industry holding things precariously together.

"Get those fishing rods ready, son," Nath instructed as he lowered the anchor in the middle of the lake. The boat bobbed lazily in the waves as they prepared to fish for the day.

It was early morning. Zack picked up the rods and opened the bait box. He looked up and caught his father's eye. His dad had aged so much in the last year. He could see it in the way Nathan moved with a slower, more deliberate task in everything he did. His father used to take him and his twin brother into the bush, running, hunting and laughing when they were younger. Now, the only energy Nathan had left was to fish. Zack loved fishing with his dad and absorbed every minute of it, but he was concerned. His dad meant everything to him.

Zack baited the lines and waited until Nath had dropped the anchor securely with a splash in the deep water. He handed Nath the baited rod and turned his attention to the remaining rod, flipping the slippery tiny fish onto the hook.

He smiled at his dad and flung his rod out into the lake, as Nath did the same. The sun would be rising soon over the watery horizon. It was still very early; the skies were just beginning to turn a lighter blue on one side. The west side was still a darker blue of night. It was so strange to Zack how that always seemed so lopsided. Daylight on one side and the night slowly slipping away on the other.

"When is this depression going to end, Pabbi?" Zack asked, using the endearing Icelandic term for father.

"I don't know, Zack," Nath replied, gazing over the lake. "I wish I had a crystal ball sometimes. I could see into the future and make better choices."

"I think you've made pretty good choices," Zack replied, his blue eyes reflecting the lake's colour.

"Yes, for some things," Nath said thoughtfully, thinking of his beautiful young wife, Maria. She was his angel. Maria had helped him to love again. Together they had birthed two strong sons, both of whom had their mother's bright blonde hair. The boys had inherited his piercing blue eyes and his tall build. He felt blessed every single day for Maria and his family. Nathan couldn't imagine his life without them.

Zack shuffled on the boat, trying to get comfortable. "Pabbi, I'm seventeen, and I was thinking about joining one of those unemployment labour camps. It would help everyone out if I got a job. Then the strain on you and mom would be less. You wouldn't have to struggle to feed me anymore. The food has become so sparse, and I don't want to become a burden on you. I'm young and strong; the camps will feed and house me."

Nath looked across at his young son, his heart skipping a beat. "Please don't," he said. "Those camps are terrible. Deplorable working conditions and even rumoured to have a communist group. I don't want you getting all messed up with that. We have enough food."

Zack grinned lopsidedly and accepted his father's words, although he wasn't sure that he would listen to his father's decision. He wanted to travel and experience his life, but Zack felt trapped by the Great Depression. It was like every door he tried to open was locked, and every door that miraculously opened had nothing behind it. He was feeling frustrated and reckless. Zack wanted to make something of his life. He yearned to show people that he was a man and that he had worth.

"Things will get better soon," Nath said. "They created the Bank of Canada just this past March. The government is changing in a good way, son. You can still work at the fishery with Mike and your cousins."

"Yeah, you're right," Zack said, slumping into the boat. He'd be stuck out here forever, he thought.

Zack closed the door quietly and stepped out onto the wood porch gingerly. He tried not to awake anyone, keeping his departure secret. He had written a short note for his mom and dad, telling them he was off to find some work and not to worry.

It was June 18, 1935. Zack felt uneasy about going against his father's wishes. He didn't want his dad to fuss. Zack always had a staunch spirit and felt spurred into action when presented with life's problems; he simply couldn't sit by and do nothing. He was once called rebellious by his mother. But it was not entirely true. Zack yearned to do the right thing and felt that without action, there would never be change.

He would come back home when the depression was over. It would save precious food for his momma and his Pabbi.

They would thank him one day.

Zack stepped quietly onto the sand and walked towards the train tracks. He didn't know where he was going, but Zack knew what he was looking for. He wanted a life he could call his own.

CHAPTER 2

Zack had been travelling for days. He kept his head down as the sun assaulted his eyes, and the dust swirled in his face. He heard a distant train rumbling and thought it might be a good idea to check it out.

During the past few days, Zack had stopped and worked in exchange for food and shelter at every farm he had come across so far. Some people knew him and opened their homes to him. But once he ate with the family, he would notice their ripped pants and old towels. The food was always small portions, and he felt bad, sometimes eating less than his body needed. The world was in much worse shape than he had ever imagined.

He wanted to help change the world, but he would definitely not be accomplishing much walking on foot. He was getting nowhere fast. The train rumbled closer and slowed as it approached the road. He watched and then made a split decision. Zack bolted and started running alongside the train. Luck was on his side as the train slowed even more. He ran hard and then leapt towards an open car. His nimble youthful body latched onto the railcar as it slowed considerably, his feet hooking securely onto the metal bars and his hands gripping the raised ladder firmly. The wind blew forcefully in his hair, and oh my, it felt good, Zack thought.

The freedom of being an adult electrified his entire body. Yes, his parents were most likely distraught and worried, but it was for the better, he thought. The train chugged along the tracks, jostling his body back and forth. Zack grabbed a bar and another until he arrived at the open car with animals. He swung himself in and sat nimbly among the stench of the animals' feces.

He smiled to himself and crouched in the dark with the fading sunlight streaking through the open train car.

He noticed a slight movement in the shadows of the train car. As his eyes adjusted, he soon realized that there were others in the animal car with him, several people, in fact.

"Where are you travelling to?" a dark shadow asked, his face barely recognizable.

"Any town that has work," Zack answered. He pushed down the fear that flitted into his mind. The sudden appearance of fellow train occupants was alarming. He had thought it was a novel idea to hop on a train. Zack now realized that he hadn't even considered that other men would be in the same position as him. He mused about it briefly as the train jostled his body gently as he sat down.

"Same here," the man said, showing parts of his face. The man's beard was uneven, and his face was dirty as if he had been living in the train car for days. He was a bit older than Zack but still young. Zack estimated the man was in his early twenties.

"Do you know where the unemployment camps are?" Zack asked confidently.

"We heard something is going on in Regina concerning the unemployment camps," the man replied. "That's where I'm heading."

A couple of the other men murmured in agreement.

"Do you have any food?" the man asked.

Zack hadn't thought about bringing food. "No, unfortunately," he said. "I've been working for free farm labour in exchange for food."

"What's your name?" the man asked.

"Zack," he replied. "What's yours?"

"Boris," the man replied, pointing to the other men. "This here is Tom, Joe and Henry. We all met on the train."

Zack nodded, "Good to meet you all."

The train rumbled along in silence for several minutes until Zack spoke again. "I'd like to go to Regina too. I'm a strong fit worker." Zack thought he was quite capable of heavy lifting. Even though he was seventeen, he had inherited his father's large muscular chest and height. Zack was just slightly over six feet tall, slim but strong. He was confident he could outperform most men in physical tasks.

"It might be a bit rough in Regina," Boris answered. "The workers are banning together to improve the wages and working conditions in the camps."

Zack pondered this. He wasn't scared; quite the opposite, he was fearless. His spirit was like a wild horse always roped to a tree. He didn't necessarily want to be part of a demonstration, although if it improved the working conditions and meant he would be secured a job, that was different. "Is it a protest?"

"Yes," Boris said simply.

"Oh," Zack replied. "Is this train going to Regina?"

"Yes, it is," Boris replied.

The train jostled along for several minutes before anyone spoke again. Zack felt lost in his thoughts. He questioned why he had left home. Was it to find work or to find trouble? He didn't know the answer. All he knew was that he was tired of doing nothing to improve the impact the Great Depression had on everyone.

"Are you still going to join us?" Boris asked.

Zack flipped his longish hair to the side. "Yeah, I'm in."

The train arrived in Regina later that evening. Boris was awakening everyone as the evening sun rested down onto the upcoming train yard in the distance. "We need to jump off now before it reaches the train yard," Boris shouted.

"Okay," Zack mumbled, barely awake. He had fallen asleep from the rhythmic train rumblings. Zack rubbed his eyes, trying to dispel the cobwebs of sleep from his brain and focus on what was happening. He brushed his dirty pants off and stood, gazing out at the rolling fields. The train was slowing down, but it was still going fast enough to concern him. "Maybe we could wait until the train slows down a bit more."

Boris glanced at him with annoyance on his face. "No," he instructed. "We need to go now." Boris swung his body towards the outside rails of the car, and the other three men joined him. They balanced themselves on the rails, watching the moving ground for an opportune time to jump.

Zack watched from the train car, unsure that he wanted to take the risk of breaking his bones on the fall.

"Come on!" Boris yelled over the rushing wind in their ears.

Zack peered ahead and was astonished to see hundreds of men gripping the rails of the train. He wasn't that great at estimating numbers, but there were many more men on this train than he had imagined, maybe even thousands. A few of them were jumping off the train. He couldn't make out if they made it or not, but he also wasn't a pushover, and he could make his own decisions for himself.

"You go, Boris," Zack shouted back. "I'll wait until we are closer. I'll meet up with you. We'll find each other."

Boris glared at Zack with malice in his eyes. "Fine," he said. "It's your choice, boy."

Zack narrowed his eyes. He hated being called a boy.

A rush of wind caught his hair as Zack peered ahead. The train was slowing. Boris and his friends jumped abruptly, landing in a grassed ditch, rolling to protect themselves from the fall. One of the men screamed, obviously hurt. Zack grimaced and watched the ground for the right opportunity. There were still several hundred men on the train, waiting to jump. The train yard was coming closer fast.

Zack wondered why it mattered if they disembarked on the train yard or in the fields. He was in a group of a hundred or more men. He decided to take the chance and wait.

The train decelerated to a slow chug, jostling him back and forth. Zack grabbed an outside railing and waited for an opportune moment. He noticed several men at the train yard already. He couldn't make out who they were but decided it was safer than breaking his legs on a fall.

He waited until the train was almost completely stopped and then jumped nimbly onto the dirt train yard. Zack landed safely and was immediately absorbed into a crowd of a thousand men as everyone jumped off the train with him. He was tall and could see over many of the men's heads, although it was confusing. Zack didn't know quite where the crowd was heading. Their shoulders were touching, and the crowd became one large moving throng of men. He had little choice but to follow.

He heard several orders from some people. "This way!" A few men pointed. "To the Square!" Several men shouted. "On to Ottawa!"

Zack didn't understand. Ottawa was directly east, in the same direction that he had just come from. He didn't have much choice but to continue onward with the crowd. The energy ebbed and flowed around him like a river carrying him to a destination that he didn't clearly understand. But what Zack cared about the most was that the workers were standing united for their rights.

The crowd moved slowly at first, then faster once they dispersed into the streets of Regina. People mostly marched together, shouting slogans and raising their fists in the air. Other people casually walked through the streets, intrigued by the influx of peaceful workers. Many local people stood by, watching the events unfold with excitement. There wasn't much else to do during a depression, after all.

Eventually, after an hour of walking, the workers arrived at Market Square. They were pushed into the square by policemen and crowd control officers, which concerned Zack, but it looked like a peaceful demonstration, so he didn't feel apprehensive. He stretched his neck out over the crowd as he suddenly heard someone speak loudly.

"We are uniting as one!" a tall, lanky man nicknamed Arthur Slim Evans shouted from a raised podium. "We have been forced to stop here in Regina. We will be allowed to send eight men onward to Ottawa to pitch our demands to the government." Several murmurs of disapproval churned through the crowd. "Do not be dismayed! We will persevere! We are achieving something! We cannot be allowed to rot in these deplorable construction camps! We are good men! We need quality work!" The mob shouted their approval. "We need wages to feed ourselves! We need medical care! We need our lives back! The On to Ottawa trek will produce change!"

The crowd erupted in joyful agreement. Hoots and hollers sounded from the trekkers.

Zack whistled and shouted. "Yeah!" He felt his entire body agree with the statements. Zack wanted his life back too. He could not just waste away doing nothing! They needed change!

Several horns sounded, and the crowd watched as the policemen waved their blow horns in the air. One policeman shouted into the round conical horn. "Eight of your men will go to Ottawa. Everyone else will remain here in Regina until a solution is reached."

Murmurs of disgruntled approval echoed through the crowd, and several men began to disperse. Zack wandered to the road and decided to try his luck at a neighbouring house. He strolled up the walkway, and the lady ran into the house, locking the door. Zack was confused. He was only trying to find shelter for the night and food in exchange for work. The lady shook her head behind the window.

He tried the next house and the next. Every time the house was shuttered, or he was politely refused. He began to feel panicky and unsure of his decision to come to Regina. He didn't know anyone here, and he didn't have anything to eat. It seemed that he had better luck in the farmyards of Manitoba than in a strange city. Zack wandered back into the square, hoping to befriend another trekker and find a way to obtain some food. His stomach growled with hunger.

As he re-entered the square, a small girl with tanned skin ran up to him from one of the houses and handed him a bun.

"Thank you," Zack replied, hungrily devouring the small bun. He waved graciously at the young girl and nodded his head in thanks.

He needed more food, or he was going to starve to death.

Zack walked closer to the empty podium and saw Boris from the train. The other three men from the train stood firmly beside Boris. Zack's hopes instantly soared; he waved and made his way over to the men. As he approached, he noticed that they were more shabbily dressed than he thought. Their pants were dreadfully ripped, and their shoes looked like they might fall apart at any minute.

"Hey!" Boris shouted. "I wondered where you had gone!"

"Just got caught up in the crowd," Zack said confidently. "Where are you guys staying for the night?"

"Over there," Boris said, pointing to a park.

Zack felt a wave of disappointment filter throughout his body. They were just as homeless as he was, he thought sadly.

"But we have some food," Boris said. "Come join us. Are you hungry, boy?"

Zack felt the annoyance of the word boy attack him again. He swallowed his pride and nodded. "Are you kidding me? I'm starving!"

"Come with us then." Boris nodded his head in the direction of the park.

Zack followed, knowing that something wasn't right. His hunger refused to abate and drove him to follow despite the intuition tugging in his gut.

They arrived at a grassy hill. It was partially muddy with trampled brownish grass. Henry, the older man, opened his jacket, revealing a stash he had been hiding and let a cluster of food fall onto the ground. The men eagerly went after it like a pack of dogs. There was a small ham, two loaves of bread, a bottle of milk, a bag of peanuts and a small bag of crackers.

Zack went after the ham, but it was snatched by Boris. Zack managed to get one of the loaves of bread and stuffed each slice in his mouth, chewing hungrily. After a while, Tom handed the milk around, and Boris passed the ham around with a warning. "Only take a little bit! I'll beat anyone who takes too big of a bite."

Zack shared his bread as well, and the entire small group of friends peacefully devoured every single morsel.

Zack felt his energy and hope return. Things were going to be alright. He had friends and a future of possible work soon.

"The demonstration is good," Boris said cheerfully. "It will help us. In a few months, we will have better work."

The other men wholeheartedly agreed as they finished off the last bites of food.

Zack nodded and swallowed the last morsel. "I completely agree," he said engagingly. "The government needs to step in and resolve the issue of the failing economy." The others looked at him and nodded. They all laid back on the hill content, with their stomachs full. Zack stretched out on the grass, his arms behind his head. A thought occurred to him. The food seemed to materialize out of thin air. "Where did you get the food, Henry?" Zack asked curiously.

The men fell silent. Henry coughed.

Boris looked at Zack. "You ask too many questions," he replied.

"What do you mean?" Zack replied innocently. "It was a simple question. Not anything else."

Henry grunted. "A family gave it to us," he said.

"Oh," Zack said. "That was very nice of them."

"Yes, it was," Boris said stiffly.

Zack nodded suspiciously but didn't say another word.

A part of Zack's mind thought they were lying. Did they steal it from a restaurant? That would be frightful. Then a worse thought occurred to him. What if they had forced the family to give them the food? Zack grunted and laid back down. He didn't agree with how these men lived, but they had helped him travel here, and they fed him. Zack would proceed cautiously. He needed these men right now and wondered again if his decisions were not so smart lately. Zack shuffled onto his side and cradled his head, thinking about where his future was heading.

The sky soon grew dark, and they all fell asleep on the grassy hill, murmuring in their sleep, wondering if their lives were about to improve or whether this was the path to destruction.

The next morning, he saw the little girl in the square again with her father and mother. She was a sweet girl with an endearing swing in her step. All the men had awoken and disappeared already. Zack had slept through it all.

He stood and wiped his hands on his pants, shuffling towards the square and approached the girl.

"Hey," Zack waved.

The girl's face lit up in a cheerful smile as she waved back.

"Thank you for the food yesterday," Zack said happily.

Her parents looked down at her, obviously not aware that she was feeding the homeless men.

Zack chuckled. "It's okay. She just gave me a bun. I am grateful for the food. Your daughter is kind," Zack said, changing his tone and addressing her father. "If you have any work that needs to be done around the yard, I would be happy to exchange work for food."

Her father narrowed his eyes and assessed the young man. "I will let you know if we have any work for you," the large man said. "We are all suffering in this depression."

"Yes, we are," Zack said, nodding in agreement.

The girl waved at him as her family ushered her to the other side of the square. Zack shuffled his feet, feeling downtrodden and lost. Hopefully, he would find his way soon.

He looked at the crowd of men forming near the square and walked to the centre as another demonstration seemed to start. There was a man with tools hanging from his belt to his left. Beside Zack, another man had a dirty coat with oil splotches on it, obviously a mechanic. Zack watched a few other men directly in front of him, with one man missing an arm. Zack thought he was likely a farmer or a woodworker. They often had accidents at work. Farther across the square, Zack spotted Boris and his friends. He waved cheerfully. They waved back.

Zack smiled as the mechanic man turned around to address him.

"Why are you here, boy?" the man asked.

The word stung at his pride again. "I'm here for work," Zack said proudly.

"Yeah," the older mechanic replied. "We all are." The man patted him on the back in a friendly gesture of acceptance.

Zack grinned. He had found solace with this group of desperate men. They were all hard-working men just looking for a chance to earn a decent living.

Chapter 3

By the morning of July 1, 1935, they had already spent several weeks in Regina, loitering and waiting for change. The crowd of single unemployed men was surprisingly peaceful and orderly. Zack was shocked that more and more residents were handing them food and doing what they could to help. They didn't have a lot of food, but it was enough. Zack's stomach growled on a daily basis, and he had lost a noticeable amount of weight.

The eight men who had left for Ottawa had come back last week, disheartened. The Canadian prime minister, R. B. Bennet, refused to bend to the trekker's demands. It was a bitter return to Regina for them. Once they had arrived back in Regina, they were told that the entire 2000 workers in the crowd were being sent to Lumsden, 30 km away, to a forced labour camp. The trekkers were insolent but still peaceful. There was no way they were going to another dirty construction camp to be treated as prisoners. Arthur Evans and other ringleaders argued in terse discussions with RCMP and other officials to no avail. The men would not accept being herded to Lumsden like animals.

The late morning sun was bright as Zack awoke to an epiphany. He needed to leave this city, he thought. There was nothing here for him. Zack bonded with the trekkers, but he sensed something terrible might happen in this crowd of disgruntled workers. Zack just wanted a decent job, although he felt there was no hope for that in Regina now. He needed to go back home, admit defeat and beg his father to accept him back. Zack had mulled over all the events of the past few weeks and realized he was not on a good path. Nothing positive had become of this, and it seemed nothing would.

He would eat something and leave today or tomorrow, Zack decided.

The police presence was increasingly concerning. Every day there seemed to be more policemen circling the streets. The square was bringing in the local residents more so than even the construction workers. He saw young children, wives and husbands walking amongst the square strolling about, looking for things to do. The families were unemployed as well, although the Canadian government was providing the married men with money. The single men were left penniless and largely ignored. It was grossly unfair, Zack thought. Being left with no job and no future fuelled his anger towards the government. How could the leaders of a vast country like Canada just refuse all the attempts the workers had made to bring this injustice to the Prime Minister's attention?

Zack brushed the dirt off his pants and slumped with his head in his hands on the exhibition grounds. Maybe something will happen today during the talks with the ringleaders.

A meeting was called for 8 p.m. that evening. Zack was excited. Maybe an agreement will be reached! Hope for a different conclusion filled his veins. Perhaps he would be able to find a job within a newly structured construction camp. He washed his face and hands in a nearby pond, wiping his face with a light scarf he found. Zack hung the scarf around his neck and straightened his shoulders.

He strolled to the exhibition grounds, feeling optimistic. He noticed thousands of trekkers watching a ball game farther away. Zack changed course and travelled towards the shouts of sports enthusiasts. He peered through the crowd; more than a thousand men were watching the ballgame. Zack joined, sitting down on the grass to watch the game with the other men.

"Maybe an agreement will be reached," a young man said, crouched with his elbows on his knees.

Another man stood, shielding his eyes from the sun. "I doubt it," he said despondently. "Government decisions never solved anything in this country."

"Evans is holding a meeting tonight," Zack said, joining in on the conversation. "Maybe he will be able to negotiate something."

"I'm not going to Lumsden," the young man replied.

"Neither am I," another man said.

Zack sat down beside the group. "Neither will I," he said. "I'm not here to be a construction prisoner."

"Exactly," the young man agreed.

"Something has to happen," another man said. "Our government is broken."

Zack nodded in agreement as the large crowd suddenly hollered at a home run. Zack jumped to his feet and shouted in joyful exuberance at the sudden victory along with thousands of other men.

The young man beside him smiled and whistled, roaring at the ballplayers. "Way to go!" he shouted.

Zack was happy to make some new friends during the game. The mood was sour but still hopeful.

Hours passed with the sun beating down on their backs as they idly watched the ball game, some accepting the bleak future, others preparing to leave, but mostly everyone was growing more and more resentful.

The sun was low on the horizon when suddenly they heard Evans shouting in the distance. "We will not accept this!" Evan's voice echoed from blocks away, his angry words carrying across the ball field.

Zack felt an eerie calm wash over him. He nudged the man beside him. "The meeting is starting," Zack said, standing.

The men joined him as they calmly walked back to Market Square to join the meeting in progress. Thousands of trekkers were preparing to leave the ball game to see what was happening.

Zack heard a policeman's whistle in the distance. Then several other whistles shrilled loudly near the Square.

Zack was confused. Why were the police using their whistles? Everything had been peaceful so far. He watched the crowd ahead of him and squinted against the setting sun to see what was happening.

Several dark-coloured vans blocking the crowd into Market Square suddenly opened their doors. Approximately three hundred policemen with steel helmets, billy clubs and baseball bats jumped out of the vans and converged onto the square. Another fifty policemen on horseback along the east and west side kept the crowd contained to the square. Several cruisers were used as blockades to keep the trekkers in the downtown core.

Evans was led off the stage in handcuffs, arrested in front of the crowd. Most of the crowd were Regina residents and their families! The local people tried scattering but were attacked by the policemen. Husbands and wives fought for their lives.

Zack picked up a few rocks and started running towards the Square as thousands of trekkers joined him. Once they arrived in the Square, it was chaos. Tear gas clouds were in the air, so he immediately covered his face with the wet scarf, thanking his luck. He tied it at the back of his neck and threw a rock at a policeman clubbing a man on the ground. The policeman went down, rubbing his head as several trekkers jumped on him, beating the policeman with chains and whatever they could get their hands on. A small girl was scooped up by her injured father as they fled the chaotic scene.

Zack found a discarded baseball bat and ran into the crowd. Testosterone fuelled his anger; families were getting beaten by the authorities! He shouted like an animal and swung at the policemen crowding around several men that were being beaten heavily with the billy clubs. The first two policemen were completely unprepared for the incoming suicidal assault.

Zack swung with lethal force, and the bat slammed into the first policeman's midsection, cracking a few ribs sharply. The policeman howled and was thrown back into the second officer. They fell into a pile on the ground as several trekkers appeared out of nowhere and amassed onto the downed policemen, kicking with savageness.

The remaining three policemen dispersed in opposite directions, obviously overcome with unexpected opposition. Zack let out another blood-curdling cry just as Boris appeared at his side. They pursued one of the policemen, chasing him into the downtown streets. Boris threw a rock and hit the officer in the shoulder. The officer slowed but didn't stop fleeing.

Zack and Boris continued pursuing until the policeman disappeared around the corner. Zack slowed down, sensing something and pulled on Boris's arm. He nodded to Boris and pulled him back. They peered ahead, struggling to catch their breath.

A wrecked cruiser was barricading the street. Several policemen hid behind it, throwing tear gas. Zack ran around a building and hid in an alcove with Boris right behind him.

"What do we do now?" Boris asked, his eyes wild.

"We wait," Zack said, tapping the baseball bat on the ground. "And watch for a good opportunity."

They peered out towards the barricade as several policemen jumped out, rushing the crowd. But the trekkers fought back hard. This was a pitched battle between policemen and men with nothing more to lose. Heads were smashed, noses were broken, blood was on every man's hands, regardless of uniform. Zack watched as the trekkers fought for their lives against an unprovoked police attack.

Zack saw an opportunity and jumped into the melee, swinging the bat. A crack sounded as the bat connected with a uniformed policeman's knees. The officer screamed in pain and crumpled to the ground just as another billy club cracked against Zack's upper shoulder. He turned around surprised, and ducked just as the policeman swung the club to his face. It grazed his ear, and Zack swung defensively at the officer's legs. The bat connected. The policeman's knees cracked sickeningly as he crumpled with his comrade on the street.

Zack straightened as a searing pain shot through his body from his injured shoulder blade. He grimaced from his painfully broken upper shoulder and looked for Boris. He found him several feet away, being beaten by two officers. Zack rushed into the fray, wielding his weapon. The policeman raised his arm against the blow, and the bat cracked into the officer's elbow, shattering it. The officer crumbled in pain but struck out wildly, swinging his billy club with his other arm. Unsteadily he swung in a wide arc, aiming for Zack's midsection.

Zack jumped out of the way just in time then rushed the policeman in the abdomen. The force of his bodyweight threw the officer into the air. Before Zack could register the victory, another policeman was on his back, hitting him relentlessly with something hard.

Then Zack heard shots fired from the cruisers. Several people fell instantly, and the policemen ducked momentarily as if they knew what was coming.

Zack couldn't believe his ears! The police were firing into the crowd! The pops of the guns were going off like fireworks.

Zack felt the policeman's arms on him, pulling him towards the parked van. Zack elbowed backwards sharply, hitting the officer blindly in the solar plexus. The man fell back in surprised pain. That was a lucky shot, Zack thought. He turned to look for Boris when he felt another billy club crack into his shoulder, splitting the bone even further. His consciousness faded briefly, and he fought to stay alert. Zack noticed that he had somehow dropped the bat. He looked down and couldn't see it. The policeman came for him with the club again, and Zack just used his fists and punched straight out, connecting with the officer's nose, sending the man's body flinging sideways.

Zack stood there for several minutes, confusion clouding his thoughts. The tear gas clouds drifted onto the square. He pulled the scarf up, but it was too late. The last thing he saw was a policeman being beaten to death. Then the world went black.

CHAPTER 4

He awoke in a strange house, with blood on the pillow and a swollen shoulder. A little girl's voice was lilting in the air. The smell of ham and soup filled the room. Despite the pain searing all over his body, his stomach growled.

"Momma," the girl said. "Can we just feed him some soup? It looks like he is waking up."

"My darling Megis," Momma said. "His shoulder blade is badly broken. He cannot lean against the bed to sit up."

"We can help him into a chair," Megis said pleadingly.

Zack moved his lips. It felt like cotton balls were in his mouth. "I can sit in a chair," he mumbled.

Megis jumped. "You're awake!"

Zack opened his eyes, focusing on the little girl. It was hard to tell how young she was, but he knew it was definitely the same girl that had given him the bun at the square. "Thank you again for your kindness," Zack said.

"What those policemen did to you men was awful!" she said, her voice pitching.

"It certainly was," he said. "My name is Zack." He held out a bloodied hand.

Megis looked at it with a moment of hesitation and then shook his hand. "You will be alright, Zack," she said. "We will feed you and mend you, but then you must go home or back to Vancouver."

"I'm from Manitoba," he said.

"Oh?"

"I came here looking for work," Zack said. "I'm originally from Gimli."

"I know Gimli," Megis said. "We went on a holiday there once. It's a beautiful place."

"Yes, it is," Zack replied. "If you ever come that way again, please ask for me. We will return the generosity. My full name is Zachary Olason."

Megis blushed. "Zachary Olason," she said, almost to herself. "Well, Zack, you are brave."

"Thank you," Zack replied. "I think reckless is the correct term."

"Those policemen were the ones that started the riot," she said, pointing out the injustice.

"Yes, I agree," Zack said, sitting up gingerly, pulling his body upright.

Megis wound her arm around his waist and helped him to stand. She was a short girl, maybe only 4 feet tall. He grabbed onto her arm and slowly walked to the kitchen table. Once he was seated securely, Megis bounded away into the cupboards grabbing a bowl and a ladle for the soup. Zack watched her spooning the hot soup into the bowl as the aroma floated over him. He could see now that she was not as young as he thought she was. Her small breasts filled out her shirt. She smiled at him, her brown eyes twinkling and brought the bowl of soup over, placing it in front of him.

Zack devoured the delicious soup like an animal, hardly breathing between spoonfuls.

Megis watched him and smiled. "You were hungry," she said, satisfyingly. "Many of the men were arrested at the square and the hospital. My father and mother dragged you here. You had saved us from a brutal police attack."

Zack searched his memory. "You must have been the first family I encountered when I initially arrived at the riot. You were the girl that was led away by your father!" Zack said, pausing momentarily, remembering the events. "How is your father? He was injured."

"Yes, he was," she said. "He is alright. A couple of bruises and contusions. He's lucky. You saved us. You are very brave, Zachary. Thank you."

Zack smiled.

"What those policemen did was wrong," Zack said.

"Yes, it was," Megis agreed.

"What happened afterwards?" Zack asked. "Do you know?"

"The policemen were arresting the fallen trekkers," she said. "The newspapers said the construction workers were even being arrested at the hospital."

"That's horrible!" Zack said, grimacing suddenly as his shoulder seared with pain.

Megis jumped to his aid and helped him return to the bed. "You need to rest, Zack," she said softly, her brow furrowing with concern. "Lie down."

"Thank you for helping me," Zack said softly.

"You are welcome, Zack," she replied. "You saved us; we couldn't leave you there to be arrested."

Zack smiled. This small girl had a big heart, he thought.

Megis smiled back. She wished there was more she could do to help this young man. After several minutes her face fell into a concerned sadness. "You have to go home soon, Zack," she said sadly. "Momma told me the newspapers said the trekkers could either return to Vancouver or return to their hometown. It's not safe here. You will get arrested if you stay."

Zack grimaced. "I will go home. It was what I was planning this morning before the riot anyways."

"Maybe I will visit someday," Megis said sincerely.

"I would like that," he said.

The train back to Manitoba was slow, and every jostle hurt his shoulder and his pride. Boris and Henry were also on the train. They had both decided to come back to Gimli to be farmhands in exchange for food and shelter. The other two men, Tom and Joe, had been arrested at the hospital. Boris and Henry were also fortunate to be brought in by local residents from the Regina Riot battlefield.

The train ride took all day. By the time they had arrived in Gimli, it was dark. Zack dreaded confronting his father. He felt like an utter failure.

He jumped nimbly off the train and stepped onto the grass, heading for the shoreline home they all shared. He left Boris and Henry in an old abandoned guest cabin near his sister Annabella's place. Annabella and Ivan would appreciate farm labour; they were growing older into their sixties soon. Zack would talk to them tomorrow and plead with them to hire the two men.

He walked all the way to the beach, and his shoes sank into the sand. It felt good to be home. He didn't know what kind of life he had here, but it was a whole lot better than what he had just come from. He inserted his key into the lock and gently opened the door. His father was sleeping on the sofa. His dad never slept on the sofa, Zack thought. He must have been sick with worry.

Zack closed the door gently, but the click still echoed loudly in the quiet house.

Nathan mumbled and opened his eyes. At first, he thought it was a dream. Then he realized he was truly awake, looking at his missing son, Zack.

Nath stood up and walked over to Zack silently, hugging him strongly. Finally, after several moments, words came to his lips. "Zack," Nath said. "You're here. I'm so glad you made it back. Welcome home, my son. We all missed you, and we love you greatly."

The traumatic events of the past few months slowly melted away as his father hugged him warmly. "I'm sorry, dad," Zack said defeatedly. "I wanted to become my own man, have my own job and feed myself. I failed horribly."

Nathan pulled him at arm's length and looked at his son's face. It was bruised and weary. Zack had a cut over his left eye, and his clothes were filthy. "You didn't fail," Nathan said. "You learned that becoming a man is hard."

Zack felt the stress of the riot leave his body in a rush and was replaced by utter love for his family. They would always be there for him, and he was immensely grateful. He struggled to maintain his composure but failed, his eyes tearing up with pent-up emotion and feelings of failure. Zack sobbed into his father's arms as he hugged his dad tightly.

"It's okay to cry," Nath said soothingly. "Only the strongest of men cry. Don't let anyone ever tell you differently." Nath hugged his son tighter. Suddenly Zack winced. He released the pressure alarmingly. "You're hurt," Nath said, concern in his voice.

"Yes," Zack said. "I believe my shoulder is broken. I was involved in the Regina Riot. I escaped just this morning on a train back here."

Nathan clucked his tongue. "Oh, my," Nath said solemnly. "Let's fix you up, my rebel son. I'll draw you a bath."

"Thank you," Zack said, wiping the tears rolling off his cheeks. He followed his father to the bathroom, feeling the traumatic Regina Riot melt into his subconscious mind. It was like a dream, almost like something that had not really happened. But it did. He had a broken shoulder to prove it.

Zack felt numb. The future was hopeless. He was a failure.

PART TWO

THE REBOUND

1938

CHAPTER 5

Zack sat in front of the backyard fire, watching the flames dance. The past few years had been rough. He was disappointed in the world, and nothing he could do would ever change it. He had started drinking alcohol after he had returned home from the riot. It numbed the pain of his failures. Whiskey was his medicine. It kept him from descending into the abyss of depression. It was a bad habit, but he couldn't see any other way to stem his reckless spirit. He thought briefly that maybe it actually fuelled his recklessness and made things worse. He immediately absolved those thoughts as heresy. He had stayed home ever since, allowing the Great Depression to kill his spirit slowly. Alcohol was what he needed right now.

Zack looked into the fire, his eyes wandering over the flames.

A pretty woman was sitting across from him. He stared at her briefly. The firelight glowed in her face, framing her long nose and her strong jaw. She stood up and shuffled her feet, sitting down a seat closer to him. She was excessively curvy in the hips giving her a pear shape that intrigued him. Her waist was extremely slim, and her shoulders narrow. She glanced at him beside the fire and curled a lock of strawberry blonde hair behind her ear. It astonished him the way she blatantly expressed her interest in him. Why would a beautiful decent woman be so intensely interested in a guy like him? He was a drunk and a troublemaker. She should be staying away from him, not flirting and shuffling closer to him. Her eyelashes fanned with desire, and she demurely looked down every time he caught her eye.

"You guys are so incredible!" she said suddenly. "Bringing a catch in of that size! Who taught you all to fish?" she asked, urging them into the conversation.

Zack looked at her as if she had just been dropped down from heaven. She appeared roughly the same age as him, 20 years old. He had just met her, but she talked to him as if she had known him for decades. "My dad Nath taught me fishing," he slurred, the excess alcohol impairing his ability to speak properly. "Boris never goes fishing. It's only me. I often go out alone now. I used to go out with my dad all the time."

"Oh!" she exclaimed nervously. "Your dad is Nath, right? Didn't he own the fishery in Gimli?"

"Yes," Zack slurred. "Pabbi had owned it at one time." He didn't like this line of questioning. He didn't want to talk about it. He just wanted to drown it all with alcohol.

"Why do you go fishing alone then?" she asked innocently, clearly interested in Zack and his history.

He took a swig of his beer and threw it in the bushes. "I don't want to talk about it," Zack said, unsteady on his feet. "Look, it's a long story, and I'm drunk. Did you want to go for a walk with me? I can take you to a beautiful spot near the beach where the moon shines down over the lake."

"Sure," she stood up, brushing her dress off. "I'm in."

Zack offered his hand to steady her.

Anita grasped his arm and teetered. She was confused. Anita had never seen him before like this. It was as if he didn't remember her or something, although she had never seen him this drunk either! They saw each other often through mutual friends, and he was a very handsome gentleman, but it seemed like the devil had come over him tonight. It must be the alcohol, she thought.

She had loved him from afar for many years. Then she had stumbled across the party last night, and he was here! She felt so lucky to have the chance to make her love for him known. Anita had fallen in love with him the night he noticed her at the town hall Christmas party and asked her to dance. They had danced for hours, but then afterwards, he had simply disappeared. Rumours floated around that he had found a girlfriend, and Anita was devastated. So many years had passed since then, and she had never really gotten over him. Then just recently, her friends had told her that he was single again. Anita was thrilled, wary and excited all at the same time. She concluded that this must be why he was so fuelled with alcohol. His heart must be mending from the break-up. She would give him time. Anita had been patient and only spoke to him briefly before, telling him that she was here for him if he ever needed to talk. But now, he was talking to her like he had never even talked to her before. It confused her. She had loved him for so long, and now he pretended not to know her? Maybe it was his grief, she concluded. Anita had waited this long; she could be patient for a while longer.

"Okay, let's go," Anita said, laughing. "It doesn't seem like anyone is interested in us."

Zack and Anita looked at the others at the party. "See you later, Boris," Zack said loudly.

He waited for a response and received none.

Boris finally raised his drunken head slowly, his eyes focusing and then closing. He mumbled something incomprehensible. A girl was sitting beside Boris on the lap of a young man, their lips locked, kissing each other passionately, oblivious to the crowd in front of them. Zack and Anita glanced at each other and chuckled. Approximately twenty young adults were crowded into the backyard, all at different stages of inebriation. Everybody seemed to be busy with their own intentions to show them any interest at all. Zack worried that they had all been accustomed to Zack's philandering, and they were all sure of the outcome tonight. He would make her his girl. He would like that if only Anita would stay with him. Usually, once women found out what a dysfunctional mess he was, they often left.

Zack laid a gentle hand on her waist. "Come on, let's go," he said. "This party is getting old. You'll love it. It is a beautiful spot. You are safe with me."

Anita smiled and slipped her hand into his.

Zack grinned at his good luck. He wasn't going to question her interest in him anymore; he would just be happy with his fate. Zack would accept it because not much mattered to him lately. He was on the verge of losing too many things in his life. His heart was suffering terribly. The world was a mess from the economic depression, and he was barely rebounding. The Regina Riot had left him disheartened and shaken. Then just when he thought that his life was slowly improving, his entire foundation began to crack. He cried most nights, although he never told anyone this. The one person he loved the most was dying, and now he was facing the reality that he would be alone in this depressing world.

"Are you okay?" she asked, concern washing over her face.

"No, not really, but I'll survive," he replied.

"What's wrong?" Anita asked.

Zack looked up to the sky. The stars glittered down on him as if in mockery. It was such a damn beautiful night, and nothing in his life was wonderful anymore. "My dad is very sick," he said softly.

Anita's heart burst open at his confession. "I'm so sorry," she cried, her arms circling around his torso and pulling him in tight. "I had no idea."

Zack relaxed and let her hug him. It felt good; he hadn't been with a woman for a long time. Her flowery smell wafted up to his nostrils and intoxicated him even further. His penis instantly hardened; he couldn't help it. She was lovely and sweet all in one. She was just what he needed right now.

"You can talk to me," Anita said softly, looking up at him with innocent blue eyes.

"I don't know if I can," he responded stonily, looking down at her. "It hurts so much, and I'm so scared of losing him. I was his baby. We did everything together. And now he can't do anything but lay in bed." The night wind blew through the trees as if his dad was right here telling him to be a gentleman. Zack had a bad-boy reputation that he didn't quite understand. All of his friends said this about him. He drank too much and had sex with all the pretty girls. He recalled his dad once telling him that one day he would come across the woman of his dreams, and she'd never even stop to say hi because he would be too drunk to notice. He looked up at the full moon and wondered if his dad's words were true. Pabbi's sickness in May had changed everything. It made him drink even more now. He had been getting into fights too. At least tonight, he hadn't gotten into a brawl. He had broken his nose twice, but most fights he won, at least. He grinned to himself drunkenly. His inebriated mind swirled all the stories and blended them into one, confusing and numbing him at the same time. "Look at the moon, honey," he said smoothly, patting her long hair against her back.

Anita looked up, and the full moon shone brightly against the black sky, beckoning them. "Oh my Lord, that is so beautiful!" she exclaimed.

Zack broke the embrace and held her hand, pulling her into the bush. "Come on; I want to show you this spot!" He stumbled briefly and then caught his balance, chuckling. "Come on, you beautiful girl."

They skipped together into the bush, laughing like kids. They were both 20 years old, although she made him feel so giddy and happy that he chuckled every time she smiled. He had just met her tonight, but he was falling for her quickly.

"This is so beautiful! Oh my Lord! Look at that moon!" she exclaimed, a radiant smile on her face.

"I used to walk on this path with my dad as a toddler," Zack said, gesturing along the overgrown path. "He would take the entire family out on day-long treks through the bush. It was his way of bonding with the lake, he would always say."

"Your dad sounds wonderful," she replied.

"He is," Zack said, growing quiet. "My mom accepted his proposal in public on a busy street right in Gimli. They said it was quite a sight! He was on one knee with a ring, and the crowd cheered."

"That is so romantic!" she said, smiling broadly.

Zack glanced back at her and pulled her closer to him. "Did I tell you how beautiful you are?" he asked, grinning his most sensual grin.

She blushed.

"Ah, honey," Zack said sweetly. "Don't be shy! You are very beautiful!"

"Thank you," she murmured, looking down.

"Look at me," he said, grabbing her chin and lifting her face to his. "You don't need to be shy. You know you are pretty, right?"

"No," she said. "I don't think I'm pretty. My legs are too big, and my nose is too long."

"Oh, sweetheart," Zack said, looking her in the eye. "You are the good kind of woman that doesn't come along too often. Remember that." He slid his hands along her shoulders all the way down her arms to her hands. "And I love your hips. They're alluring in a very sexy way."

She glanced up at him demurely, her eyes saying so much but her lips forming no words. Zack was pulled into her aura with a force he had never felt before. Her lips were glistening with moisture. His head lowered slightly to her mouth. He needed to kiss this woman. She tilted her head up, urging him to take her. His lips touched hers, and he closed his eyes, relishing in the sensations.

Both their bodies shuddered with sexual electricity. It was more than just a drunken kiss. It was passionate and lovely. Her mouth tasted like moonshine and syrup. He entered her mouth with his tongue, probing hers. She yielded to him easily, melting in his arms. Zack felt her arms go slack as she lovingly melted in his warm embrace. He had no idea what he was doing right, but he loved the effect it had on her.

He really liked her. Something about Anita was so very different.

Zack rubbed his hands along her back and waist as they kissed. She arched her back and pressed her breasts against his chest. Her physical urgency had an immediate effect on him. His groin twitched. Her mouth was wet and inviting. He kissed her deeply with his hand behind her head, holding her steady.

She swayed briefly, and he wondered if it was because of the alcohol or the sexual chemistry coursing between them. He held her tight, intend on keeping her safe in his arms.

He walked with her farther into the beautifully treed path, both of them holding hands. They stopped and kissed, then continued walking. They repeated this sensual dance until, finally, he couldn't stand the tension any longer, and he removed his shirt. He could see her eyes glowing in the night, watching his every move. He pecked her lips and pulled her towards him. She quickly melted in his arms. He combed his fingers through her hair and kissed her fully, mumbling between breaths. "You are so beautiful, Anita." His hands wound around her waist, and she moaned heavily.

"Yes," she murmured. "I've been waiting for you for so long."

Zack felt the sexual energy racing through his system like a potent drug that he no longer had any control over. He wanted her to make the next move. He wanted to know for certain that this was what she truly wanted. Zack wanted her so badly that his groin hurt, but he needed to know that she wanted him back. That confirmation was what made it feel right.

Her hands lifted to his jaw as she kissed him. They broke the kiss and looked into each other's eyes in the late-night darkness. "It's a full moon," he said, gesturing with his head. "Look."

Anita turned her head towards the lake. The full moon rose over the calm bluish blackness. He hugged her tightly as they gazed at the moon shining onto the lake.

"It's so beautiful," she said. "I've never seen such a calm moonlit night."

"I'm happy that I'm spending it with you," he said.

"Really?" she said, genuinely surprised. "That makes me very happy hearing you say that."

"It's like I've known you for years," he said, slurring the words with a low husky tone.

"Yes, I was just going to say the same," she said. "You have no idea how long I've been waiting for this moment." She stumbled briefly, and Zack caught her.

"Let's sit down, honey," he said, pulling her to a rock outcropping near the lake. He helped her sit on the rock and sat beside her. She looked at his bare chest as if he was an apparition. Then she started leaning towards him. He wondered what she had in mind. Then her touch electrified him. Her fingers danced along his naked pecs and started sliding all along his chest, stomach and near his beltline. She knelt before him and started worshipping him. It was his turn to melt. This woman had a remarkable effect on him. She lowered her lips to his chest and started kissing his pecs, little loving kisses all over his naked skin. He had never been worshipped like this before, and Zack melted in her arms. She sucked at his hard nipples, and he gasped, surprised but pleased with the exquisite feeling. Zack watched her intently, his erection growing fully in his pants. He needed to straighten his crumbled penis. He nonchalantly slid his hand in his pants and rearranged his penis, so it wasn't so rigidly uncomfortable.

Anita took this as an invitation and pulled her shirt over her head, revealing her small perky breasts. They pointed at him and curved slightly up to the sky. Zack reached out and touched her skin, both of his hands engulfing her breasts fully and gently squeezing them. She moaned heavily and pressed against him urgently. He lifted her up into his arms and carried her effortlessly into a more secluded spot, kissing her deeply, pulling away only to remove her skirt. He lay down their clothes as a blanket and lowered her gently onto it. Her eyes glowed in the darkness as her breath came out hoarse and panting. He wanted this woman so badly, and she wanted him back. He loosened his belt.

Suddenly her fingers were all over him, helping him. She was fumbling with the zipper, feeling his skin, slipping her small hands into his pants. Zack pulled his pants off roughly and the discarded clothing pooled at his feet. He kicked the offending garment away onto the pathway as he caught a tantalizing view of Anita lying naked on the path, stretched out on a pink skirt. His penis jumped and urged him to claim this woman as his.

He mounted her with his large six-foot frame, and she was barely visible underneath him anymore. She was small, probably only five foot two inches. She gasped as he engulfed her with his large body. He hovered above her and kissed her lips gently, waiting until the moment was right. Her kisses became urgent as he lowered his penis to her entrance. He groaned as his penis nudged her vagina. Her kisses became impatient, and her breathing came out in short heavy pants.

"Please," she breathed in his ear.

He pressed his penis inside her vagina and felt her tight walls push against him. He slid into her body slowly, feeling every inch of movement. The feeling was so incredibly exquisite, and he feared he would immediately lose control. Zack bit his lip to hold back from the sensation. He could feel her intense grip all around him. She grasped onto his shoulders, and her powerful legs wrapped around his waist. He thrust deeper into her wetness, held it there for a moment, then slowly pulled back out.

She gasped in ecstasy, pushing her hips up to meet him. He gratified her by thrusting into her again. The moonlight glowed on his naked shoulders as he languorously made love to her. Anita gazed at the stars glinting above them as if the planets had all aligned together for this moment. It was surreal.

Hours passed as they continued this slow dance of love. Time had somehow slipped away from them both. They floated on a cloud of pleasure and bonded like none other. Zack was amazed and yet extremely grateful for these moments suspended in time. It was like they were deposited onto this piece of land in a fairy-tale dimension, almost as if they were on a completely different planet. The bluish darkness, the moon and the stars were so incredible. Her womanly scent wafted up through his nostrils, and he breathed her in. He was developing feelings for this woman at an astonishing rate. She met him with every sway and thrust back as they tangoed together on the dirt path. He vowed if she stayed with him that he would heed his father's advice and quit drinking. Zack would be a good man for this woman. He crossed his fingers that she wouldn't leave as quickly as the others have.

She smiled up at him. "The moon and the stars," she breathed. "It's surreal."

"It feels out of this world," he agreed, gently sliding out of her, then in again.

She moaned deeply, and her legs began vibrating.

Zack couldn't hold back any longer. He gazed into her eyes under the moonlight, and he felt connected with her so wholly and uniquely. She clutched her arms tightly around his torso and buried her face in his shoulder. Her moans vibrated throughout his entire body. He felt his semen rush to his penis, and he struggled to react in time. He pulled out quickly but not fast enough. He was afraid that he had ejaculated partially inside of her.

Anita gasped, "Why did you pull out?"

Zack kissed her deeply. "You'll get pregnant if I don't."

"But I want you," she said, mumbling something incomprehensible.

Zack felt a glow of love spread throughout his body. "You really want me?"

"Of course, babe," she said, cuddling into his shoulder as a shudder released throughout her body.

"I'll be here for you," Zack said slowly. "I want you to stay with me."

"I will," Anita said, her body feeling so incredibly satisfied, like something important had just happened to them both.

"I'll be a good man," Zack said, his emotions bubbling up to the surface.

Anita kissed him in agreement.

Zack tasted her honey lips, and his heart soared. She liked him! He would clean up his act starting now. He wasn't going to let a good woman like her get away. Zack relaxed his body beside her, looking up at the moon. "It's a full moon."

"Yes, it is," Anita said in wonderment. "The sky, the waves, the stars, it's all so incredibly beautiful. I've never felt like this before. It's like something happened tonight. Something special."

Zack gazed into her eyes in the bluish blackness. "Yes, hon," he said. "We met tonight. I'll never forget this first night."

Anita nodded, but something disturbed her. He had said something that wasn't right. Her brain didn't process it right away, although she filed it away subconsciously for something to think about in the future. "Can we go back to your place? My parents are home tonight. I'd rather not wake them."

"Definitely, my sweetheart," Zack stood, pulling his pants back on. He held his hand out and pulled her up. She stood up swiftly and propelled into his arms. He hugged her tight. "We can go to my dad's old cottage. Let's go, beautiful."

❦

He awoke on cloud nine. They had slept at the small cottage he shared with his brother Adam. His brother wasn't home this weekend. The brothers alternated weeks; Adam was taking care of Pabbi this time. Every other week Zack had off, he suppressed his emotions with alcohol, but Adam chose to bury himself in his job. Adam was working towards a political career like his father, Nath, had done. He was surveying land, marking off regions for future developments and attending council meetings. He was hoping to get elected as mayor in a few years.

Zack was much different from his identical twin brother. Zack didn't like politics, always preferring physical revolt to solve the country's problems and preferring heavy labour as his outlet for work. Zack naturally worked with Mike and Vira at the fishing business, but he had been falling apart lately with his erratic behaviour. He was going to change that today.

Zack opened his eyes and smelled the wonderful female scent beside him. He laid an arm over Anita and pulled her close into him, kissing her naked shoulder. They had made love several more times throughout the night. His head throbbed from the morning after effect of the alcohol, but he still felt gloriously happy. He had somehow found a special woman, and she was in his arms.

Anita groaned.

"Good morning," Zack whispered.

Anita opened her eyes slowly. "Mmm," she replied lazily. "Good morning, Adam. Oh my Lord, my head hurts. It's like heaven waking up in your arms, though."

Zack froze at the mention of his brother's name.

"My head hurts," she said. "Is that normal? I don't normally drink that much."

Zack felt his throat constrict. Did she just call him Adam? Was it a mistake? Maybe she had him confused with Adam.

It was fine, he thought, trying to stem the rising panic in his throat. Most people confuse them both.

"Are you okay?" she asked, turning her head to look at him.

Zack wasn't sure what to say. He didn't want to let her go. He wanted this moment to last forever. It was only one night, but Zack felt more connected to this woman than any other girl he had ever met. "I'm okay," he said, trying to think of what to say. "Yeah, it's normal to have a little headache."

"Are you sure everything is okay?" she said. "You sound unsure." Anita sat up, crossed her legs and caressed her hand along his young beard. "I've been waiting a long time to be with you, Adam. I know that I shouldn't be saying this so early, but I really want it to last between us."

Zack's heart sunk, and his chest hurt like it was somehow imploding upon itself. "Anita," he said slowly. "I'm Zack, Adam's twin brother."

Anita gasped and pulled away.

Zack clung to her. "Please listen to me," he said. "I really like you, Anita. I haven't felt like this about anyone before. What we experienced last night was special; it was like we were on a different planet. I had no idea you thought I was Adam. You never called me Adam."

"Yes, I did," she said, her voice uncertain. "I thought I did."

"No, you didn't," he said. "I would have heard it right away and stopped everything from progressing."

"I didn't know Adam had a twin brother," Anita said, looking at his face. "You are identical twins."

"Yes, we are," Zack answered.

She moved to get off the bed.

"No, Anita," he pleaded. "Please don't do this. We can build something. I don't want to lose you."

Anita stood, her face pale and ashamed. Her mouth dropped open as if to say something profound, and then her lips closed. She pulled her shirt over her head and searched the floor for her skirt.

"Don't go, Anita," Zack begged.

She turned to look hard at him, her legs still naked. "I'm in love with Adam. I'm so sorry, Zack. I had no idea." She burst into tears and covered her face. "I have to find my panties and skirt. I have to go home." She rummaged along the floor until she found her clothes, quickly slipping them on and pulled open the door.

Zack swung his long legs over the edge of the bed. His heart hammered in his chest. The only woman he had fallen in love with didn't even want him. It was all a stupid mistake.

"I'm sorry," Anita cried, tears streaming down her cheeks. "Bye, Zack."

The door shut quietly behind her as Zack felt his entire world implode.

Chapter 6

The fishery business was starting to recover slowly. Mike and Vira Kozak had taken it over from Nathan ten years ago, right before the Great Depression. They were lucky with the timing; they had worked hard at Vira's farm and sold it before the economic collapse. Neither Mike nor Vira had the passion necessary to be Ukrainian farmers. They were both a mix of Icelandic and Ukrainian, their parents immigrating amongst the mass European exodus. Ukraine farmers were eager to escape Austro-Hungarian rule before and during WWI. Plenty of Kozaks had remained in Ukraine from Mike's father's side of the family. Several years back, they had received distressing news in 1933 that a terrible Soviet famine had killed many of their relatives back home. One brave cousin had escaped and made it to Canada. Anton Kozak was helping in the fishing boats today. He was one of the hardest workers Mike had ever employed. The man had miraculously escaped from Ukraine in a bold crash through the Romanian gates in 1933, half alive and emaciated. He was accepted into Canada as a refugee shortly afterwards.

"Hand me those nets," Mike said, his dark blonde hair blowing in a gust of wind. He wore it long nowadays, and it suited him with a sexy mature look. "I'll take the nets to the shore to dry."

Anton whipped his cowlick down smoothly and bundled the nets, handing them towards Mike. "I'll help you take them to the beach," he said, his thick Ukrainian accent slurring his words.

Mike marvelled at how much Anton looked like his dad. The deep green eyes and blondish hair looked like his father Ivan had been duplicated; even the cowlick was the same. Mike chuckled to himself because he looked very similar to his grandpa, Nath and nothing like his father. "Thanks, Anton," Mike said, gesturing with the nets towards the shore, flipping his hair to the side. "This way."

His father, Ivan and his mother, Annabella, were in their sixties now, growing much older, but his grandfather, Nathan, worried him the most. He had turned eighty this year, and his heart valves were malfunctioning, leaving him suddenly bedridden and weak. It pained Mike to see his grandad this way. Nathan had been such a strong, robust man all his life and to be reduced to a weak senior citizen was something that Mike could barely accept as reality.

"How's your Afi doing?" Anton asked gently, referring to Mike's grandad with the endearing Icelandic term.

Mike moved the nets gently to the racks and spread them with Anton's help. "He's not doing well, Anton," Mike said, rubbing his short beard. "We've been doing all that we can for him. His heart isn't functioning well anymore."

"I'm sorry," Anton replied.

"Thank you," Mike said. "It's been tough on us all."

Mike heard the warehouse door slam from across the beach. "Oh, someone is at the shop. Can you finish laying out the nets? I'll be right back."

"Sure," Anton said, pulling the nets carefully across the old stands. They had continued using the old wooden racks from forty years ago. They had rebuilt the antique frames and improved the designs but still preferred to dry them on shore. The quality of the nets stayed firmer when they were allowed to dry completely.

Mike reached the fish store and opened the front door, shocked to see Zachary Olason standing there. "Zack," he said. "You made it in today. I was wondering if you were coming in at all, so I called Anton to help today." Mike paused, sensing something troubling about Zack's demeanour. "Are you okay? You look sick."

"I'm not sick," Zack replied. "I just had a rough night."

"Another one of those?"

"It's more than just drinking too much," Zack stated, staring blankly at the wall for a multi-second. "But I'll recover."

"Well, grab some pails and wash those boats out then," Mike said, gesturing with his hands towards the dock. "They need a good cleaning."

"Okay, I'll do that," Zack said, his shoulders slumping slightly.

"Are you sure that you're okay?" Mike asked. "You seem tired."

"I am tired," Zack replied. "Of life mostly." He looked up at Mike, a weary cloud of grief crossing his face. "You know when your hopes get up just because one little thing happened? Especially when you're looking for hope." He blinked slowly.

"I haven't been dealing with Pabbi's bad heart very well, and I guess I'm just clinging to things that simply aren't there."

"Come here," Mike said firmly, grabbing his arm and hugging Zack tightly. "We've all been upset about Afi. I love him like he was my dad too. He's still with us miraculously. We need to be grateful for that, at least."

"Yeah, but for how long?" Zack said. "Will he survive another year or just another month?"

"The doctors don't know," Mike replied softly. "Some people live longer than others. It depends on how badly his heart valves are damaged. They have no way of predicting that."

"I know," Zack said. "I just wish I'd stop looking for hope because there is none."

"That's not true," Mike said. "There's hope everywhere around you. On the sand, in the smiles of strangers around you and even out on the lake."

Zack looked at Mike sadly. "Maybe for some people," he said.

"Cheer up, Zack," Mike said, slapping his shoulder. "I'll give you extra work today to keep your mind off of things." Mike grabbed a bucket and followed Zack out to the boats. Mike had a noticeable limp on his left leg. The German stick grenade that had taken him out of WWI had left him with this deformity. Mike thought he was extremely lucky, considering that the doctors told him that he would never walk again.

His wife, Vira, had been his rock of support. She helped him walk every day for that first year. She was his salvation, his hope and his everything. The war nightmares had ravaged his mind for years, waking him in a sweat, shouting military commands. She was patient and so incredibly loving that it made his heart hurt sometimes just to know that he was loved. He didn't know what he did to deserve such a wonderful wife, but he was extremely grateful for her.

After the birth of their first son, Eli, the cloud of trauma started to lift. Mike began seeing the world in a different way. He had a purpose. He had his family to protect and serve now, not the entire world anymore. They had four more children together afterwards. The nightmares became just dreams, and the limp was just a sore left leg. He smiled as he thought about how his life had turned around.

But seeing Nath suffering with his failing heart was like a rug being yanked from underneath him. Nathan was always his grandpa, his best friend and his mentor. He couldn't even grasp what life would be like without him. Mike was a strong man because of his grandpa's influence. How could he possibly lose Nath?

"I was just thinking, Zack," Mike said.

Zack turned and looked at Mike, snatching the pail from his hands. "What were you thinking about?" he asked.

"I was just thinking about how important Afi is to us," Mike said solemnly. "He's been so much a part of my life. He moulded me and taught me everything I know today."

Zack nodded. "I know," he said. "I feel the same. I look up to him too. He's a strong man in so many different ways. I always tried to be like him. I was always his favourite."

"That's the thing, Zack," Mike said. "I think everyone was his favourite. It is just the kind of man he is. Everyone is special to him."

Zack nodded, hefting the pails into the boat. "True," he said, agreeing.

"Yeah, well," Mike said. "Let's wash these boats clean and go fishing tonight. It's what Afi would want us to do." Mike smiled at a distant memory. "Did you know he was so happy when I took over the fishery?"

"I was still only ten years old," Zack replied. "But I remember. He was delighted that you and Vira took it over."

"It was what he always wanted," Mike replied. "When I had told him many years ago that I was joining the Great War, he was deeply disturbed. He asked me to think twice. He asked why I didn't want just to get married and take over the fishery." Mike washed the boat with his strong arms, pulling his sleeves up. "I told him that I would be back and go fishing with him after I did my duty as a sniper. And I did it, I came back, barely."

"Oh, so he wanted you to take over twenty years ago?" Zack mused, running the numbers through his head. "Before I was born!"

"Yeah," Mike answered. "Your mom wasn't pregnant until after I got back, and they all finished building the summer home. That was one of the best days of my life. Everything seemed so hopeful and full of light."

"You were a tough soldier," Zack said admiringly.

"War is not what you think it is," Mike said. "It is not a world of bravery and heroes. What I had discovered about war is that it's just a stinking pile of rotting flesh and death everywhere you look. I was lucky to make it back home alive."

Zack nodded, but he wasn't convinced. He knew of the mental anguish Mike had gone through coming back and living a normal life. He had heard of all the gruesome stories. A stubborn part of him still thought that the way to peace was through revolt and violence. He kept it to himself as he finished cleaning the boats. His time would come one day when the world would need him again.

∿

Nath lay on the bed, looking up at the ceiling. Maria had fallen asleep in the bed beside him. He loved her so incredibly much. She was his best friend and his lover. He felt so unbelievably blessed to be married to her for a glorious twenty years. He felt a cough bubble up in his throat. He tried to hold it back, so he didn't wake Maria, but it was futile. The cough rasped out of his lungs, and the pain in his chest seared throughout his body.

Maria awoke suddenly and jumped to get him some water.

"It's alright, babe," Nath said, between coughs. "Lie down."

"No, I'm getting you some water, hold on." Maria ran to the kitchen and returned with a glass of water, holding it to his lips. "I don't want to lose you," Maria said, looking into his eyes. The man she had fallen in love with so many years ago was withering away in front of her eyes.

"I'm not going anywhere yet," he said.

"You better not," she said, curling into him and hugging him tightly.

The front door opened, and he heard one of his sons come in. The floor boards creaked with every step in a specific way signalling to him that it was Zack. Funny how he knew his sons so well, Nath thought.

"Pabbi," Zack said as he poked his head into the bedroom. "I'm going to make you some of that herbal tea you love. Hi Mom." He kissed his mom on the cheek. "How are you feeling, Dad?" Zack sat down on the chair and rubbed his father's frail arm.

"I've felt better," Nath said, laughing lightly. "How have you been doing, Zack? Have you been cutting back on the alcohol?"

"A little bit," Zack lied.

Nath narrowed his eyes at his son. "Don't ever think lying to me will go unnoticed."

Zack nodded his head to the side.

"You need to stop this, Zack," Nath said. "I've told you many times that life may be difficult, but drinking will make it worse. You need to stop, Zack."

"Well, I was going to stop a few days ago," he replied.

"What happened?"

"Ah, nothing," Zack said. "I just met a girl, and I hoped that she would be the one. But it was just a mistake."

"I told you before," Nath said. "No woman will stay with a man who drinks too much. You have to save yourself, Zack. Nobody can do this for you."

"I know," Zack said.

Nath laid his head back on the pillow and sighed. "Zack," he said. "Life is never easy. Nobody ever promised you an easy path. Your momma once told me that we never really appreciate the light until we've known the dark and lived in its trenches." Nath smiled and patted her leg beside him. "She was right."

Zack smiled admiringly at his mom and dad. He wanted a love like they had, something pure, genuine and family-minded.

Maria kissed Nath on the forehead and jumped out of bed. "You're still a silly romantic," she cooed.

Zack laughed and patted his father's arm. "Yep, Momma's right," he said.

"Nothing wrong with believing in forever," Nathan replied.

"I guess so," Zack said. "Sometimes it's hard to believe that when everything in your life proves differently."

"True," Nathan replied. "But that's just how you perceive life to be. One small change in how you view the world is sometimes all you need."

Zack looked up to the ceiling. "Maybe."

"It's tough growing up," Nath said. "I know. I had to do it too. We all had to. Everyone's path is different. Just try to make sure you don't set it on fire."

Zack exhaled heavily. "I'm trying, Pabbi."

"I know, son," Nath said. "I know."

CHAPTER 7

Adam was tired. He had been working steadily for the past few weeks in his position of assistant reeve. He had been putting a lot of time into achieving his goal of becoming reeve in the future. People liked him. He was a stable professional with an analytical mind. He was charismatic like his father, Nath, and he felt strongly that the way out of the world's problems was through government.

Adam and his brother were close, but lately, Zack had grown distant and moody. He didn't quite know why. Adam cared about his brother but didn't understand him. His penchant for violence and drinking was not something that was part of Adam's life, nor did he want it to be. Adam still loved his brother but felt that he was destined to live a better life than that. It pained him to see Zack suffering through his emotions the way he did. His brother was always a wild spirit and more emotional than him, but they were identical twins and bonded from birth. It disturbed him that Zack was becoming so distant.

He would have to remind himself to spend more quality time with him.

Adam closed the town hall door and stepped out onto the dirt road, his footsteps crunching the loose rocks methodically as he walked home. It was an hour's walk to the cottage at Willow Point, where Adam and Zack lived. It was Zack's turn to stay with Pabbi, so he'd have the cabin to himself all week.

It was a dusty, hot afternoon in the summer, and he could feel the sweat forming on his collar already. He should have sipped some water before leaving work. The heat could be dangerously hot in the summers. Adam crossed the street and waved at Anton, who was walking on the other side.

As he approached, Anton waved back and smiled. "Heading home?"

"Yeah, all done for the day," Adam replied, combing his fingers through his short-cropped blonde hair. "How was the fishing today?"

"It was good," Anton said, pronouncing the words in broken English. "I enjoy my time with Mike and his family. But this heat scares the fish away. We have to sail farther and farther up to the northern parts of Lake Winnipeg."

"Be careful with that," Adam said. "My dad always tells us the story of the 1876 storm which had killed three young fishermen, shattering the wreckage of the boats along the northern shores. They never even found the bodies." Adam shook his head solemnly. "Lake Winnipeg is like an apparition from heaven one day then turning into the beast of evil the next."

"I have witnessed the beautiful sunrises," Anton replied, his eyes growing wide in shock. "I do not look forward to meeting the beasts of evil."

"It is just a saying," Adam said. "The storms are truly terrible here."

"I will be careful."

Adam slapped his back. "You are doing fine," he said. "So, do you like it here in Canada?"

"Oh, yes," Anton said, smoothing the pesky cowlick on the crown of his head. "Very much so. The famine almost killed me in Ukraine."

"I heard of that!" Adam replied. "You are so lucky to get out alive!"

"So many people died," Anton said, shaking his head. "My mother and father. All of my siblings. All dead. It is a miracle I survived."

"The universe needs you," Adam said. "Keep your chin up. You have all of your extended family here."

"Yes, I am grateful for that," Anton said, smiling. They both walked in silence for a while. Anton often walked with Adam halfway to his home. They travelled the same road to their homes every day.

Several other people were walking home as well. A small rush-hour crowd formed with people on bicycles; some of the residents walked, and a few cars travelled on the road too. Among the crowd was a slim woman that Adam knew. He waved. She noticed him with a surprised glance and demurely looked up, waving back. She seemed shy, Adam thought. He gestured for her to cross the road to join them. She smiled and shook her head no.

Adam grimaced. Why was she acting like this? He had liked her for several weeks now, and he knew she had a crush on him for years. "I'll be right back, Anton," he said as he crossed the street towards Anita.

Anita looked shocked and nervous. He really couldn't understand her. Women confused him. "Anita," he said. "How have you been doing? I haven't seen you in over a month. Do you take a different way home now?"

"Oh no, I just, umm, had a few weeks off," she said, not looking him in the eye.

What the devil is wrong with her? Adam couldn't make sense of it. "Well, I will walk with you then," he said, waving bye to Anton and then returning his attention to Anita. "Are you okay? You seem out of sorts."

"I haven't been feeling too well lately," she replied. "I'm probably just tired from working at the post office today."

Adam's brow creased in concern. "Are you alright?" he asked.

"I'm fine," she lied. "Probably just coming down with a summer cold." Anita shielded her eyes from the sun. "You cut your hair," she pointed out.

"I did," he responded confidently. "Do you like it?"

"Yes, you look good," she replied thoughtfully.

"Thanks," Adam said. He looked up at the sun and tried to think of something else to keep her talking. "Can I walk you home, Anita?"

"Okay," she replied nervously. They walked on for several yards before Anita spoke again. "Anything new happening at the town hall?"

"Yes," Adam replied. "We are discussing many different options to reinforce the fishing pier and the lighthouse to protect it from more flooding and ice jams in the winter. It is a difficult problem with no feasible solution. We have added much rock and cement to the shoreline parts of the pier, but as it extends farther out towards the lighthouse, it becomes more vulnerable," Adam said, gesturing with his hands to encompass the vastness of the lake. "So far, the lighthouse has been standing up to the elements, but I feel it is only a matter of time before it is destroyed by the ice jams."

"Why do you think that? It's been holding up so far," she asked, interested in Adam's passion for politics.

"Well," he said. "Mostly because it extends quite far out into the lake on wooden boards, which was a problem with the original dock until we added more rocks and cement underneath closer to shore. One bad flood or ice jam, the entire wooden dock is lifted away and claimed by the sea."

"So, what do you propose?"

"I am trying to push the making of an island where the lighthouse sits," Adam said, rubbing his thin beard. "My idea is the entire dock doesn't need to be made out of earth, but if we built a strong island where the lighthouse sits, then nothing can wash it away."

"What did the council say?"

"They said it was near impossible," Adam said dejectedly. "And too expensive."

Anita looked down in thought. "Oh," she said. "So, you've had a frustrating day."

"Yes, exactly," he said. "I know the island is what will eventually need to be done, but nobody wants to listen to me now. Unfortunately, it will take a horrible flood or winter storm to destroy everything; then they'll do something." Adam sighed and looked up to the skies. "Sometimes, I think I am too idealistic and want to change the world too much."

"I think it's admirable that you want to make a difference in this world," she said.

Adam smiled. "That's the sweetest thing anyone has ever said to me."

She smiled back, her eyes crinkling and her lips lifting.

He liked the way her face looked when she smiled. "You are beautiful," Adam said suddenly. "I hope you know that."

She blushed and looked down at her toes. "Thank you," she said.

Adam brushed his hand along hers as they walked. The sun was glowing in the west over the farm fields in the distance, an orange sphere scattering its rays amongst the clouds. They walked for several minutes in silence, appreciating the view. The summer sun would not completely set for several more hours, he knew. The scattering rays were best at the hour before sunset, especially tonight. He wondered if Anita would join him to watch the sun set.

He liked her. He was attracted to her for a very long time; he just wasn't able to show it. Adam had become embroiled in a bad relationship with another woman, and it took an entire year for it to end finally. He wasn't sure if he was ready to take the plunge with another woman yet, but he was convinced that it would be with Anita. That Christmas dance so long ago had stuck in his memory. He had always felt close to her in a strange sort of paranormal way.

Adam looked down at her and brushed his hand along hers again. She smiled. Then he slipped his hand into hers. She looked up at him and grinned sheepishly. She likes me back, he thought.

"I have a question, Anita," Adam said as they walked hand in hand for several feet.

"Yes, what is it, Adam?" she asked.

He grinned handsomely. "Since the sun will be setting so beautifully tonight," he said. "Would you join me to watch it set along Willow Point?"

Her face beamed into the biggest smile he had ever seen. "Definitely! I would love that!"

"Okay!" he exclaimed happily. "So, I will walk you home first. I will wait until you change out of your work clothes, and then we will walk to Willow Point together."

"That sounds perfect," she said, her heart lifting.

Zack sat on his father's sofa, cradling a beer, looking out over the lake. The large white Olason house on the lake was now one of the oldest in town. So many tourists and Winnipeggers had built kit homes in the area for their summer cottages. During the summer, the population of Gimli increased ten-fold. Zack didn't mind, but the house looked older than everything around it now. He loved the old house and the lake. It was in his veins, just like the lake was in his father's blood. He lived and breathed the open sea like all the other Olason's before him.

But he was still unhappy. He yearned to fix the world's problems. Zack had failed so many times and was spiralling into a well of depression. He couldn't find meaningful work except fishing with the family business. Zack couldn't stop his father from dying either, and to make it all worse, he couldn't be with Anita.

It was just one night, but he had fallen in love with her, ready to give up his wild ways and start a family with her, just like that.

Zack shook his head and gazed out at the lake. How could he have thought so naively?

He should forget her. But he couldn't. She had said that she loved Adam. It pierced his heart when she said that. He looked identical to his brother! Why couldn't she just choose him? What was so special about Adam?

It all seemed so unfair.

He watched as a bald eagle soared down onto the lake, scooping up a fish with graceful ease. Zack shouted excitedly, "Mom!"

Maria poked her head into the living room, her waist-length blonde hair gracing her back. She had aged well, not much grey and only a few wrinkles. Maria was nineteen years younger than his father, but she still became pregnant with the twins in her late thirties. "What is it?" she asked curiously.

"Look!" Zack pointed out towards the lake. "An eagle!"

"Oh my Lord!" she said. "Would you look at that?" She smiled, her eyes wrinkling at the corners sweetly. "That strong hunter is at it again. I wonder whether it's the same eagle I keep seeing or if there is a family of eagles around the shoreline."

"Probably more than one," he said, his gaze drifting out to the lake again.

Maria tilted her head to the side, sensing something was disturbing her son. She walked over and sat on the opposite armchair in front of the large window. "A penny for your thoughts?" she asked.

"Ah," Zack said, throwing his head back. "Not much to say, except I always seem never to get a break in life. It's a recurring story. I'm stuck. I can't change anything even if I tried."

Maria nodded. "Why do you think that?"

"Oh, Mom," he said. "You know that I failed during the Regina Riot. I failed at finding a job, finding a woman and pretty much everything else."

"You didn't fail," Maria said, leaning back in the armchair, gazing out at the lake with her son.

"What do you mean?" he asked.

"You tried to force change in the world, Zack," she said. "That's admirable. I was extremely worried about you and distraught, but when you came home, I was proud of you. You set out in an unknown world and made a big effort to change your life and the world."

"But I failed," he replied quickly.

"You did not," Maria said slowly. "You showed to yourself that you have the courage to make change happen. R. Bennett lost the election after the riot. He was not an effective leader. Change finally happened, maybe not in the way you had intended, but it did happen. The economy is slowly recovering, and the labour camps were disbanded." She stood up, walked to the sofa and put her hand on his shoulder. "You did more than many other people would have done."

"Thanks, Mom," Zack said.

Maria patted his shoulder. "And you will find a woman soon. Don't rush it. It will happen naturally one day."

"It seems like every girl I fall in love with doesn't love me back," he said.

"That's because you haven't met your special person yet," Maria said.

Zack scowled. "I don't think there is anyone special out there for me. I thought there was at one time, but I was wrong."

Maria smoothed his hair. "Did I ever tell you about your dad and me?"

"Many times," Zack said, chuckling.

"Well, I'm going to tell you again, but there are some things you never heard before." Maria sat down on the sofa at Zack's feet and started massaging his foot. "When I met your dad, we both felt the same as you do now." She looked up, and her eyes were transported back to twenty years ago. "I had just lost my first husband a few years back and came to Gimli for a change. Nathan had lived thirty-nine years as a widower alone, without attempting to fall in love again. Thirty-nine years, Zack!" She shook her head incredulously. "So, we were both widowers.

And you know what? It turned out that he was my special person. He understood me like no one else, and I understood him like no other woman ever had." She massaged his foot and concentrated for a bit, then looked at her son. "Believe me, Zack. There is someone out there made just for you. Don't ever stop believing."

"I hope so," Zack said, his head bobbing lazily back as her massaging fingers lulled him to sleep.

Maria watched her son fall asleep on the sofa and smiled. He will find his special woman soon, she thought. Then I'll have to let him go a little bit more. A tear escaped from her eye and ran down her cheek. Her twin boys meant so much to her. She loved them with every ounce of her soul.

"Come on! It'll be setting soon!" Adam shouted, pulling her hand through the bushes. The sun was setting quicker than he thought. They had talked for hours as she fed him at her parent's house. Anita had made a ham lentil soup. It was so nice being absorbed in their mutual interest in politics and enjoying each other's company. Time seemed to vanish when he spent moments with her. When he looked outside at the fading day, he realized with a jolt that they would miss the sunset if they didn't hurry. It was as if the clocks didn't keep time anymore. It just all stood still while they enjoyed each others' company.

"I'm hurrying!" she said, giggling as she followed Adam through the thick bushes. The summer wind blew through the branches and filled them both with the dewy scent of a hot summer night.

"I know a wonderful spot!" he shrieked. "You'll love it!"

Anita laughed wholeheartedly. She felt so weightless when she was with him. Her feet crunched softly in the bush as they scrambled along the path. As Adam jumped onto a trail and pulled her hand excitedly, she suddenly stopped in shock.

"What is it?" he asked, confused at her sudden hesitancy.

Anita looked down at the trail in the bushes. It looked similar to the path that she and Zack had made love on. Her heart shattered. Anita had hurt him so much; she knew this. She glanced at Adam. He was the man she had always been in love with all this time. She couldn't forsake this kind of love over a simple mistake of identity. "No, it's nothing," she said. "I just think I've been on this path before."

"Oh, it's beautiful," he said. "My mom and dad used to bring my brother and me here as kids."

Anita shuffled closer to Adam and held his hand firmly. "Let's see this sunset," she said.

Adam pulled her excitedly towards a small dock. They ran on the beach until they reached the shoreline. Adam pulled his boots off and then his socks, tossing them onto the sand. Anita followed his actions, pulling her shoes and socks off too. They stepped onto the dock barefoot and walked to the very end. The sun was very low on the horizon. Adam was right; it was very close to setting.

"After you, my beautiful lady," he said, gesturing to the rough wooden dock as a place to sit. "Have a seat, my beautiful."

Anita smiled and sat on the offered spot. He joined her and hugged her close as they dangled their bare feet off the pier. The sun glowed in a magnificent ball of reddish-orange light. The rays bounced off the clouds above the sun, painting the sky with purple and pink reflections everywhere.

"Oh my!" Anita exclaimed. "The sunset is exceptional tonight! You were right. How did you know?"

"Oh, sometimes, it's just the clouds or the weather. I don't really know. I think the lake is in my blood. I can sense a beautiful sunset coming miles away."

Anita smiled at his profound words while she gazed at the kaleidoscope of colours stretching for miles.

"You are the most beautiful woman I've ever met, Anita," Adam said abruptly, almost as if he was thinking aloud.

"Thank you," she said. "You are a very handsome man, Adam. I'm a little shocked that you would want me."

"Of course, I would," he said. "Don't be silly." He leaned back on his hands and felt the chemistry igniting between them. He turned his head and saw her eyes gazing dreamily at him. Adam leaned closer and pulled her chin to his. Her lips looked so luscious and soft. He bent ever so slightly nearer and then softly kissed her lips. The electricity danced through his entire system, like something important had happened tonight. His body was on fire as he pulled her closer to him. One of her hands lifted into the air and wrapped around his back, pulling him into her body heat. They kissed like this for hours, happily embraced in each other's heat.

Time must have stopped because the night was descending quickly, and darkness was surrounding them. Adam blinked and wondered what kind of magic was happening tonight. "Time doesn't seem to exist when I'm with you," he said.

She cuddled into his chest, just a fraction of an inch, impossibly closer. "I feel the same, Adam," she said, her words muffled into his chest.

CHAPTER 8

Zack pulled out his rifle, joining Mike and his cousins as they stalked deer in the forest. It was an early autumn morning, and the air was crisp and cool. Mike had a way of limping through the forest soundlessly that was eerie and unnerving. He knew this forest like an expert knew his craft. The first few years Mike had gone back to hunting, he had experienced severe war flashbacks. Nath had come with him and talked him down to reality. His grandpa would reassure him that it was okay; gunshots while hunting were normal. He would also tell him to breathe and focus on where he was. Mike would smell the trees and listen to the birds. He concentrated on slowing his breathing and told himself repeatedly that it was just his past giving him anxiety; reality was something entirely different. When Mike had recovered, Nath would hug him slowly and tell him that it was okay to feel this way. He was a brave soldier, but he was no longer that soldier. Mike Kozak was a hunter, a fisherman and a father. He had come back to who he was before the war and even better.

Mike was immensely grateful for his grandpa. There were moments when he didn't know what he would do without him. But Mike also knew that the future was constantly changing, and he was a strong man, capable of great things.

Mike was here with his sons Eli and Julian, passing on his hunting skills to the next generation. Zack had joined the group as well. Mike felt gifted to hunt again without being paralyzed with flashbacks. He still had the immediate physical response when he heard a gunshot. His heart would hammer into his throat, and his hands would shake. Only now, Mike knew it was coming and accepted the trauma in his mind as a fixture of his being. His response was what mattered, and he knew this all too well now. Mike was pleased that every hunting trip became easier and easier.

"Dad," Eli whispered. "Are you okay?"

"Yeah, son," Mike replied, swallowing. "I'm fine. Let's go to the clearing that Afi showed us. We can get a male deer today if they are out."

Eli nodded, motioning Julian and Zack to follow. Eli was only two years younger than Zack. They had become close relatives, often shooting together. Zack picked up his gun bag and headed into the forest with his relatives. He wanted to be here to support Mike because he knew how much the man struggled in the past, taking his sons out hunting. Zack was a reassuring adult presence.

"Mike," Zack said in a quiet voice. "Did you bring your old Ross rifle?"

"I sure did," Mike replied. "I never go hunting without it."

"I love that old gun!" the younger boy, Julian, shouted to everyone's surprise.

"Shh!" Mike scolded. "Lower your voice, son. You're going to alert the deer to our position."

Julian blushed embarrassingly. He was only seventeen years old; he didn't know any better. "Sorry, Dad," he whispered.

Mike patted him on the back, reassuring him. "Mistakes are always made," he said. "Try to learn from them. If the deer are gone when we get there, we will have to return next week. They will be spooked for a while."

Julian frowned sadly. "I hope not," he whispered.

The group of men walked further into the forest as a gentle rain began to fall. The summer precipitation was welcome after a few hot weeks. The humidity was high near the lake; all four men were sweating from the sauna-like heat. The drops of rain that fell on their backs were a blessing.

Mike started crouching in the shrubs, peering out into the clearing with the group. He turned and placed his fingers on his lips, gesturing to keep quiet. Eli crouched just like his dad and waved Zack over to Julian's position. Zack crept soundlessly to the large oak tree where Julian hunkered behind.

Eli was the shooter today. Everyone else was backup. If Eli didn't get the first shot, then Zack would shoot second, then Mike and then Julian. They had agreed to the order before-hand. Although it was mostly an unnecessary precaution, Eli was an expert marksman like his dad.

A young group of bachelor deer foraged in the clearing. Two of the bucks were relatively young, the other two adolescents. The largest buck nodded his head angrily at the group. He would most likely leave the bachelor group soon. His territorial nature would soon get the best of him.

Eli raised the old Ross M-10 rifle. Nathan had given the gun to Mike for his 16th birthday many, many years ago. It was the family's prized possession. They had other guns now, but the old M-10 had a special place on the gunrack at home over the deer head in the living room. Mike took exceptional care of the old gun, oiling the wood and cleaning the weapon meticulously. Eli felt honoured to be the shooter today with his dad's rifle.

Eli crouched his neck down, peering through the sight at the bucks. He felt the butt of the rifle snugly against his shoulder as the older buck came into view. He steadied his aim, closed one eye and calculated the distance at approximately 200 yards. It would be a comfortably close shot with the Ross rifle. He could shoot well over 300 yards and still be accurate.

Eli exhaled slowly. He felt the calm come over him. Eli fired.

The bullet cracked through the air and hit the buck in the heart.

The buck looked at the group as if he didn't understand what was going on. The younger deer jumped away into the bush. The buck wavered as if to join the exodus, then suddenly fell.

"Perfect shot, son!" Mike exclaimed loudly as his heart hammered relentlessly from the rifle shot.

They all ran to the fallen buck. Zack examined the animal and determined that it was killed instantly. He shook his head incredulously. Eli was an incredible marksman. Mike could shoot at 200 yards also and be pretty darn good, but this kid was amazing. Zack laid his bag out, removed his knife and began the bloody job of field dressing. This didn't disturb him at all. Some men didn't have the stomach for it, Zack knew. Julian looked away. Zack continued slicing the buck open.

Mike joined him with shaky hands as they prepared the deer for transport. Zack watched over Mike closely. "I can do this," Zack said calmly.

"It's okay," Mike replied. "The more I do it, the better it gets."

Zack nodded, still watching Mike with concern. He didn't know what war memories were like, but they affected some men very badly. He cared about Mike and hated seeing him go through the pain of the past.

"Let's finish and get this deer meat in the truck," Mike said calmly, but his hands still shook.

Zack began to tie everything up to prepare for transport as the boys went back to retrieve the truck. The buck was bigger than he'd thought and would make for excellent meals.

Zack smiled and hugged Mike's left shoulder. "This is the best catch of the month!" Zack exclaimed.

The family ate fish while the deer carcass hung in the shed. Annabella passed the potatoes to her sons. "Don't eat it all! Save some for your sisters!" she chastised.

Annabella had aged gracefully; she was in her sixties now. Her face was still full of youthful optimism, and her eyes still glowed with the rare sapphire blue glint of the Olason's. She was Swampy Cree and half Icelandic with tanned skin and long black hair. Her daughter Katya looked exactly like her, but her other daughter Natalie had blond hair and green eyes like her dad, Ivan. Annabella was so proud of her children. She felt blessed to have a wonderful husband that still loved her and a large family to keep her busy.

Zack was sitting at the table, too, enjoying dinner with his half-sister and her family. His dark blonde wavy hair was lighter than Nath's, but his eyes were the same blue as hers. She loved her brothers so much, although lately, they had been growing apart. She didn't quite understand why.

"Where has Adam been lately?" Annabella asked.

"He's been working at town council quite a bit recently," Zack answered.

"Is he still living at the old cottage with you?" Ivan asked.

"Yes," Zack said. "Although, we exchange weeks staying at the house with Dad, helping Mom."

"You are good sons," Ivan replied.

"Thanks," Zack said as he pushed a mouthful of potatoes in his mouth. He chewed gratefully. Food was becoming more available, and the economy was slowly recovering. Boris still worked for Annabella on the weekends in exchange for fish and vegetables. His friend had also secured a job with a local blacksmith, making horseshoes. It was good work, and Zack was jealous, much better than the fishery or the construction camps.

Eli spoke next. "How did you learn to field-dress an animal so well?"

"My dad taught us," Zack replied. "Hunting is much more than just shooting the animal; he used to say." Zack looked down, momentarily overcome with emotion.

Annabella smiled softly. "He'll pull through, Zack. Pabbi is a strong man, tougher than you know."

Ivan nodded in agreement.

"I hope so," Zack said unconvincingly.

Zack finished his food and stood with his plate, helping to clear the dishes. They all came together as a family, cleaning up the kitchen and drinking beer. Annabella glared at Zack several times with a warning look conveying that he should not drink excessively with her kids present. He nodded and agreed silently, cradling the beer all night.

Once everyone had gone to bed, he stretched out on the sofa and stared across at the wood panel walls. He loved his sister and his parents so much. He loved his brother too, but he felt guilty. He had unforgettable sex with the woman who was in love with Adam. And Zack had cherished every single minute of it. There was something seriously wrong with that. He found it very difficult to let her go so his brother could have her.

Zack turned out the light, grabbed the blanket and laid down fully on the sofa. He felt his body sink into the couch and relaxed as the night encapsulated his thoughts. He moved his hand absentmindedly over his groin, and it tingled. His mind immediately jumped to images of Anita. Zack grunted and moved onto his side. He had to get that woman out of his head. She wasn't his.

The night sky and the smell of the grass filtered into his nostrils as a woman moaned underneath him. She writhed and clutched him in ecstasy as he released part of his semen inside of her. He felt the energy drain from his scrotum as he pulled out quickly and laid beside her, cuddling in the most wholesome way with the stars shining above their heads.

His eyes blinked open and stared at the blank ceiling.

Why couldn't he just forget about her? Why did his heart torture him over and over? They had only known each other for one night. He should know better.

He had to go to his dad's place today. Zack ran his fingers through his shoulder-length hair and sat up, pulling on his socks.

Annabella was already in the kitchen.

"Oh, you surprised me," Zack said. "Why are you up so early?"

"I was worried about Pabbi," she said.

"I am, too," Zack said.

"He will make it, right?" Annabella asked.

"All we can do is hope," Zack said, pulling his jacket onto his shoulders. "I have to go to dad's and help out today. It's my week to be with mom and dad. Momma said she has some shopping to do, and she doesn't want to leave him alone."

"Okay, Zack," Annabella said, moving swiftly across the room, hugging Zack warmly. "You go take care of dad." A tear escaped from her eye as she let him go.

"Thank you for dinner, Bella," he said, closing the door behind him.

He trudged through the grass fields towards the road. The sun was rising, and he loved the scent of the early morning dew. He didn't tell Annabella, but the reason he awoke early was so he could walk in the forest with his thoughts. He ventured east into the heavy forest and felt the calm come over him. He knew that one day he'd lose his father. He just didn't want it to be now. The trees swayed with the wind as the waves crashed along the shoreline.

The wind was stronger as he neared the lake. It blew in his face and whispered stories about the ghosts of his ancestors. So much went on here in this land that was once called New Iceland. There was so much strength and bravery, love and loss. He thought maybe one day that he could be as strong as his father. He felt weak some days, though, like he wasn't fit for human consumption. His crutch was alcohol, and he knew it made him a bad choice for everybody, his family, his friends and his lovers. He told himself that he would quit one day when he had a damn good reason.

He thought the reason had been Anita. But it was a lie, a fallacy. Anita was a story that had no happy ending. It had started with such beautiful imagery but had ended suddenly, like a bullet in the chest of the buck.

He had fallen just like the buck, too, dead in his tracks.

A gust of wind blew in his face, making him stoop his head down.

A realization dawned on him. He had somehow fallen in love with Anita.

It couldn't be, he told himself. He had only known her for one night. But that night would forever be burned in his memory. He couldn't let go because it was the best sex he had ever had.

Zack rubbed his hands along his face, starting from his forehead and then over his brow, pressing into his temples, trying to push the memory somehow away. Maybe she will come back to him? Perhaps she will realize that she loved Zack and not Adam.

He sat down on a large beach rock and watched the waves crash up on the beach, wondering why life had so many questions and so few answers. The waves pulled the sand from the beach and washed it away into the lake with every wave. His life was just like that, Zack thought. Every question was washed away into the water just as he thought he had the answer.

CHAPTER 9

Adam walked quickly out of his house. He had a bouquet of flowers in his hands. Adam was going to surprise her today. He walked to the 1937 Ford, opening the door and placed the flowers gently inside the vehicle. Adam slid into the driver's seat and slammed the door. The vehicle was Mike's, and he had borrowed it yesterday, saying hi to his brother briefly. Zack and Mike had gone hunting with the truck last weekend, and Adam had to wash the blood off the cab.

He wanted to impress Anita, and he had a plan formulating in his head. He hoped she would say yes. He pulled into her property, shifting down and then sliding it into neutral as he slammed on the brake. The truck took him a while to learn how to drive it. The small gas pedal was on the floor; beside it was the brake and clutch. It took considerable pressure on the brake to stop and strong arms to steer the vehicle. It was a dark green colour, and Mike had bought it new for the entire family to use. It was primarily used for transporting supplies and farming, but occasionally Mike had driven to Winnipeg with Annabella.

Adam had spent the entire evening washing the truck, and it looked impressive. It was a V-8 and was capable of considerable speed, even reaching 65 miles per hour. The three-speed manual was hard to learn, but everyone had eventually mastered it. There were not many vehicles on the roads in Gimli or on the highways, unlike Winnipeg, which had countless cars and trucks.

Adam pushed the emergency brake down with his foot and stepped out of the truck with the flowers in his arms. A small smile crept on his lips as he walked up to her door. He knocked and waited in anticipation.

He heard several soft footsteps creaking the floorboards, then the door opened, and Anita popped her head out, wearing a small knee-length nightgown.

Her hair was a mess, her eyes sleepy, and she was disorientated. "Adam?" she said, confused. "What is this?" She pointed to the flowers in his arms.

He smiled broadly. "I thought I would surprise you," he said, holding the flowers out for her. "I picked them near the cottage. The blue flowers have grown there forever. I don't know what they are called, but they look like a small lily. I picked them for you." He placed them in her arms. It was quite a large bunch of flowers, and some fell out of her grasp. Adam bent down and picked up the fallen flowers as he continued talking. "I just thought I would let you know how much you have brightened my life." He placed the errant lilies in her arms and saw her lips tremble.

He held onto her arms and looked into her eyes. They were moist with tears. "What's wrong, Anita?" he asked. "Did I do something wrong?"

"No," she replied, her voice breaking. "I have never met a man as sweet as you."

"Oh," Adam exclaimed. "Then that's a good thing!" He stepped into the house. "Let me help you put these flowers in some water."

He held her arm, and they walked into the kitchen together. Anita opened the tap and ran some water into a vase. Adam was pleased with the advent of indoor plumbing and water pumps in the Gimli houses. It was a huge improvement to the quality of life in Gimli. The Willow Point cottage that Adam and his brother lived in still didn't have running water. Pabbi was considering installing a water pump earlier this year. The brothers would have to do it themselves, and Adam was keenly interested in how the systems worked. He watched as she shut off the tap and the pump noise stopped. "How long have you had running water here?" he asked.

"Oh, just a few years ago," she replied. "My dad had installed the pump and the plumbing underneath."

"Pabbi and Mike have running water, too," he said proudly. "We will be installing a pump at our cottage soon. We were hoping this year, but Pabbi fell ill."

"I'm sorry about your dad," she replied, her eyes glowing with sincerity.

Adam leaned forward, placing his large hands on her cheeks and kissed her gently. She responded instantly, her arms circling around his waist. His tongue slipped into her mouth, and he felt her melt into his arms.

He broke the kiss. "I missed you," he said. "I know that sounds silly because I just walked home with you a few days ago. It seems like every time I see you, my heart glows."

She blinked demurely, her lashes fluttering. "I missed you too."

He felt the heat increasing between their bodies. Something pulled him into her warmth, he wasn't sure what it was, but

Adam needed to kiss her again. She opened her mouth easily. His tongue entered her warm mouth. His hands moved along her body, lingering on the sides of her breasts. Adam noticed her breathing rapidly increased, so he left his hands there. She squirmed in his arms, pushing her breasts into him. Adam moved his hands slightly lower and lightly danced his fingertips along her hips. She moaned.

He kissed her deeper. He couldn't control himself. Her responses compelled him to continue finding more spots to touch and kiss.

Anita ran her fingers in his hair as they kissed passionately in the kitchen. He walked them together to the countertop and leaned her against the wood cupboards so he could continue kissing her. Adam's hands wandered down to her buttocks and her legs, smoothing the thin nightgown against her bare skin. She arched her back and moaned.

He was quite astonished that she was responding so sensually towards him, then he realized she was naked underneath her gown. His hands slid over her buttocks, and he didn't feel any panties. He brought his hands up to the sides of her breasts again and noticed she was without a brassiere as well.

Now he understood.

She had just woken up and was nearly naked in his arms. His brain stopped working, and his hormones took over. His penis grew stiffly erect, and he lifted her onto the counter as they continued kissing urgently, her legs spreading around him.

"Yes," she groaned as he positioned his hips between her legs.

Adam felt utterly pulled into her scent, her smooth skin, then her sweet sex smell wafted up to his nostrils, and he lost all control. He lifted her gown up around her waist, dropped his pants and made love to her right there in the kitchen in the morning sunlight.

Zack pulled his father up in bed and helped him to stand. He circled his long arms under his father's armpits and pulled him to standing.

Nath leaned against his son, steadying himself.

"Are you ready?" Zack asked.

"Yes," Nath said softly. "I can make it. I've been feeling better today."

"Okay, let's take it one step at a time," Zack answered as he walked carefully with his dad into the living room, towards the sofa. The sunlight was beaming through the large picture windows facing the lake. "Not too far now. You're doing good, Pabbi!"

Nath focused on his feet, putting one foot in front of the other as they both walked across the dining area towards the front room. "Thank you, son," Nath said. "It's hard for me, you know, to be weak like this after so many years of being the strong, tough man."

"You still are the strong man, Pabbi," Zack said. "To me and everyone who knows us."

"I wish I could help you with the plumbing at the cottage," Nath said. "And the fishing, hunting, everything I used to do with you."

"Don't worry," Zack said. "Mike said he'd help us to get the well in the correct spot and set up the pump and plumbing. Besides, you worked hard all your life, and it's our turn now."

Nath felt tears well in his eyes. "You're a good son," he said softly.

They neared the sofa, and Zack gently grasped his armpits again, allowing Nath to use him as a crutch. His father gently lowered his frail body onto the sofa slowly and deliberately. Once Nath was positioned comfortably, Zack pulled an armchair over and sat with his father, watching the boats out on the lake.

"I miss being on a boat," Nath said reflectively.

"I know," Zack responded. "I miss being on a boat with you."

The sunlight shimmered off the lake, glinting against the boats. It was a beautiful summer afternoon, not too hot and not too windy. "One day, I won't be here anymore, Zack," Nath said. "Promise me that you will take care of your mother."

"Don't talk like that," Zack said. "I don't want to lose you."

"But it's inevitable," Nath said. "I am old. I will die. I can't live forever. I'm eighty years old. I'm lucky to have lived this long."

"I know," Zack said, at a loss for words.

"Promise me to take care of my beautiful Maria," Nath said.

"I'll take care of mom," Zack promised.

"Good," Nath said. "Now, let's watch the boats."

Mike pulled the truck into the short driveway with Zack in the front seat with him. "We have everything we need for the plumbing," Mike said as he parked the truck. "Hopefully, we are not missing anything for the well or the pump. It would be nice if Adam is home to help us."

"He should be," Zack answered. "I've been taking care of Pabbi all week, and I need to go back to work soon."

"We will take the water pump together since it's the heaviest item," Mike said, pulling the tail gate down. "Hold the heavier end, and we will haul this monster to the cottage. Too bad there's no driveway to the house. We need to fix that next year and get some dirt to fill in for a decent path for vehicles."

"Okay, I got it," Zack said as he lifted the heavier end. "Grab your end." Mike grabbed the other end as they grunted and wrestled the awkward water pump off of the truck. When they were steady enough, they walked the pump all the way onto the back deck, cursing at the heavy weight.

Finally, they let it go on the deck and rested. "I'm going to get a beer," Zack said.

"Please don't drink right now," Mike said. "I need you sober while we do this."

Zack nodded shamefully. "Okay, I'll get some water for both of us."

Zack entered the back door, jiggling the keys in the lock. "That's weird. Usually, we don't lock the back door. Adam must not be home."

Zack opened the door and heard something, a voice. It alarmed him at first; then, he realized it was his brother. He must still be sleeping and just woke up. Why did he lock the door then? It seemed strange. It wasn't like him. "Adam!" Zack shouted.

A bunch of muffled voices and rustling sounded in the back bedroom.

"Hey, Adam!" Zack shouted, stomping towards the cathedral ceiling main living area. "Mike is here. Get up! It's afternoon. We need your help with the new plumbing system. We're installing it today. Where are you?"

"Coming! Hold on!" Adam shouted back.

Another muffled voice sounded, a small whisper. Zack tilted his head. Was there someone else here?

Zack was getting angry, especially after lifting that heavy pump onto the deck, and his brother was still sleeping! He walked angrily into the large cathedral main room and stopped dead in his tracks.

Anita was standing behind Adam in a nightgown. Her hair was all messy, and she looked so damn beautiful, his jaw dropped. Zack's entire body reacted in shock; at first, he didn't know what he was seeing, then his love turned to anger. He looked at his brother in a jealous rage. Adam was just dressed in pyjama pants, obviously hastily thrown on.

"Hey, sorry," Adam said, looking down embarrassingly. "I didn't know we were doing this today." He wrapped his arm around Anita's shoulder and introduced her. "Oh, Zack, this is Anita. She is my future wife. Sorry, I didn't mean to introduce you this way."

Zack took a deep breath in. He wanted to smash his brother's face. He told himself that he couldn't. It wasn't his place. Then he looked at Anita, and she wouldn't look him in the eye. The hurt kicked him in the chest all over again. "Yes," Zack blurted out before he could think. "We already met before. Hi, Anita."

Adam frowned. "Where did you meet before?"

Anita finally looked up. "We met at a party a few weeks ago. I thought Zack was you." She laughed nervously. "But Zack explained that he was your twin brother, so we laughed and had a few drinks. I got a ride back home with my brother. Nothing special, just a weird night." She looked at Zack, her eyes burning into his, pleading with him not to tell.

Zack felt his entire head throb. He tried to think hard. She was obviously lying for a damn good reason. He didn't know what to say. He looked at his brother as he kissed Anita on the top of her head.

Adam smiled happily. "I love her," he said. "We're going to marry."

Zack's hands started to shake, and he knew that he should just let her go, but he still loved her. He didn't know what to do. All he knew was that at this moment, he needed to leave. Zack immediately pivoted on his foot and turned back towards the kitchen; he left abruptly, shouting behind him. "I'm happy for you both!" Zack sneered scornfully.

He slammed the back door hard.

Mike looked up, alarmed. "What's going on?"

"Nothing," Zack said. "Adam has a woman over. They're barely dressed. Let's just get to work and get this plumbing in. He can go fuck himself! I don't want his help."

CHAPTER 10

Zack looked into the fire, standing unsteadily. He had his arm around another girl tonight. She looked like Anita, Zack thought suddenly, then abandoned the thought as mind trickery. He was still unreasonably mad at Adam, and the worst thing was that his brother had no idea why. Zack didn't care. His emotions were raw and his heart broken. From this day on, he was going to start being selfish.

And he was going to start with this woman in his arms. Zack leaned his head towards her and kissed her hair.

She smiled and looked up at him dreamy-eyed.

He couldn't even remember her name.

He threw his empty beer in the bushes, grabbed her waist and pulled her towards the road. They both walked drunkenly to the car. Zack had left after installing the plumbing at the cottage. Adam had eventually come outside to help while Zack strained to keep his mouth shut. He wanted to yell at his brother and punch him for taking Anita from him. But his rational mind knew it was wrong. Anita had told him the minute she had found out that he wasn't Adam. She had been in love with Adam for some time. Zack was just a mistake.

He looked up to the sky, remembering the disturbing images of Anita and Adam barely clothed. He pulled out a cigarette and lit it, blowing the plume of smoke at the sky as if to say, who cares.

But Zack did care. That was the problem.

After the entire day of plumbing mishaps, they had the job nearly done. They still had to drill and hook up the drains, but all the piping and pumps were installed. Zack had said he would finish the job with Mike tomorrow. He didn't need his brother's help. Adam left confused in the evening. It was Adam's week to stay at Pabbi's house anyways.

After a long emotional day, Zack had ended up at Boris's backyard drinking beer all night. Boris's car was a solid 1930 Model A. The old vehicle was nothing like Mike's new truck, but it worked fine. Boris let Zack borrow the small car occasionally. It sat in the driveway, beckoning them as they stumbled their way around the house.

Zack stood unsteadily. He told himself that it was well past midnight and he should be going home, but all the jealousy and testosterone was still stinging throughout his body.

He stopped on the path, looking up at the stars and had a flashback of Anita naked on the ground with him. He threw his cigarette down, stamped it out and pulled the woman closer to him. He kissed her roughly. She responded immediately, wrapping her arms around his waist and kissing him back with passion. She was a good kisser, Zack thought.

"Come, let's go for a ride to my cottage," Zack said, pulling her arm towards the vehicle.

She giggled and followed, her blonde curls bobbing behind her.

Zack opened the car door and helped her in. As she sat down, the look in her eye caught his. She looked down demurely as if ashamed of the sexual thought that had just crossed her mind. Zack understood that look completely, and his penis hardened instantly. He kissed her strongly again. She responded immediately, kissing him with intensity. She turned her body to the opened door, and her legs splayed open. Zack didn't wait for any further invitation. They immediately began fumbling with each other's clothes. She reached for his pants and found his zipper, struggling with it. Zack took control and unzipped his pants as she pulled them down his hips. Zack kissed her passionately as he fumbled with her dress until he found her panties. Zack pulled them to the side and positioned his penis at her entrance. He towered over her, still half-standing, then leaned over her, ducking his head into the Model A. He felt his penis slide into her wetness and groaned at the luscious sensation. Zack panted on her shoulder for a few seconds, then lost all control and started pumping into her like a starved animal. She groaned beneath him, totally consumed by his male energy.

"You're so beautiful, honey," Zack murmured as she squirmed with passion beneath him. He could feel her vagina begin to grip him. Zack felt his control slip away, and he pulled out suddenly as she cried out for more. He ejaculated in a sloppy mess all over her legs and the car seat.

"Sorry," Zack moaned. "It's been a long night. Let me take you to my place, and we can do this right." He kissed her, zippered up his pants and walked around the vehicle to the driver's side.

He lit a cigarette and started the car, adjusting the idle and spark. He released the clutch and pushed the gas. The car moved, chugging along down the dirt road. Zack's eyesight felt funny like it was somehow blurred. He blinked and inhaled the smoke from his cigarette. "We'll be home in no time," he said. "Motor vehicles are the best invention since home plumbing."

Zack glanced over at her. She was smiling, but her eyes were glazed over from the sexual surge of hormones and alcohol. He grinned. Well, at least, they both had too much to drink, and they were both satisfied, Zack thought. He looked down at his lap just as the end of his cigarette fell onto his pants. Zack jumped and yelled, swatting at the burning red ball.

Suddenly, the girl was yelling something.

"Watch out!" she yelled hysterically.

Zack looked up, but it was too late to react.

The car slammed into the tree and threw both of them forward. They weren't going very fast, but the impact still hurt. The girl had a bloody spot on her forehead, but she seemed to be alright. "Oh my God! Are you okay?" Zack asked.

"Yes," she giggled nervously. "I'm okay."

"We can walk the rest of the way," Zack said, turning off the vehicle and hopping out, opening her door. They spilled out of the Model A and wandered onto the road stumbling in each other's arms.

It seemed they had walked for a long time before they reached the cottage. The lights were out, and everything was dark. Zack opened the back door. It was open this time. They tripped and fell into the cottage, laughing hysterically. She began kissing him again, the cold kitchen floor against his back. She unzipped his pants quickly and started sucking on his penis, a bit too roughly.

"Hey, let's go to my bed, beautiful," Zack said, pulling her up and stumbling through the house with her. They crashed into some chairs, then fell on the bed laughing as she tore at his shirt and pulled his pants off. He gripped her blouse and pulled it over her head as her tiny breasts popped out. She immediately climbed on top of him and started grinding her hips onto him. Zack kissed her forehead as she guided his penis into her. He felt himself sliding into her wetness as she rocked fully on top of him. She created a rhythm with her body, grinding into him. Zack grabbed her waist and pushed his hips upwards, deepening her thrusts.

Her breasts dangled in his face as her sweaty body ground above him. Zack strained to catch a nipple in his mouth. He missed multiple times but finally managed to suck on one nipple momentarily. Zack tried thrusting deeper, but the position wasn't working for him. His penis softened slightly, and he wasn't sure why.

Zack asserted control and shifted her off of him. He grasped his large hands onto her waist, turning her away from him. Zack pulled her hips backwards, lifting her lithe body onto her hands and knees. She laughed as he manhandled her. He kissed her back and slid his hands along her smooth skin, delighting in her curvy figure. Zack smoothed his hands over her luscious buttocks and couldn't control himself any longer. He crouched behind her and slid his penis into her vagina, pumping into her as her buttocks jiggled with every push.

Her sweet buttocks beckoned him to push harder.

"Say my name!" she cried.

"Hon," he said. "You're so pretty."

He grasped her butt cheeks, squeezing them roughly and immersed his entire penis into her deeply. She yelped.

"Sorry," he said and pulled back.

He slid gently into her as her backside jiggled yet again. He became hypnotized by her buttocks. He didn't know if it was because he was drunk or his testosterone was having fun with him. He felt his imminent orgasm grip his mind with ridiculous thoughts of releasing deep inside her. His animal instinct took over, and he immersed his penis fully inside of her again and held it there. He inhaled sharply and couldn't stop himself. He released a full load of his seed inside her deeply, groaning like an animal.

"Ahh," she groaned as if heaven had just happened inside of her.

He collapsed onto her panting as they splayed onto the bed. He kissed her neck and her cheek lovingly. "You're so beautiful," he said drunkenly.

"You're so handsome, Zack," she slurred sexily.

Zack slid off of her and pulled her small body into his, cuddling her warmly in a spoon position. "You feel so good, sweetheart, thank you," Zack said, his words slurring. He felt his arms and legs weaken as he enveloped her entire body into his, hugging her warmly.

She murmured something incomprehensible then they both fell asleep into a deep drunken slumber.

The morning rays filtered through the living room and awoke him. He moved his arms and felt the cold bed beside him and a pillow. His cloudy mind recalled the events of the previous night in strange fragmented pieces as if it was a movie and some scenes were missing. Then he heard her in the back, the out-house door slamming shut. Her footsteps gently padded back onto the deck and into the house. He watched as she entered the bedroom, removed his oversized coat and climbed back into bed naked.

He cuddled his arms around her, pulling her into his warm skin. She squirmed and turned her head towards him.

"You never said my name," she said accusingly. "Not once. I like hearing my name when you are close."

Zack swallowed hard. He searched his memory and couldn't recall her name. He felt foolish and stupid. "I didn't know that was what you liked," Zack said, trying to avoid a confrontation.

"I asked you to say my name," she said.

"I know," Zack said. "I'm sorry."

The morning air was cool in the cottage, and she turned away silently.

Zack crossed his fingers and made a mental note to find out her name as soon as possible. How could he forget such a simple thing? Hopefully, she lets it go, he thought.

"You don't even remember my name, do you?" she accused.

Zack was silent. He didn't know what to say. Admitting such a travesty was paramount to committing relationship suicide.

She sat up.

"Please," Zack said. "Just let it go. Fall back asleep with me. We can discuss it when we are both wide awake."

"Say my name," she demanded. "Then I'll go back to sleep."

Zack exhaled, not knowing what to say. He thought it had started with a J sound. "Joanne?"

She jumped up as if stung by a scorpion and threw the first thing she was able to get her hands on. Zack's belt flew across the bed. He ducked as the leather strap hit his arm.

"You had sex with me and didn't even know my name!" she screamed. "My name is Grace! That's my name!" She grabbed her blouse hastily and threw it over her head, pulling it down. She pulled her skirt on angrily and stood. "Not that it matters now. I'm leaving!"

"No, don't leave," Zack said guiltily. "I'm sorry. I was drunk. I want you to stay."

She looked back at him as if momentarily deciding if she should stay, then turned on her heel and stormed out, slamming the door behind her.

Zack rubbed his face and buried his bearded chin in the pillow. Why do women always leave him the morning after? Why can't he keep a woman for longer than one night? He groaned and curled into a ball, chastising himself for being a stupid man.

Boris stomped up the deck and knocked angrily on the front door. "Get up!" he yelled through the entrance. "Or I will kick this door down!" He banged his knuckles violently on the wood, like a hammer smashing through the door. "Get up, Zack!"

Zack jumped out of bed in alarm, wondering what else he had done wrong. He pulled his pyjama bottoms on and ran for the door, yanking it open. Before he could think, Boris struck out with a sucker punch, his fist connecting with Zack's nose. Zack cried out as the sickening crunch of his nose breaking reverberated through his skull. He fell to the floor like a dead weight.

Zack awoke a few seconds later with the room spinning. "What did I do?" Zack yelled from his stuffed bloody nose.

"You smashed up my car, you imbecile!" Boris yelled angrily. "I found it wrapped around a tree. You had taken it out last night with that girl." He pounced on Zack and lifted his fist again.

"Stop!" Zack screamed. "I'll fix it! I'll fix the car!" Zack's memory played back portions of the night, the cigarette and the tree, but he couldn't explain how he had arrived at the cottage. "I am good with cars. I'll fix it brand new, Boris. I'm sorry!"

Boris lowered his fist and stood up. "Get up, Zack. You're a mess." He held out his hand and pulled Zack up. "Go wash up and get dressed. You have a lot of work to get started. My car is damaged badly."

Zack rose up to standing, feeling slightly nauseous. "Okay, Okay," he said. "Let me get a coffee." He pulled his shirt on and shuffled into the kitchen to find where he had put the coffee. Zack shook his head and wiped his bloody nose on a towel. He looked at the blood smeared on the cloth.

He needed to quit drinking.

CHAPTER 11

Zack wiped the grease on his pants and looked up across the dusty farm field. A trickle of sweat streamed down his face, balancing on the end of his crooked nose. It had been two months. Zack was almost finished the repairs to Boris's Model A. He had banged out the dents and replaced the radiator with a used one from a local mechanic shop. He had also fabricated a new wheel well of metal and attached it to the vehicle surprisingly well. All it needed was some paint. Zack would figure out a way to do this next step. He wiped his brow and cursed himself once again for the single night of debauchery that had resulted in two months of work. Although, it all did have a positive side. He was getting hired by the local mechanic, Bob, to fix boat engines. He was so impressed by Zack's skill and dedication that he was to start the following Monday.

But Zack was still unhappy. He lost the girl. He lost trust from his friends, and he proved to himself that he should not drink anymore.

He had only drunk once or twice a week since that one night, but each time he questioned his limits and was wary of losing control again. Boris was still mad at him, but they had reconciled tentatively.

Zack looked up as a distant motor rumbled from the highway. He squinted and couldn't see who it was.

The sun was bright and low in the unusually hot autumn afternoon. He recognized that motor. It was the common sound of a powerful V8. Zack walked closer to the front lawn of Boris's house. The Model A had been parked in the field beside his friend's house. It was towed there two months ago and had not moved until just yesterday when he had finally got the car working. Zack had driven it to the driveway and was ecstatic that he had managed to fix the radiator satisfactorily.

The noise grew closer and closer until Zack saw the dark green Fork Truck that he loved so much. It was Mike! He was happy to see him. It had been a while since they had talked. He walked towards the road but was astonished to see his mother, Maria, in the passenger seat. She didn't look happy.

What could possibly cause his mother to visit him at Boris's? Zack instantly worried that something bad had happened to Pabbi but quickly abolished the thought because his mom looked angry. The hair stood up on the back of his neck. He didn't like it when his mother was mad. The rare times she was angry with him, it was always for a very good reason. His stomach recoiled as he walked up to the truck. The wheels stopped, and Mike jumped out.

"Mike!" Zack yelled happily. "I haven't seen you for a while."

"I've been busy working," Mike replied. "Umm, Zack, your mom needs to speak to you immediately."

"What's wrong?" Zack said, his hair completely standing up on end and a shiver spreading down his spine. He had a premonition that he would remember this day for the rest of his life.

Maria stepped gracefully out of the truck with a scowl on her face. "I am not happy with you, Zachary Olason!"

Zack stayed silent. He knew better than to speak when his mom was angry.

She walked over to him and stood dangerously close to him. "Remember that one night of fun you had?" she said, her eyes flashing angrily. "I hope you remember it for a very long time!"

"What now?" Zack said pleadingly.

"Don't you what now me!" she yelled. She took two calming breaths, then spilled out her anger. "A woman came to my door this afternoon. Her daughter, Grace, has been sent to the nunnery. She is pregnant, Zack!" Maria inhaled sharply. "They said the child is yours."

Zack's knees felt weak and wobbly. He leaned his hand against the truck to steady himself.

She continued on. "I told Grace's mother that if you are the father, I will adopt my grandchild and raise the baby with your help."

Zack's jaw dropped. He was going to be a father? How could this be? One night and oh, yes, now he remembered. The image of Grace's buttocks came into his mind, and he looked down, ashamed. He ran his hands through his hair in distress.

Maria caught the guilty look on Zack's face. "So, it's true!" she said. "You are the father! You know this Grace woman?"

"Yes," Zack said quietly. "I know Grace." He looked up at his angry mother. "I am, most likely the father." His voice cracked, and he swallowed hard.

"Well, then," Maria said, her voice growing calm. "You will be learning how to be a parent soon." She walked away resignedly towards the truck passenger door while Mike held it open for her. "Maybe this is a good time to stop drinking, Zack."

She slammed the door and looked away as Mike walked around the front of the truck, passing by Zack. He whispered in Zack's ear, "You messed up good this time. I'll be here for you if you need me."

Zack watched Mike return to the driver's seat, waving nimbly, then pull out of the driveway, the V8 engine roaring onto the highway. Zack wasn't aware how long he had been standing there, but when he had finally stopped staring into the distance, it was sunset.

Today felt like a turning point. Zack could still hear his mother's words echo in his head. One night of fun that he would remember for a very long time.

And he still loved his brother's future wife.

PART THREE

WARS

1939-1940

CHAPTER 12

Zack tried to keep his back straight while rocking his baby to sleep. The rocking chair creaked rhythmically as his daughter, Josie, quieted in his arms. She was two months old. Momma said she was a good baby. Zack thought she cried a lot, but he had never had a baby before, so he honestly didn't know. He fell in love with her the first day he met her. The mother, Grace, was furious with Zack and rightly so. She blamed him for her eight months of captivity at the nunnery. He was sad that she hated him. He would have married her if she wasn't so volatile towards him.

Nath snored quietly as he turned over in his bed. Zack looked up, examining his father's face worriedly. He looked fine. Lately, Nath had been improving, and Zack was thrilled with this. He speculated whether having a baby in the house had strengthened Nath's will to live.

He smiled down at the sleeping baby in his lap. Josie was a gift from heaven, Zack thought. Even though her arrival was strewn with conflict, she had single-handedly improved everyone's life. Zack had stopped drinking entirely and worked at the mechanic shop fixing boat engines full-time now. He worked on several fishing tugs fixing the steam engines and even some newer diesel engines. Zack had quickly become a valuable boat mechanic. He had developed an uncanny aptitude for fixing mechanical problems. He loved boats and fishing, so he was becoming happily content with his lot in life.

He was trying his best to be a good father and a better person. He worked hard and spent his evenings with his daughter. He hadn't fallen in love with another woman, although it seemed the love he felt for his daughter filled that gap easily. Zack looked out of the window gazing at the lake's whitecaps. It was early July. The clouds were raining down hard today, and it made him feel like the skies were crying for all of his lost loves. He wondered if he still loved Anita. At his deepest moments, he acknowledged that he harboured many feelings for her. But they were family now. Anita and Adam had a surprise early pregnancy, delivering the baby in April 1939. In his gut, he wondered if Anita had ever told Adam that she had the best sex ever with Zack. He concluded that she had not; Anita had most likely continued burying the secret since there was no reason to upset her happy marriage. Zack cared for her enough to set her free in his heart. After all, Anita was now his sister-in-law. She was part of the family as well as their new baby boy, Bjorn. He loved his nephew. Zack saw Bjorn only a few times; he was only one month older than Josie.

Zack pondered the dates, and something didn't quite add up, but he soon lost track of the thought once his mom arrived home. He heard the front door click close, and several paper grocery bags set down. Zack stopped rocking and gently stood, trying not to disturb the baby. He swayed with her in his arms to the lace-covered bassinet and placed her gently inside. She grunted sweetly, and half smiled in her sleep.

Zack grinned broadly, love spilling out of his heart to this sweet little girl.

"Zack," Maria whispered. "Come help me with groceries. I picked up many new fruits and vegetables from Annabella's farm."

Zack turned his head and straightened, pushing his fingers to his lips. "Shh," he whispered. "She just got to sleep."

"Okay," she lowered her voice to a quiet whisper. "Come help me. I need help."

Zack nodded and left the baby's room, and walked into the kitchen. "Wow, you bought a lot of food!"

"Annabella had leftover carrots from the last year's season," Maria said. "She also gave us some new strawberries. They're small but sweet and delicious. The rest of the grains and stuff I had to buy at the grocery. There are more bags in the car."

Zack sauntered out towards the repaired Model A that he had purchased for his mom. He had bought it as a wreck, and since learning from fixing Boris's car, he knew that he had the skills to reassemble the Model A's. Zack purchased parts from the wreckers and fixed everything, even tinkering with the engine until it ran smoothly. He even painted it the same dark green colour as Mike's truck. His mom was thrilled when he gave it to her. She had been surprised and elated, asking what she did to deserve such a gift. He had told her that she was the best mom ever and had rescued his daughter from an orphanage. It was the least he could do. They had hugged and reconciled. It seemed his baby girl was knitting the entire family back together, just by being born.

Zack grabbed the remaining bags from the trunk and prepared to slam it shut. The trunk never seemed to close properly without being slammed, which perturbed him greatly. He bent down for the millionth time and checked the hinges, shaking his head at the problem. It wasn't the time to fix the trunk, but the issue tugged at him as if he had somehow missed something.

He liked mechanics because he could solve problems. Zack could fix almost anything now, although he was much better at motors than body parts. He scowled at the stubborn trunk and slammed it, the issue still nagging at him.

Zack walked into the house with the bags of food. "Mom," he said happily. "Here's the last of the groceries."

"Zack!" A voice hollered through the back door of the mechanic shop. Zack looked up and was happy to see it was Mike. He had grown quite close to Mike, and they often ate lunch together. The mechanic shop was right beside the fishery warehouse. The main work was the fishing boats since almost all of them were now motorized. There were still the old sailboats, but they were mostly used as pleasure crafts. The fishing boats were all steam or diesel engines. The mechanic shop was busy.

"I need help with one of our boats," Mike said, walking in confidently with his youngest daughter, Nina. She was a beautiful girl, but she was always interested in male things, no matter how much her mother Vira tried instilling her with feminine pursuits. Nina insisted on following her dad to the fishery every day during the summer. Mike had his arm around her shoulders as they walked into the back of the shop.

Her eyes brightened as she saw the partially disassembled engine on the iron work table. "Is that the new diesel engine?"

Zack chuckled. She was always inquisitive about such things. "Yes, it is!" he replied passionately. "I prefer to work on the diesel engines rather than the old steam engines. They are better built, in so many ways."

Her eyes glittered as Zack showed her details of the diesel engine. Even Mike showed interest, and they all huddled around the engine block, inspecting all the components.

Mike laughed, "Nina seems to have a keen interest in mechanics."

"Well, maybe one day, I can show her how to fix these engines," Zack said, smiling.

"Would you really do that?" she asked, her youthful teen-age energy making her feet skip from one side to the other.

"As long as your dad is okay with it!" he replied happily.

Mike smiled. "I guess it couldn't hurt anything. Just don't tell your mother. She has dreams of you becoming a seamstress or a midwife."

"Never!" Nina shrieked.

"I know, I know," Mike replied gleefully. "Oh yeah, that reminds me, Zack. A girl came into the fishery this morning looking for you. She asked for Zachary Olason like it was a formal thing or something. She had said her family was vacationing in Gimli for the summer, and you had invited her to find you. She said that she knew you from the Regina Riot."

Zack stood straight up in shock, almost banging his head on the overhead rack. "Was her name Megis?"

"Yes!" Mike replied. "That was her name! A very unusual but pretty name."

"Oh my Lord!" Zack exclaimed. "I thought I'd never hear from her again. Her father and their family had rescued me from the aftermath of the Riot. Megis had nursed and fed me before instructing me to flee the city. That little girl had saved me from prison."

"Umm," Mike said. "She's no longer a little girl, Zack." Mike looked at his daughter and nodded his head towards the large bay door, urging Zack to join him in a private discussion.

Zack was confused. He followed Mike to the door while Nina was completely absorbed in the engine parts.

"What is it?" Zack asked.

"Megis is a beautiful sweet girl," Mike said quietly. "I told her that you work next door. She said that she'd be stopping by after lunch. She seemed very interested in finding you."

"Oh?" Zack said.

"Well, you'll be meeting her soon," Mike said. "I suggest you clean up a bit. You're a dirty, greasy mess!"

Zack washed his face in the bathroom and looked in the mirror. He was getting older, and his beard was full now. His blonde hair was longer than socially acceptable, but Zack didn't care. He liked it long. His body was in great shape at the age of twenty-one. Zack was stronger now than ever before. He pulled his dirty coveralls off and realized in dismay that he was wearing an old pair of trousers and a ripped shirt underneath. Oh, well, she'll have to like him for who he is, Zack thought.

He left the washroom and cleaned up his workspace a bit, putting away tools and busying himself. Zack looked at his hands and cursed. He was just getting himself all greasy again.

The front shop door chimed. The office was bleak and unimpressive. It was nothing more than just a bench and an old rusty desk with motor parts on it. Zack cringed. He looked up, caught a glimpse of her wavy black hair, and instantly felt butterflies swarm in his stomach. It was strange how someone from the past can illicit such a response. She was just a small girl when he last saw her. He hadn't thought anything back then. He braced himself for the shock of seeing her grown up.

"Hello?" Megis called out, her smooth feminine voice echoing into the shop.

Zack wiped his dirty hands on his pants and stepped out of the back.

Megis was beautiful but not in the normal sense of pretty. Her black wavy hair rested at the apex of her shoulders and bounced when she turned around. She was a very sweet girl with a kind demeanour that seemed to emanate from her. She was a little taller than he had last remembered, but not by much. At over six feet, Zack towered over her. Megis had a petite body with slim arms and legs; he estimated she was not even five feet tall. Her face was oval with lightly tanned skin. But it was her large brown eyes that hit him like a hammer. They were the most beautiful eyes he had ever seen. They bore right through him like she somehow knew his inner passions. Well, it was true that she knew him from a long time ago when he was only seventeen, Zack thought.

He smiled nervously. "Hi, Megis," Zack said. "It's been such a long time! The last time I saw you, you were so much younger."

She laughed softly, her voice sending shivers through his skin. "Everyone thought that," Megis said, her voice calming and inviting. "I always looked younger than I was."

Zack smiled. "Let me guess," he said. "You're nineteen now?"

She laughed heartily. "How did you guess?" Megis replied, her dimples creasing on her cheeks.

"Just stupid luck," Zack said, chuckling. "So, you were fifteen when we first met in Regina?" He struggled to maintain his composure as her dimples and eyes mesmerized him.

"Yes!" she said happily. "Many people had always mistaken me for ten years old back then. It's hilarious."

"Well, you don't look ten years old now," Zack said. "You are very beautiful."

Megis blushed unexpectedly. "Thank you," she said bashfully.

Zack wanted to grab her and kiss her right now, but he constrained himself. He would just scare her away, he thought, chuckling to himself. Zack smiled and tried to pull himself out of his funk. "What are you doing in Gimli?" he asked curiously. "Did your family finally come out here for vacation?"

"Yes!" she replied, delighted to change the subject. "We have been here for a few days. We rented a cottage out on Willow Island for two weeks."

"Willow Island?" Zack said, surprised. "That's where I live. My family still calls it Willow Point. It was renamed to Willow Island many years ago. My dad was one of the original settlers at Willow Point."

"Really?" she replied. "That's so interesting! What country did he come from?"

"Iceland," he replied.

"Oh my!" she exclaimed. "That's a far journey!"

"It was, believe me," Zack said, chuckling. "We have heard the stories over and over again since we were born."

"I'd like to hear those stories one day," Megis said sweetly.

"I would love to tell you," Zack said softly. "Maybe you can come over for a coffee around the fire. Willow Island is a very small community. I am most likely one of your neighbours."

"I would love that," she replied. "If you have a piece of paper, I can write down where we are staying."

Zack rustled through the desk, spurred by a rush of adrenaline. He must find a piece of paper! "Hold on," he said, disappearing in the back. "I'll get something to write on." He ripped a flap off a cardboard box and returned with a lead pencil in hand. "I found something!" He smiled broadly as if he had just won a prize.

Megis laughed sweetly. Her laugh was infectious, and Zack found that he couldn't stop grinning. She grabbed the pencil and scrawled out the address in pretty cursive writing with hoops and swirls.

"There!" she said proudly.

"I love your writing," Zack said. "How long did you go to school for?"

She stood proudly, her shoulders back and her small breasts pushed out towards him. "I finished grade nine!" she replied proudly. "I did the best in English class, even though my first language was an Ojibwa dialect."

"You are native?" Zack asked wondrously.

"Yes, partially," she replied. "My biological mother was Plains Cree, and my father was a British soldier. I am adopted."

"Oh my!" he replied. "We have so much to talk about!" Zack smiled, placing his large hand on her arm happily. "My half-sister is part Cree as well!"

"You are joking!"

"No, I am telling you the truth," he responded. "My dad fell in love with a beautiful Swampy Cree woman named Anwa when he landed here back in 1875."

"Swampy Cree!" Megis shrieked, her hand covering her mouth in shock. "The entire village of Swampy Cree's had perished during the smallpox epidemic!"

"Yes," Zack said, astonished. "You know the local history!" He glanced down in respect. "Unfortunately, she passed away soon after my half-sister was born."

"That's terrible," she said solemnly. "I'm so sorry, and yes, I studied history."

"I never met her," Zack said. "Although my dad talked about her a lot and taught us some of the ways of the natives. I'm impressed at your knowledge."

"Oh my," Megis exclaimed. "That's so amazing. Thank you. What did you learn about the native way of living?"

"Mostly hunting and fishing," he said. "And to never give up on true love."

"Oh?" Megis said, her eyes lowering demurely.

"Yes," Zack said. "My dad never remarried for a very long time. Then he met my mother out of the blue at a post office!" Zack chuckled. "He said it was love at first sight. They've been together ever since."

"That's so beautiful," she said softly.

A few moments of awkward silence filled the room as Zack pondered what to say next. He wondered if he could see her tonight. He was anxious to continue this conversation with this intelligent, pretty woman. Zack feared if he pushed to meet with her tonight that it would be construed as too eager. What should he say?

She smiled and seemed to sense his turmoil. "Can you stop by tonight at around ten o'clock to pick me up?" Megis smiled, then instantly realized that she had just blurted out an invitation. Megis blushed and looked down, trying to hide her embarrassment. "Umm, sorry. It's just that my parents are very controlling and they usually get rather sleepy by ten o'clock. It's the only time I can sneak out without having to give them lengthy explanations." She chuckled sweetly.

Zack's eyes creased with joy as his face broke out in a happy grin. "I will most definitely be there at ten o'clock tonight! Don't be sorry. I would love to spend the night talking to you."

"Okay," she said, smiling back. "Well then, I guess I will see you tonight." She placed her hand on the door knob and turned to go.

"Wait," Zack said.

"I have to go," she replied sadly. "My parents will be back from the market soon."

"I just wanted to ask if I could give you a hug," he asked. "It has been a long while since I saw you last."

"Yes," she said. "It has. I would like that."

Zack rushed over and wrapped his large arms around her, almost engulfing her petite body entirely. She nuzzled her jaw into his chest, smelling his manly scent. Megis felt strangely safe and content in his arms, almost like she was coming home finally. This confused her because she had never lived in Gimli before, although it felt so incredible being in his arms. She murmured something unintelligible.

Zack pulled away and released her. "Go to your parents," he said. "They must be waiting."

Megis nodded. Thankfully, he hadn't heard what she had said. Megis was disturbed that she had just blurted out her feelings. She didn't know Zachary Olason that well, but for some reason, it seemed her heart thought otherwise. "Yes," Megis said. "It was so nice seeing you again, Zachary. We can continue our conversation tonight. I am looking forward to it."

"Yes," Zack said, opening the door for her. "So am I."

"Until then," Megis replied, walking away slowly, waving behind her.

She mused quietly to herself as she walked faster to meet her parents at the car. She had murmured to Zachary Olason that she had been waiting a long time for him. It both shocked her heart and made it sing at the same time.

Zack had cleaned himself in the new bathroom, trimming his beard and changed into clean trousers and a white shirt. He smiled at himself in the mirror. He looked good. Zack brushed his teeth and gargled to get his mouth smelling fresh. At the door, he dropped a deer bone for the dog. Pepper was a stray dog that Zack had found curled up on his back deck a few days ago. He was skinny, and at first, Zack had feared that the dog was vicious or rabid. Zack had ignored the animal at first, but then after dinner one day, he had placed his leftovers on a plate and left it outside. He heard the dog quickly chomp the meal down within minutes.

The dog didn't leave, always sleeping at the door. Zack started feeding him leftovers every night. He called him Pepper because of the dog's coat. It was black and white, sort of like an older man's beard. Maybe he would train him as a hunting dog, Zack thought.

"I'll be back, Pepper," Zack said. "Protect the fort." He stepped off the deck and walked on the grass into the bush. He knew precisely where Megis was staying. He didn't even need the address. He knew Willow Island better than anyone. She was staying at Iva and Norman's cottage. They were two elderly settlers that had moved to Winnipeg. Their cottage was almost always rented to vacationers.

Zack inhaled the crisp night air. It was an unusually cool summer night. It had been raining for a few days, which had cooled everything off. He stepped into the dark forest, his feet squishing onto the moist ground. Sometimes, Willow Island became so humid that swampy areas would collect water. The ground table rose threateningly in certain years of heavy snow melt and summer rains. This year was a normal year, and he felt grateful. There was always the threat of flooding, and nobody wanted that. Nice weather meant more tourists and more dollars spent in the local economy.

Zack felt the darkness close in around him as the sunset fell below the horizon. It was a comforting feeling. The forest was his friend. He had learned from his past here, searched for answers and sought solitude here. Zack skipped over a downed tree expertly and swiped a branch out of the way. He knew his way distinctly, even in the darkness.

He peered through the trees and saw the cottage in the distance. He quickened his step with his heart hopeful. He liked Megis. She was sweet, kind and pretty. He enjoyed talking to her immensely. She was engaging and interesting, unlike many other people.

After several minutes, he arrived at the cottage. Zack stepped onto the front step quietly and heard a rustle. He paused cautiously and listened. Wolves were still a problem in the area, so he had to remain vigilant. But it wasn't a wolf. He could tell by the movements. It was a human.

"Zack," she whispered from the bushes. "Don't go onto the deck. I'm here."

Zack removed his foot from the step and ventured towards the bushes. Within seconds, he could see Megis, her lithe female body standing at the edge of the bushes.

"Don't wake my parents," she said. "Let's just go to your place for that coffee and a fire."

"Okay," Zack replied, lowering his voice to a whisper. "This way." He grabbed her hand and led her out into the forest. "Watch your step, and don't let go of my hand."

She followed, gripping his hand as they meandered through the bushes and trees. "Have you always lived on Willow Island?" Megis asked.

"Not always," he answered. "My father, Nath, had built a grand house near the fishery for us all. We lived there as a family for my entire childhood. Two years ago, I moved out here with my brother. The family always owned the cottage out here. They built it back in 1917, and it still stands strong."

"Is your brother younger than you?" she asked.

Zack laughed. "We are identical twins," he said. "My momma said that I was born first, so technically, I'm older."

"Oh my!" she exclaimed, laughing. "You are identical twins!"

"Yeah," he said. "Most people can tell us apart now. My brother Adam wears his hair short, and I like my hair long."

"I think it looks good on you," she said absentmindedly.

"Thank you," Zack said thoughtfully. Her hand was warm in his palm. It felt good to touch her. "We are here. It's too dark to see, but that is the main lakeside cottage that my parents built in 1917 and deeper in the bush over there is the guest cabin. That was the original cabin that my dad lived in when he first arrived here in Canada. Mike says it has Anwa's ghost in it. I have never felt anything, but he has always maintained that he senses something in there."

Her brown eyes widened as she strained to look into the bushes.

"I will show you in the morning if you like," he offered.

"I would like that," Megis said.

Zack brought her to the firepit on the beach.

She widened her eyes and spread her arms out. "Oh my Lord," Megis exclaimed. "This is beautiful. Do you know how beautiful this is? Look at the stars!" She pointed in the sky as if it was a miracle.

Zack chuckled. "Yes," he agreed. "The stars are beautiful. I used to stare at them at night wondering what my life meant."

"The stars are so clear here!" Megis said, looking around with her head reached up to the sky. "Can we just look at the stars for a while before starting the fire?"

"Okay, let me just get a blanket, so we don't get sand in our hair," he said.

"I don't mind sand in my hair," she giggled.

Zack laughed, "Okay." He pulled her gently down to the sand, and they both stretched out, their hands clasped together. The stars twinkled and shined brightly. There was no moon tonight, so the blackness contrasted brilliantly with the bright stars. There were so many stars that it seemed an infinite number, something nobody could ever count. Zack pointed to a brighter star closer along the horizon. "My mother says that star is another planet. Maybe Venus."

"That one?" Megis said, pointing into the night.

"Yes," he said. Zack pointed to another group of stars directly above them. "I think somewhere in those group of stars is the Big Dipper. It looks like a big scoop."

"Oh!" she exclaimed. "I see it!"

Zack laughed and squeezed her hand. "I really enjoy spending time with you," he said. Zack was just thinking that; did he really say it?

"I enjoy spending time with you too, Zack," she said. "It feels so comfortable."

"I thought the same thing," he said. Zack leaned up on one elbow and curled towards her on his side. "Do you ever look at the stars and wonder why you are here? We are so small when compared to the wondrous sky. What is our purpose here?"

"I think of that all the time," Megis replied. "I wonder if we all have predetermined paths or it's all just random occurrences. I'd like to think we all mean something to this universe."

"I hope so too," Zack responded. He laid back down and stared up at the stars in silence with her. With their hands still joined, they examined the stars, letting the beautiful display fill their hearts with possibilities and impossible questions.

"Look!" she squealed, pointing to the east. A shooting star streaked the star-dusted sky in the distance.

"I saw it!" Zack exclaimed, laughing. "We both saw it!"

"You're special, Zack," she said abruptly. Megis never could control what her mind thought and what she said. She chastised herself for speaking too soon.

"Thank you," Zack replied. "I think you're special too. I have never met a woman quite like you."

She smiled and propped her elbow up, looking at him with her brown eyes glimmering darkly in the night. Zack propped his elbow up and met her halfway. His hand fluttered to her chin as he held her like this, suspended in time. Finally, he said, "May I kiss you?"

"Yes," she responded, her voice fluttering.

Zack leaned in closer and then closed his eyes, kissing her soft lips. His body shivered instantly from the electric currents of her sensuality connecting with his. He kissed her mouth again, softly, lingering with the tip of his lips.

It felt so right like he was finally doing something that was the most endearing thing he had ever done. It was like all the stars above them had aligned for this moment, his lips on hers and her body against his. He felt light-headed and giddy, his heart opening up like a flower closed for so many years. Zack was ecstatic and joyful at the same time. He thought Megis was such a wonderful, kind and intelligent person. She was better than any woman he had ever met before.

He pecked her lips and pulled away, looking into her eyes. "I've never met a woman like you before," Zack said. "You care about people."

She smiled and leaned forward, kissing his lips gently. "Thank you," Megis said. "I cared about you ever since I saw you wandering in the Market Square."

"You did," he confirmed. The silence filled the darkness between them for several moments, and they felt comfortable with it. Zack wrapped his arms around her, pulling her into his embrace. He kissed her forehead and snuggled closer, her small body disappearing in his warmth. "You smell good," he said.

"So do you," Megis replied, murmuring into his shirt.

"I want to take you fishing someday," Zack said aimlessly. "Can I take you fishing?" Zack kissed her forehead again.

"I would love that," she replied.

"Okay," he said. "That's what we will do the day after tomorrow. I'll show you the cabin and all of Willow Island's beaches tomorrow." Zack inhaled her scent as his emotions floated on a cloud of happiness. "I will get the fire going soon. I really like laying under the stars with you."

"So do I," she said. "I can stay here all night just hugging you and gazing at the sky."

Zack exhaled and smiled. He liked Megis; he liked her a lot.

Adam turned over on his side, trying to sleep. The baby had been crying on and off all night. He didn't know whether Bjorn was hungry, had a messy diaper or was simply tired. Everything he did wasn't helping. Anita grabbed the baby and latched him onto her breast. He suckled greedily, and then within moments, he quieted down. Adam began drifting off to sleep.

"Babe," Anita whispered.

"What, sweetheart?" he replied.

Anita held Bjorn in her grasp, looking down at his blond head. She was concentrating on a memory, her gaze filtering out into space. The image in her mind tugged at her. Anita had to tell him the truth. She had to tell him about Zack. It would fester inside of her until it rotted her stomach. But Anita was afraid. She didn't want to risk losing Adam.

After several moments of silence, Adam turned towards her and propped up a pillow lazily. "Is everything alright?" he mumbled sleepily.

Anita watched Bjorn fall asleep on her breast. He was a wonderful baby. He cried a lot, but she was so grateful for the easy delivery and the joy of having a baby to share with Adam. Although, there was an important detail that tugged at her, which Adam needed to know. It was more serious than just the fact that she had made love to his brother under the stars. It was a difficult subject, and Anita wasn't sure if there would ever be a good time to bring it up.

She gazed into Adam's dark blue eyes. "I just wanted you to know how much I love you, Adam," she said softly. "You mean everything to me."

"My sweetheart," Adam replied. "I love you too, babe. Now put Bjorn in the bassinet and try to sleep."

Anita leaned over and laid Bjorn into his small wooden bed, rocking him until he lay fully asleep. She returned to the bed and cuddled Adam's back, spooning him. It wasn't the right moment. She would wait until another time. She had to be open and honest with him. Anita couldn't hide her secrets forever.

The morning dew bubbled on the grass as the birds chirped happily. Zack led Megis to the cabin as promised. They walked through the overgrown path to the front door.

"I need to cut this grass," Zack pointed out. "I will do that tonight after dinner."

He jiggled the skeleton key into the lock and pushed the old door open. The hinges creaked as if it wasn't opened often. "I don't know why it always makes that sound," Zack said. "I have oiled those hinges over and over again. We actually use this cabin quite a lot during summer family gatherings, and we rent it out occasionally." He stepped inside, inspecting the hinge curiously. "This door always squeaks, no matter what I do."

He held Megis's right hand and walked with her inside the small cabin. Zack strode over to a window and pulled open the curtains, letting the sunshine in. "It smells a little musty sometimes," Zack said, opening the window. "I need to air it out."

Megis stood captivated by the historic cottage. She gazed up at the ceiling and all around her at the simple but elegant furnishings. A small wooden desk with an old inkwell stood in the corner. A small double-framed bed was tucked sweetly in the opposite corner. A large warm blanket and pillows graced the bed. "It's beautiful in here," Megis said, walking into the small kitchen. "Was this the house that your dad and Anwa shared?"

"Yes," Zack answered. "It was the first home they had lived in together."

"Oh, my," Megis exclaimed, enthralled with the story and the old home. "An old wood stove! This must be the original wood stove they used!" She ran her hands along the charred black surface as a chill ran up her spine.

"Yes!" Zack said proudly. "It is one of the original stoves they had brought with them from Iceland."

"So beautiful!" Megis said softly as the chilling feeling spread throughout her arms. "I haven't seen something like this in my entire life."

"I'm so glad you like it," Zack said. "I maintain it myself, mostly for my dad and the vacation renters now. When I was younger, my dad always came out here with us and took care of the cabin meticulously. He grieved for many years after Anwa's death. He said learning to love again was the hardest thing he ever had to do. My dad rebuilt the cabin slowly over the years, log by log. He continued to care for it until just a few years ago. He's getting elderly now, so I thought I'd take over the tradition for him. It means a lot to him."

Megis felt her emotions bubble up unexpectedly, and her eyes moistened. "You are such a good son, Zack," she said passionately. "I'm sure your dad appreciates the effort you put into this beautiful home of his past."

Zack smiled. "I never thought of it that way," he replied. "I guess you're right." He opened another window as an instant breeze lifted the curtains and rushed through the small house. "Thank you for saying that. I haven't always been the best person."

Megis smiled as the breeze wafted through the cottage. "Of course, you're a good person, Zack," she affirmed. "I knew that the first day I met you."

"You did?" he asked incredulously.

"Yes," Megis replied. "That's why I gave you the bun."

"You're very sweet," Zack said softly.

"It was the least I could do for a strong young man trying to change the world," she said, reaching out to open another window.

Zack reached around her and jiggled the crescent lock to the open position. "Sometimes these old locks stick," he said, trying to stem the emotions from taking hold of his heart. He hugged her warmly from behind as the window finally opened. "Thank you for saying that. I always thought I had failed horribly during the riot."

She turned in his embrace and looked deeply into his blue eyes. She leaned upward and kissed his lips gently, a spark jumping through their bodies. Megis pulled back gently. "You were definitely not a failure," she said, her voice thick. "Not too many men in this world have the insane amount of courage like you do."

Zack smiled, feeling his chest pull and his emotions flooding his heart. He had thought that nobody in the world could ever see anything positive about his rebel spirit. But somehow, Megis did. He hugged her warmly and buried her head into his chest, kissing her hair. "You make me feel special," he said, his voice thickening with emotion. "Thank you."

Megis kissed his chest and allowed the energy of the cabin and the surroundings to filter through them and around them. It was a lovely feeling. The chills were gone, she noticed, replaced with a sense of warmth and tenderness.

Zack kissed her head again. "I like you, Megis," he said softly. "I am going to take you to the beautiful deserted beaches on the island next."

CHAPTER 13

The fishing was good today. Zack was glad. He had an intense desire to impress Megis and make her believe that he was the best fisherman around these parts, which he was. He had inherited the Olason fishing blood. Zack knew where to fish, what time of day and what method. Today he had the fishing rods. He handed Megis one as they sat on the rocks at Sandy Hook, a point just south of Willow Island. There were some rocks that jutted out into the lake that formed a natural fishing point.

They had borrowed two of Annabella's horses and had travelled here earlier this morning. It was a lovely ride, and he was astonished that Megis knew how to ride horseback.

"Of course," she said. "My parents always took me to ride the horses at Regina Beach. I love horses."

"You have many skills," Zack said, running his fingers through his thick hair, staring up at the sun.

"Not really," Megis said. "I was raised mostly as a city girl. My parents were really good to me, though. They couldn't have children, so they found me at the orphanage and adopted me immediately."

"How old were you?" Zack asked.

"Only a toddler," she replied. "I don't remember. My adopted parents are the only parents I have ever known."

"Well, they did a great job," he said.

Megis smiled sheepishly and kissed him on the lips briefly. "Thank you."

Zack showed her how to thread the bait on the rod and wound the line up. He loved watching her tiny fingers working on the fishing line and the way she moved. "When you are ready," he instructed. "I will throw your line out for you." He whipped his arm back and forward, throwing his line out far. "See, like this. You'll slowly start to wind the fishing line back in. If you feel a tug, wind it faster. You might have a fish."

She finished baiting her line, and he threw her line out, handing the rod back to her. "Yes," he instructed, watching her. "That's right. Wind it back slowly."

She followed his instructions, intent on doing her best at her first time fishing.

Zack mused on their similarities. "My daughter is adopted as well," he blurted out.

"You have a daughter?" she said, surprised.

"Yeah," he replied, coughing nervously. "I used to drink a bit too much. During a party, I had an accident with a girl, and well, she became pregnant and hated me for it." Zack gazed across the lake. "Josie will be three months old soon. My mother adopted her right away from the orphanage. I still get to be with my biological daughter every day. She's a sweetheart."

"That's so wonderful!" Megis said. "Can I meet her one day?"

"Of course," he said. "If you want to."

"Of course, I want to," she said. "Why would you think I wouldn't?"

Zack shuffled his buttocks on the rock. "I thought maybe you'd be mad at me for impregnating a girl."

"No," Megis said. "Accidents happen."

"I was a different person back then," Zack said, pulling the line slowly in. "I changed so much after meeting my daughter for the first time. I quit drinking, and do you know what astonished me the most? That I did it for myself."

"I'm glad," she said, pulling in her line. Suddenly the line went taut, and Megis struggled to hold the rod steady.

Zack jumped up and wrapped his arms around her guiding her hands. He helped her wind it back and tugged against the fish. The rod began to bend with force. "You got one!" he exclaimed. "Keep winding it! I have a hold on the rod. This one's not getting away!"

"Oh my Lord!" she exclaimed happily as the fish flopped out of the water, splashing and fighting.

Zack reeled in the rest of the rod and clubbed the fish. He held it up for her to see. "A nice size! It's a whitefish!" He handed her the rod and slipped the fish into a bag. "We can have fish for lunch! Would you join me?"

"Definitely!" she said.

"Okay," Zack said, pulling his rod in and packing up his fishing kit. "Let's get this all together and return to the cottage for a fire."

Megis helped pack up the bait and fishing supplies while Zack grabbed the rods and the fish. They walked together into the bushes towards the horses. Megis hopped onto her horse and slung the fishing supplies in a small bag over her shoulder as Zack packed up the rods. They trotted on the horses back towards Willow Point, past the crashing waves and the beautiful rays of the hot summer sun. They began sweating in the humid heat, the forest acting like a furnace.

He watched her buttocks bounce off the horse with every trot. She had a tiny backside, but it fit her body. She was small all over, and he thought it was quite attractive. Her shoulder-length hair bounced on her upper neck with every movement on the horse.

She turned around suddenly, catching him staring. She smiled, oblivious to his admiring eyes. "Do you think we could do this again before I go?"

"When are you leaving?" he asked.

"Oh," she said. "Not for awhile. We just arrived five days ago. We won't be leaving for another ten days."

Zack thought of what this meant. "I don't want you to go," he whispered to himself. Did he really say that aloud? Zack looked down sheepishly.

She smiled to herself, looking ahead. Megis had caught the emotion behind his endearing words but pretended not to notice. "I'll come back!" she shouted gleefully.

Zack felt disappointed, and he didn't quite know why. He had only spent a few days with this woman. But something was tugging at him, an important piece of information that would help him sort things out.

Then it came to him like an epiphany.

He hadn't had sex with her yet!

It wasn't like he didn't want to. Zack definitely wanted to. Something was different. He couldn't quite figure out why but for some reason, he wanted to wait and take it slow with Megis. He cared about her, and he was developing more and more feelings for her every day.

"I want you to come back," Zack said. "I mean, I really enjoy spending time with you. You're fun and a kind person. I really like you."

She grinned and looked back again, trying to hide her emotions. "I really like you too," Megis replied.

The late morning sun was quickly turning into a hot summer day. Zack's shoulders began to sting from the sun's rays. "Let's get back home quickly before we burn," he said.

The horses travelled for another six miles before they arrived at the cottage nestled in the bushes. "Let's unload the fish and supplies," he said. "I will get this fish cooking right away."

Megis dismounted and took the large fish bag towards the cottage while Zack grabbed the fishing supplies. Pepper jumped happily out of his dog house to greet them.

"Oh, you have a dog!" Megis exclaimed.

"Sort of," Zack explained. "He was a stray that just kept coming back. I fed him and built him a dog house. He recently disappeared for a few days, but he just came back last night, thankfully. His name is Pepper."

Megis patted the dog as Pepper energetically greeted her.

"Stay," Zack firmly said to Pepper. The dog dutifully obeyed and stayed at the dog house, whining.

Zack wound his arm around her waist, walking up the steps to the cottage. He held the door open for Megis.

The house was empty. Adam and Anita had moved out a few months ago, finding their own home in Gimli. Adam was making enough money at the town hall to afford a house to rent for his new family. Zack was glad they moved out. He couldn't live with them, choosing to stay at his parent's house until they had left.

He watched Megis put the fish in the sink and started gutting it. Zack was impressed. She had skills far better than any other woman he had ever met.

"I will put away the fishing supplies," Zack said. "And I will get the cast iron pan on the stove and start frying this fish. My dad showed me the best way to cook a fish, so it turns out moist and delicious."

"You are a good man, Zack," she said. "You know how to cook; you're a gentleman, and you keep a clean house too."

Zack laughed loudly. "Thanks," he said. "I'm not clean all the time, but I try." He bent down to grab the cast iron pan as Megis watched his muscled arms rummaging in the cupboards. He pulled out matches and placed the pan on the woodstove, throwing several logs in and lighting the match. The fire started quickly, warming the pan with oil within a few minutes. He whipped an egg, then dipped the fillets in the mixture, breading them before placing them in the sizzling pan. She handed him more fillets as she cut them one by one. They worked as a team, sometimes lightly touching each other, occasionally brushing a light kiss here and there.

Megis smiled and stood on her tiptoes, kissing his lips fully.

He bent down and kissed her as he held her waist. "I enjoy spending time with you," he said. "Just like this. No pressure or wild, crazy nights, just normal things, like cooking and fishing."

"I love it too," she said, smiling, as they waited for the fish to cook.

They ate ravenously and smiled at each other over dinner. Soon after, they moved to the sofa.

"Can we just cuddle?" Megis asked. "I love the way that feels with you. It's so comfortable like I was made to fit in your arms."

"I was just about to say the same thing," he said.

They curled into each others' arms smoothly, like she was designed just for him. Her leg flopped over his thigh as he embraced her in a full-body hug. Her scent was all over him. Megis was touching his skin, on his hand, his arm and his face. It felt so lovely to bond with someone in this physical way. He wanted this woman to be his. He wondered what he had to do to make her stay.

"See, I fit perfectly in your arms," Megis murmured.

She nuzzled her nose against his chest as he hummed an old Native song softly. It was a wistful song with some happy notes.

His father had hummed the song to Zack ever since he was a baby and all through his childhood. Zack knew the melody well.

Once he had finished the ballad, Megis looked up at him. "Where did you learn that song?" she asked.

"It was an old Native tune that Anwa, my late stepmother, had sung to my father," Zack replied. "My dad always said that it soothed me as a baby when I was upset."

"Oh," Megis said softly. "I thought it was a Native song! I may have heard something like it before; I'm unsure where, though. It's very lovely."

"Yes," Zack said. "I was told Anwa was a gentle, lovely soul, very similar to my own mother. My dad was heartbroken for a very long time. He always said that my mom was his angel. My mom is nineteen years younger than my father."

"Oh? Well, you have a wonderful family," she said. "Age doesn't mean anything when you're truly in love."

Zack smiled and kissed the top of her head. "I'm glad you think so." He wrapped his arms tighter around her petite body and encapsulated her in his warmth. She snuggled into him closer, her nose now completely buried into his chest. He liked this feeling when he was holding her. Zack hadn't felt this way about another woman. Actually, he hadn't even known a woman like her before. Zack felt his emotions bubbling up to the surface, and he fought to keep them down. He wondered if this was the woman for him. Zack always hoped he would meet someone very special, a woman who took the time to be with him and accept all his faults.

He hummed the song again, wondering if she would stay. Zack wasn't in a position to tell her that she should stay with him and not travel back with her parents. His heart thumped hard in his chest when he thought that she could leave, just like every other girl had. Zack tried to purge the negative thoughts from his head and just focus on the moment. He had a beautiful woman in his arms that he cared about immensely.

That was enough for now.

"Is it alright if I take Megis out for a boat ride tomorrow?" Zack asked her parents. They were a lovely couple. Her dad was a large gentle giant, and her mom was petite like her. She had long brown hair always wrapped up in a bun. They had never been able to have children, so Megis was their pride and joy.

Her dad, Joseph, placed his fork down and chewed thoughtfully. They had invited Zack over for dinner to get a better sense of what kind of man he was. Their daughter was quite enchanted by him. "Do you have a safe boat? Is it motorized or just sails?" Joseph asked between mouthfuls.

Zack nodded. "Yes, it's motorized," he said. "It's a four-person fishing boat, a very safe vessel. It was once used by the fishery, but they have since grown far too big for such small vessels. It was my favourite boat, so I took it over. I go fishing once a week, sometimes more. I was raised in a fishing boat by my father, so I know the lake better than anyone else."

"Oh, well, that is comforting. I suppose it should be alright for Megis to go out on the boat with you. What time tomorrow?" Joseph said, coughing roughly.

"Are you okay?" her mother patted his back.

"Just a piece of food going down the wrong tube," he said, coughing hard to the side.

Megis looked from her dad to Zack, concerned but hopeful that her father would accept her boyfriend. They had spent many days together, often spending every single day in each other's arms. They would laugh, talk and cuddle. Every night, she would return to her parent's rental home. Every morning, she would eat quickly and leave the cottage, crossing the street to awaken Zack.

He had taken a week off of work to spend more time with her. The mechanic shop was busy, but Zack was due for some vacation time. He found that he was quickly becoming accustomed to seeing her face every morning. It cheered his soul. He felt very happy and hopeful.

"I was thinking approximately 10 am?" Zack replied.

"I guess that would be okay," her father said, coughing slightly, trying to clear his throat.

"Great!" Zack said enthusiastically. "I'll be here tomorrow at 10 am with my truck." Zack was incredibly proud of his truck. It was an old wrecked 1930 Ford that he had fixed from scrap parts. He had bought it for almost nothing, rebuilt the motor and even repainted it.

Megis smiled proudly as they all finished dinner, and Zack left late that night, walking home alone. He thought that he might be falling in love with Megis. He looked down as his footsteps crunched onto the dirt road. Zack could see his home from their cottage; it was that close. He didn't want to leave tonight. Something inside his heart wanted to stay with her every morning and every night. It was like seeing her all day and evening wasn't enough anymore. Zack wanted her to be sleeping in his bed as well. But he knew that would be impossible with her parents always here.

Zack opened the back door, pausing to pat Pepper's head affectionately and then stepped into the dark cottage. He wandered around inside the house, finally removed his clothing, masturbated and fell asleep on the sofa, his mind filled with warm thoughts of her naked skin against his.

The truck bounced over the rough dirt roads heading out of Willow Island. Megis's hair flew all over the place, the thick waves bouncing in the wind. They had all the windows down and the fresh lake air whipped through the truck. The radio was on, playing a comedy show. Megis laughed as they listened to the lame jokes. Her eyes reflected the sun and turned a lighter shade of brown, mesmerizing him. Zack had to tell himself to keep his eyes on the road. She looked absolutely stunning today.

Megis was wearing a pair of feminine high-waisted sailor pants tucked into black boots with a loose white blouse. Women didn't wear pants often, but when they did, it was quite fashionable. Her parents had bought her the beige-coloured sailor pants in Gimli a few days ago, and she was thrilled to have an opportunity to use them.

"You look stunning," Zack said, glancing sideways as he drove to the main road, the dirt road kicking up a dust cloud in the truck's wake. "I love those pants."

"Thank you!" she exclaimed. "I'm excited to go out in your boat."

"You'll love it," Zack said, smiling. "How is it that you are here with me after so many years? I am amazed that we found each other again!"

"I know!" she said. "It's so strange how we met again after all those years." She had to almost shout over the loud truck and wind noise.

"You are going to love this!" Zack said excitedly. "I have brought some fishing rods just in case, but I will most likely just take you across the lake. It's a nice calm day, good for a boat ride."

"I am excited!"

Zack laughed. He was excited too. He wanted to whisk her away on a boat, in his truck, anywhere really. It didn't matter what they did; he enjoyed her immensely.

He slowed the truck down as they approached the main road to Gimli. He turned right and accelerated on the provincial trunk highway. The wind wafted a scent of her woman smell, and Zack felt giddy. He smiled broadly, his cheeks almost hurting. "You smell so pretty," he said.

"Thank you!" Megis said. "I washed my hair last night with a perfumed soap."

Zack smiled. "You are the most beautiful woman I've ever met, inside and out." He kept his eyes on the road and glanced over briefly, noticing that she grew quiet. "Did I say something wrong?" he asked.

"No, quite the opposite," Megis responded. "No one has ever said that to me before."

"Oh?" he said. "Well, it's the truth."

The road curved, and the truck's wheels gripped firmly onto the road as they approached Gimli. When he travelled by truck, it was barely a five-minute drive to the town. Zack turned on Main Street and headed straight to the pier. He felt a sense of déjà vu come over him, as if his ancestors may have done the very same thing that he was doing today. After all, the lake was in their blood.

As the pier came into view, he smiled. Zack was taking his girlfriend on a boat ride! It was serene and fulfilling, as if the world of Zachery Olason was a giant puzzle and Megis was the piece he had been missing for so long. His father, grandfather, cousins and relatives had all gone out on this lake before him and had fallen in love too. It filled him with an exhilarating sense of belonging and fulfillment. He loved his heritage and felt happy today.

Zack braked and parked the truck, pushing the emergency brake down with his foot. He jumped out of the vehicle and walked around the truck, opening the door for Megis. She smiled sweetly and kissed him on the lips. Zack hugged her waist and kissed her back, pulling her closer. His testosterone increased instantly, sparking his veins with electricity. They kissed deeply and spontaneously right there in front of everybody. A few people hid their faces on the busy dock, obviously uncomfortable. Zack felt eyes on his back. He kissed her more gently and then scooped her into his arms, placing her gently down on the sidewalk. She giggled loudly, drawing more attention.

"I think people are looking at us," Zack said.

"Oh, I'm sorry," Megis said. "I didn't realize."

"Don't be sorry," he said. "It's their problem, not ours. Let's get the boat, my beautiful girl." He grabbed her hand and led her to the fishery, where his boat was tied up on the dock. As they neared the dock, Adam was walking out of the fishery with Anita and Bjorn. "Adam!" Zack exclaimed, bending down to the little baby in Anita's arms. "Bjorn, my favourite cute little nephew!"

Anita stared at Megis and then glanced at Adam. Zack followed her gaze and straightened. "Oh, Adam!" Zack said. "This is my girlfriend, Megis." He hugged her waist and kissed her forehead.

"Hello, Megis," Adam said, shaking her hand. "I am Adam's twin brother."

"Oh!" Megis said. "Zack had mentioned that he had an identical twin brother! You look so different. Maybe it is the haircuts."

"Yes, most likely," Adam said, chuckling arrogantly. "I cut my hair just recently. My brother still hasn't."

Zack stared at him confidently. "I prefer my hair the way it is," he said.

Adam's face dropped into a frown. "Well, we were just on our way home. We were picking up some fish for the week and some vegetables from the market. What are you two doing?"

"I'm taking Megis on a boat ride," Zack said proudly.

At that moment, Bjorn started to fuss, and Anita struggled with him, placing him onto her shoulder, patting his back and rocking with her feet back and forth. "Okay, have fun," Adam said. "It looks like our little prince needs to take a nap soon. See you later." Adam touched Anita's waist and guided her to the car with a box of fish in his arms. "Be safe on the lake," he called to his brother.

"Of course, I will," Zack replied, watching his brother rush his family to the car.

"That's your brother?" Megis said. "You seem so very different from each other."

"Do you think so?" he said. "Some people can't tell us apart."

"Maybe it's just how I view you. Adam is a completely different personality from you, and his hair is very short." She smiled and followed his eyes towards the boats. "He doesn't seem much like you at all, except the facial features and eyes."

"Well, I will take that as a compliment," Zack said. "We've had a strained relationship lately."

"Why?"

"Oh, it's nothing," he lied. "Just stupid brother stuff."

She smiled and kissed him on the shoulder. "Okay," she said. "Let's go to the dock and see your boat."

They walked hand in hand around to the back of the fishery, located the blue boat and untied it. "You get in first," Zack instructed. "I will untie it fully and step in last."

He helped her on board the boat, gracefully holding her hand as her small feet stepped onto the vessel. She sat down obediently, watching him untie the rope. His long muscular legs fascinated her. He was so much taller than her and stronger too.

He flipped his hair to the side, smiled at her and stepped into the boat in a rush. They drifted away from the dock. Zack watched the pier float into the distance as he pulled the starter rope on the small outboard motor. The engine rumbled to life, blowing a small plume of smoke out and propelling the boat towards the middle of the lake.

The water splashed as they sped forward. It was a calm day, and the boat slipped into the lake, splitting the water into a wake behind them. Megis was smiling, and her hair was whipping back with the wind.

Zack steered the boat east and pulled Megis closer to his side, kissing her on the forehead. When they neared the other side of the lake, Zack slowed the boat towards an isolated beach.

"It's so beautiful here!" Megis shouted over the loud motor.

"I love it out here," Zack said. "It's where I go to be at peace with myself."

Zack turned off the motor and let the boat drift towards the deserted sandy beach. They floated and admired the scenery.

Megis dipped her hand in the water lazily.

Zack watched her sensually caress the water absentmindedly. It made him think about sex with her. They hadn't had sex yet. He wasn't even sure why. He just enjoyed every second with her and didn't want to push it. He wanted this girl forever, not just a weekend.

"What are you thinking?" she asked.

Zack grinned. "I was thinking about how nice it will feel when we decide to make love."

"I think about that often too," Megis said.

"You do?" he asked.

"Yes," she said. "Of course. All the time."

"What things do you think about?"

"I think about you naked on top of me," she replied.

His penis grew in his shorts. "Oh," he said dumbly.

"Can we have sex one day?" she asked shyly.

Zack swallowed hard. "Yes," he said, his voice hoarse.

The boat floated and lapped at the gentle waves. The sun was hot today.

"When?" Megis asked.

"We can do that whenever you like," he said nervously.

"Oh," she said, her voice growing husky.

Zack kissed her head and wrapped his arms around her. His skin touched hers, and they both felt so peaceful and connected that it felt unreal. They were floating and cuddling. The world was silent around them except for the sounds of the lake.

"Can we do that tonight?" she asked.

Zack swallowed as his penis grew fully erect. "Yes," he said. "We can do that."

"Okay, good," Megis said, giggling nervously. "I'm a virgin," she added.

"Oh," Zack said.

"Does that bother you?"

"No, not at all," he replied.

"It bothers me, sometimes," she said. "I worry that I won't know how to be a good lover."

Zack hugged her tighter. "You are already everything I've ever wanted, so I doubt it would make a difference."

Megis smiled and snuggled into his chest. She turned her head and looked up at him. "I'm everything you've wanted?" she asked, her voice cracking.

"Yes, baby," Zack said slowly, choosing his words deliberately. "You're beautiful, kind and spontaneous." The boat rocked back and forth over the gentle waves. "I actually think I'm falling in love with you."

She turned fully around and kissed him on the lips. His entire body responded instantly, and his emotions felt raw. Could she really be the woman for him? He laid his hand on her chin, pulling her closer and gazed into her eyes.

"I think I'm falling in love with you too, Zack," Megis said, gazing deeply into his watery blue eyes.

They kissed again. Their emotions mixed in with their desire, creating a different kind of chemistry. Zack had never felt this way before. It was an attraction on a different level. His body, mind and heart wanted every single piece of her. He wanted it all; sex, cuddling, talking, sharing and quiet moments together with this woman. His heart soared into the blue sky, and he briefly wondered if it might crash again like all the other times.

"Stay with me, Megis," Zack said. "I don't want you to leave."

Megis smoothed his arm with her hand. "I have to go back with my parents, babe," she said. "But I will come back. I will pack my bags and return to Gimli to come be with you." She swallowed. "If that's what you want, I mean."

"That's what I want, Megis," he said. "You can live with me."

They kissed again, sealing their agreement as the waves rocked them gently and dreams of the future flooded both of their minds. Not another word was spoken because they both knew it was meant to be.

The night air cooled the forest as Zack and Megis returned home. The humidity was high, making it feel like he was in a steam hut. The moist air flattened Megis's hair against her head and curled the ends up. She smiled, the curls protruding into her face. It made her look even cuter, Zack thought. He held her hand and walked with her towards the back door. Pepper barked happily, jumping on Zack's legs. "Down, Pepper!" he scolded. Zack opened the door with a mischievous glint in his eye and then suddenly scooped her up into his arms, chuckling.

She yelped and laughed wholeheartedly. "What are you doing, silly?"

"I am carrying the person I love," he said gleefully.

Megis squealed in delight, wrapping her arms around his neck, holding on. His arms were under her legs, and she was lighter than he thought. He quickly kicked the door closed and kissed her. It felt so wonderful! His entire body was firing jolts of happy hormones to every extremity. Zack wanted to make love to this woman so badly; he briefly wondered if he would lose control right here, standing in the kitchen.

Zack rushed with her into the living room, then the bedroom, as his mind urged him to claim her as his woman soon. He briefly wondered if she meant much more to him than just a girlfriend. Emotions and hope flooded his chest as he lay her down on the bed. The realization hit him as hard as a hammer. He wanted her as his wife. He didn't want her to leave at all. Zack somehow knew at the bottom of his soul that Megis was the woman he had been waiting for all this time. The screw-ups, the parties, the illegitimate child, the drinking and the recovery all led to this moment of time. The past and present all collided in a rush of emotion that took him by surprise. Zack kissed her gently and unbuttoned her blouse, slipping it off of her arms. He understood now why he had to go through all the past mistakes. Zack would never be with her if it weren't for the Regina Riot. The past was only a road that led him to the present. And he was deliriously happy that the path led him right to Megis.

Her hair was splayed all over. Megis smiled sensually, then reached behind her back and unclasped her brassiere. Her small breasts jumped out perkily, saying hello to his eyes. He instantly grabbed them both in his hands and squeezed them. Megis moaned heavily and threw her head back into the mattress. Zack removed all his clothing quickly, throwing the blankets haphazardly over to the side and positioned her gently to the middle. He kissed her softly as she fumbled to remove her sailor pants. Zack helped her and slid the fashionable pants down her legs, pulling each boot off and throwing them all onto the floor. His eyes locked onto her naked body. She was small, almost skinny, with a very tiny waist and narrow hips. Her legs were very slim, and the apex of her thighs was glistening with moisture. Zack reached his hand to her vagina and touched her lightly.

Megis followed his roaming eyes as he slipped one finger inside her. She groaned heavily, and her head rolled back.

Zack felt his control quickly slipping away as her scent wafted up to his nostrils. She smelled so exquisitely feminine. He had an irresistible desire to taste his fingers. So he did, slipping one finger into his mouth. "Mmm," he said. She tasted like butter with a touch of honey.

Megis moaned and gazed at his naked body, her eyes hooded. "Zack," she said softly. "I want you."

Zack felt a strong urge to please her. He wanted her to be completely satisfied. Zack pulled her legs down towards him and wound her knees over his shoulders as he positioned his mouth to her vagina. The pleasant smell of sex overcame him and sent him into a cloud of desire. His tongue darted out at her vagina and tasted her honey.

Megis cried out in ecstasy and stretched out her neck, melting into the bed.

His wet tongue swiped at her genitals again, licking and tasting her inner woman. Her instant responses to his licks spurred him on even faster. It was urgent now; he had to help her get to the place of no return. Zack wrapped his arms around her buttocks and held her body tight against his face, burying his chin and his lips into her vagina.

Megis moaned and wiggled in his grasp, but he somehow knew not to let go. He continued his gentle lapping of her vagina and fought her wiggling, pulling her closer and closer into his face.

"Ah," she cried out suddenly.

Her legs wrapped tightly around his shoulders and her fingers coiled into his hair. Zack felt an urgency like none other. He furiously lapped and licked, starting from the bottom of her inner labia to the top and back, repeating the rhythmic movements over and over again, increasing with speed as her fingers tightened in his hair. Megis began to press his head against her vagina. He stuck his tongue fully into her wetness and gripped her buttocks fiercely.

Her body was as tense as a tightrope, and Zack felt an urgency to relieve her of this extreme tension. He must lick her until she releases his hair. Zack knew this instinctively. He had never before tasted a woman's genitals, but it was a wonderful taste, and he found that he loved it. Her flavour was deliciously arousing, and his penis responded by sticking out into the side of the mattress.

He could feel her body begin to vibrate, and he knew that he must do something. He squeezed her buttocks rhythmically in time with his licks and held on even tighter. A gush of fluid released on his chin, and he felt her body vibrate in his arms.

She cried out loudly, "Zack!"

He murmured into her vagina and felt her relax suddenly. Small involuntary tremors spread throughout her legs. "Oh my God, Megis," he murmured. "You are so beautiful."

She shuffled her torso away from him and pulled him up to her face. Megis wiped the liquid from his chin and kissed him gently. "You are wonderful, Zack," she said, her voice thick. Her hands caressed his wet beard, and she lovingly traced one finger all the way down to his chest, a zigzag pattern.

Zack felt the electricity soar throughout his body at her touch. His own urgency began to take hold of his senses. He needed her now.

His entire body felt like it was on fire, sending warmth to all his limbs. "I love you, Megis," he murmured, positioning his penis at her entrance.

"I love you, Zack," she replied.

He pushed into her tight entrance and felt resistance. Zack pushed harder until he felt something give way. His penis slid slowly inside her. The snug warmth surrounded him like a loving blanket. It felt like heaven. His mind floated above him, not requiring any more thought, leaving only his physical body in power. He moved his hips, sliding slowly into her, then out.

She gasped and clutched onto him.

"It's okay, baby," he said, his voice caressing her mind. "Relax. Breathe."

Megis exhaled slowly into his shoulder as he rocked gently into her.

"Look at me," he said.

She opened her eyes and gazed into his watery blue depths.

"I have a lot of feelings for you," Zack said sensually, his voice husky and strong. "I want to give you everything."

"Yes," she responded. "So do I."

Zack balanced his weight on her leg and slowly slid his penis out of her vagina, then re-entered her just as slowly. He continued this methodical movement over and over until he felt himself reach an apex. It came on suddenly without warning, and Zack immediately snapped back into time. He didn't want to cause her any pain like he had Anita or Grace. Zack pulled out suddenly and released onto the sheets.

Megis gasped. "Oh!" she cried as if she didn't want him to leave her warmth. "Babe?"

"I'm sorry," he said. "I don't want to cause you to get pregnant. Not now. Definitely sometime in the future. But I just," Zack paused, stopping and burying his face into her neck. "I love you, and I don't want anything bad to happen."

"Oh, sweetheart," she said, wrapping her arms around him and lacing her fingers through his hair. "I love you too."

Zack felt his body melt into hers as if they were one. His arms felt rubbery, and he slid to the side, pulling her tiny body into his. Megis rested her head against his arm and inhaled the scent of sex all around them. Zack caressed her hair and hummed. The native song came from his lips easily, humming the tune that his ancestors had heard many years before. The mournful soothing tune caressed them both, lulling them into a deep sleep. Their bodies remained entwined with legs and arms tightly wrapped around each other in a state of loving bliss. Megis's head snuggled into his shoulder. She accepted this man as hers, and in return, Zack welcomed her as his woman too. The night enveloped them both and promised them a future filled with hope.

Chapter 14

They awoke to sunshine every morning until the end of the week, making love every night and every morning. It felt so blissful and happy that Zack had to pinch himself to believe it was real. Megis had told her parents that she was in love with Zack and would be moving to Gimli shortly after. Zack was amazed that his life was finally turning around for the better.

They were so good for each other. Nothing seemed to be in their way. For once, his life was easy. Zack wondered if it would last or be taken away from him. Every woman had left him the morning after, but Megis stayed. She loved him! He felt blessed and grateful for this small woman's influence on him.

Megis was sleeping beside him, and he was watching her sleep. Her chest was rising ever so slightly with every breath. Zack smiled and traced his fingers gently over her naked back, swirling tiny designs of love onto her skin. She murmured and rolled over, facing him.

"Good morning," Megis mumbled lazily.

"Good morning, beautiful," Zack replied happily. "You look so lovely in the mornings with your crazy wild hair."

She chuckled. "No, I don't," she said.

"Yes, you really do!" Zack insisted.

"Mmm, okay," Megis replied, cuddling into his arms tightly. She buried her head into his chest. "We only have one day left before I have to leave with my parents. I don't want to go."

"Then don't," he said simply.

"I have to," Megis said. "I need my clothes and personal items from home."

"Maybe I should go with you then," Zack said, trying to keep the plea out of his voice.

"But you can't," Megis said. "You have to work. You can't sacrifice your job right now. You've taken too much time off already for me."

Zack frowned. "You are right," he agreed. "When will you come back?"

"A week or two," she replied. "I think that will be enough time to pack and move my stuff out here."

"Alright," he said despondently. Zack had hoped that he could go with her to Regina and help her move everything in one weekend. He felt dismayed and disappointed. Zack loved her more than any woman he had ever met, and his heart ached to be with her permanently. He understood that she had a life back in Regina with her parents, and she needed time to progress out to Gimli to be with him. Zack felt apprehensive like he was somehow holding his breath until she committed to him. He thought of their lives and what it would be like together. Zack would love to marry and have children with her. His parents would be ecstatic to have more grandchildren. It might even help Pabbi live longer. Nath seemed to be doing so much better since they adopted Josie. Adam brought Bjorn over occasionally too. Every time the babies were awake, Nath was moving around the house, alert and busy. Young children changed a family dynamic so much, Zack mused. He wanted Megis to be a part of his family.

A thought occurred to him. "You haven't met my daughter, Josie, yet," Zack said, rubbing his beard. "Did you want to see her today? We could spend the day with her."

"Yes!" she exclaimed happily.

"Oh!" he replied, surprised at her enthusiasm. "She's only a baby. But she did start smiling just a few weeks ago! What a moment that was!" Zack smiled broadly, his face brightening up. "Okay, well, let's go now. I'll get the car ready."

"I love babies! I can't wait!" Megis said.

Zack parked the truck on the dirt driveway in front of his parent's house. He walked around the vehicle and opened the door for Megis, holding her hand. Zack was beginning to realize that he absolutely adored her. Every step she took, every word she spoke, he absorbed it all and relished in her company. His heartstrings tugged at the thought of her leaving the morning after tomorrow. He tried not to think about it. He didn't want to lose her by appearing too needy.

Zack walked with her up the steps to the front door. He had introduced Megis to his mom previously at the cottage, but Megis had not met his father yet. He knocked on the door briefly and opened the door, poking his head into the front entrance. "Momma?" he said loudly.

Steps sounded through the house as Maria made her way to the front. "Zack?" she shouted. "Is that you?" Maria shuffled in the back bedroom until finally, she appeared in a robe with messy hair.

"Mom?" Zack said, surprised. "Have you been sleeping this late in the afternoon?"

"Umm," Maria said, stammering. "Yes, I took a nap with your dad."

Zack chuckled to himself. His parents were always a loving couple, often touching each other and sleeping together every night. "Mom," he said, gesturing with his arm around Megis's waist. "You remember Megis?"

"Yes, I do!" Maria said, smiling. "How are you, Megis? Are you enjoying your vacation in Gimli?"

"Yes, extremely," Megis replied. "The beaches are beautiful here, and Zack even took me fishing and boating. The lake takes my breath away. It is so beautiful."

"I'm glad you are having a wonderful time," Maria said, her eyes glowing happily. She looked around the room and gestured to the kitchen. "Fix yourself something to drink. I'll get dressed into something more appropriate. Josie will be getting up soon from her nap." She paused and turned back. "We have adopted a baby just recently." She looked to Zack and back at Megis, not sure if she knew.

"I told her that Josie is my daughter."

"Oh, good," Maria said softly. "She's a beautiful baby, and we are delighted to have her brighten our household."

As if on cue, a muffled cry and fidget of blankets sounded down the hall. "That is her," Maria said, disappearing back into the bedrooms. "I'll be right back!"

Zack pulled Megis towards him and hugged her in the kitchen. "Let's find some tea," he said. "My father makes his own herbal teas from dried fruits and maple syrup. I'm not sure what else is in those teas, but some of them are even medicinal."

"Where did he learn that?" Megis asked.

"From Anwa," Zack said thoughtfully. "She had passed down some native tea remedies."

"I love that!" Megis said happily. "Can I see which types of tea he has?"

"Sure," Zack said, gesturing to the cupboard of tea tins with loose dried leaves. "We can just put a teaspoon of tea leaves in a metal tea strainer and make a pot for all of us. Just pick one that we'll all like."

"Can I smell them?"

"Definitely," Zack replied, opening the first metal container.

Megis leaned forward and inhaled. It smelled of lemon and earthy tones. She nodded to the next one. Zack opened it as she smelled the second tea concoction.

"This one smells like mint!" she exclaimed. "And something else."

Zack smiled. It was his favourite. "It's vanilla mint."

"I like that one," she said decisively.

Zack grinned broadly. She knew his favourites without even asking him because she liked them herself.

Josie's cry filled the room suddenly as Maria returned into the living room with the baby in her arms. Josie was fussing and fidgeting. "Zack," Maria said urgently. "Please prepare her milk."

"Yes, momma," he replied, grabbing the cleansed glass bottles. Zack rummaged in the cupboard, taking out a can of evaporated milk and corn syrup. He opened the can of milk, measured the water and poured a small amount of corn syrup into a one-litre glass milk container. He secured the lid and shook it until the formula was well mixed.

Megis watched him intently. She was impressed that her man was such a knowledgeable father at the age of 21.

Zack poured the prepared formula into one of the small glass feeding bottles and secured a rubber nipple on the cap. He warmed it briefly in a pot of water on the stove. When he was finished, he tested the temperature on his wrist and handed it to his mother.

"Did you want to feed her today?" Maria asked. "You haven't been around lately. She misses you."

"Sure," Zack said, gently lifting the baby out of Maria's arms and sitting on the sofa with Josie.

Megis followed him to the sofa and sat beside him while he fed his daughter. "You're a good daddy," she said admiringly.

"Thank you," Zack said softly as he tilted the bottle to the baby's lips. Josie sucked eagerly at the nipple and held onto his large index finger.

Moments later, Nath shuffled into the living room.

"Babe," Maria said, rushing to his side. "You're awake."

"Yes, I am," Nath said quietly, noticing Megis on the sofa. He walked slowly to the sofa with Maria's arms around him. Nath sat down gingerly. "And who is this beautiful young woman you have brought home, Zack?"

Zack smiled across at his father. "Dad, this is my girlfriend, Megis. Megis, this is my father, Nathan."

Nath leaned forward briefly and nodded. "Nice to meet you. So how long have you two been together?"

Megis smiled. Something about the elderly man made her smile brighter. "We actually met years ago during the Regina Riot," Megis said, twirling the ends of her hair nervously.

"Oh!" Maria interrupted. "I didn't know that! You didn't tell us much about that time, Zack."

"Megis was the daughter of the family that had sheltered me after the riot," Zack responded. "We hadn't met again until her family came to Gimli for vacation. We've been staying together for the last two weeks, Mom. Megis is going to move here."

Nath smiled broadly. "Is that so?" he said, grinning. "You don't know how happy I am to hear this, my son." Nath shuffled over to make space for Maria. She promptly sat beside him snugly. "It's been a long road for you, Zack, and making a move from Regina to Gimli is a big step for a young girl. Is your family moving out here as well?"

"No, sir," Megis said softly. "I'm moving here to start a life with Zack."

Nathan felt love for his son flood over him. "I'm so happy for you, Zack," Nath said, pushing the grey strands of hair from his eyes. He still kept his hair longish but had cut it more recently because it was getting much thinner. "You've had a tough few years, Zack. You deserve happiness now."

Zack looked up from his baby daughter and tried to shield his eyes from the emotion bubbling up. "Yes," Zack said. "I sure hope so." He wanted to ask Megis to marry him but was hesitant until she moved here. Zack felt apprehensive and unsure. He didn't want her to leave. Josie finished her bottle of milk, and Zack placed it on the side table, then positioned a small towel onto his shoulder, pulling her onto his chest and tapping on her tiny back rhythmically.

Megis watched him intently, fascinated by how his persona turned into a lovely father so quickly. She smiled and wondered if they would have children someday.

Josie burped suddenly and spit up some milk on his shoulder.

"That's a good girl," Zack said, wiping her mouth and cradling her.

Maria smiled. "I'm delighted for you both. You make a good couple. I can see it in your eyes."

Zack looked up from the baby, addressing his parents. "I am relieved that you both met Megis before she left," he said. "Megis means a lot to me."

"When are you moving?" Nath asked Megis.

"I am hoping in a couple of weeks," Megis answered.

The room fell silent for a moment.

"Well, I hope the move goes well," Nath said, sliding his arm around Maria. "When you meet the right person, you need to keep them close." Nath kissed Maria's shoulder gently. "Maria was the light in my life when I met her during that autumn day at the post office. She just came out of the blue and brightened my entire life with the love I felt for her."

Maria smiled and hugged him. "You did the same for me too, my sweet."

"You met at a post office!" Megis said, remembering the story Zack had told her.

"Yes," Nath laughed. "It was the most random chance meeting ever. I thank the universe for her every day."

"That's so sweet!" Megis said.

"My parents have always been crazy romantics," Zack said, laughing. "It's almost embarrassing."

At that moment, a knock sounded on the door.

"Oh, that's Annabella," Nath said, rubbing his grey beard stubble. "She told me she would be dropping by with her daughters to help with the baby."

Maria stood and approached the door as it opened.

Annabella poked her head inside. "Maria," she said warmly, reaching out and hugging her stepmother. She glanced over at Nath as her two daughters, husband and granddaughter, walked in behind her. "Pabbi! You look so much better!" Annabella exclaimed.

Her daughters, Katya and Natalie, nodded in agreement. "Afi," Katya exclaimed, walking over to the sofa where Zack sat with Josie. "Mom is right! The colour is back in your face, Afi."

"I have this beautiful baby to thank," Nath said. "And my supportive family."

Ivan grabbed the bag of food from Annabella's hands and placed it on the counter. "I will get the rest from the car," he said, kissing Bella on the lips.

"Ivan," Nath said happily. "Nice to see you again. Be careful with the step in the front. I have to replace one of the rotting boards."

"I will take a look at it," Ivan said. "I can fix it next week."

"You're a good son-in-law," Nath said as Ivan left, looking across the room at his granddaughters. "Come here, you!" Nath smiled broadly at Katya. "I haven't seen you for so long. I still remember when you were a toddler, we made oat bars, and you ate them all!"

Katya smiled and rushed over to Nathan, hugging and kissing him on the forehead. "I was a handful," she laughed, her long black hair falling forward. "I remembered you telling Mike that all kids are trouble. It's part of growing up." Katya smiled, her brown eyes glittering. She was the only one in the family with brown eyes, most likely the gene from Anwa's side of the family. "We are all grown up now and know all too well how much trouble our kids are." Katya chuckled as her teenage daughter, Lulu, rolled her eyes. "Lulu is still trouble! Natalie and I are almost forty now, Afi!"

Natalie looked more like her Ukrainian father with blonde hair and green eyes. She embraced her grandfather too. "How's the baby, Afi?" Natalie asked.

"She's a wonderful baby," Nath replied. "She doesn't fuss much at all. She must know that she's loved."

"I'm so glad," Annabella said, rummaging in the grocery bag and placing food in the cupboards. "I brought some homemade potato salad, soups and some more canned milk for Josie. Ivan and I are going to leave Katya and Natalie here with you for the day so they can help out with the baby." Annabella stretched her neck out around the kitchen archway, noticing Megis sitting beside Zack. "Zack, are you going to introduce us?"

"Oh!" Zack said, absorbed in the conversation and people. "Yes, this is my girlfriend, Megis! Sweetheart, this is my sister, Annabella, her husband, Ivan, and her daughters, Natalie and Katya. And of course, their granddaughter, Lulu."

Megis smiled, "Hi, it's a pleasure to meet everyone."

Zack hugged her warmly. "They are all wonderful family. A very large family, sometimes I get the names all mixed up, but you'll get used to it." Zack laughed.

"Wonderful to meet you, Megis," Annabella replied. "It looks like Zack finally found a good woman."

Megis grinned broadly. "I think the world of him. Always have."

Zack hugged Megis's waist as Katya took the baby out of his arms.

"I'm going to change her diaper," Katya said, cooing. "You have a stinky bum, you pretty little lady." She walked out to the back bedroom with Josie.

"Well, I think you should stay for dinner with us tonight, Megis," Maria said, smiling. "So we can get to know you better before you leave."

Zack felt a sudden pain in his chest as the thought of her leaving struck him temporarily. He blinked and tried not to dwell on it.

Megis smiled. "I would love that."

"Perfect," Nathan said.

"I brought some deer meat too," Annabella said. "Mike gave it to me to bring over. We can have a feast. I can bring a chicken to roast later on when Ivan and I return." She leaned over and hugged her father. "We will be back."

Ivan brought the last bag in and hugged Nath. "You are looking really good today," Ivan said. "Don't worry about that step. I'll have it fixed in no time."

Annabella laced her fingers into Ivan's and waved at everyone with her free hand. "Nice meeting you, Megis," she called. "We'll see you all later!"

Megis and Zack waved with the rest of the family as everyone settled in. Zack kissed Megis on the forehead. He loved his woman more and more every day. It felt so right having her by his side.

Zack ran his fingers along her neckline and watched her breathing rise and fall in her chest. He thought she was the most beautiful person in the world. He adored her. They had a wonderful dinner with the entire family; even Mike and his children had shown up. It was the most beautiful warm feeling sharing his new girlfriend with his family.

Things were finally starting to get better. He had a steady job, his father's health was improving, his family was supportive, and he had fallen in love with a wonderful lady. All he needed was for her to move into his house. His mom and dad had agreed to rent the cottage to him for a lesser amount if he kept up the yard and house repairs. It was his home now. Adam had his life with Anita and rarely came by. Zack never thought of Anita anymore. The only woman his heart yearned for was Megis, and he wanted to keep it that way.

Megis rolled over and moaned.

He kissed her hair. "I love you," he said softly.

She murmured in response. "I love you, too."

Zack watched her pack her clothes and felt apprehension grow in his heart. Her father was coughing in the other room, so Megis closed the door. He handed her the cute sailor pants, and she folded them into the suitcase.

She smiled. "I will never forget that beautiful boat ride."

"We will have plenty more of those," he said.

Megis tiptoed and kissed him on the lips. "I sure hope so," she said gleefully.

The room grew silent as the weight of Megis's departure fell hard on Zack's shoulders.

"I don't want you to go," he said abruptly. "I know it's not rational. I know you have to go back home one last time." Zack looked at his toes, wondering how much to say, how much not to say. "I just don't want to lose you."

"You're not losing me," she said. "Don't worry, baby. I'll be back before you know it."

"Okay," Zack said, exhaling lightly. "You're right."

"I will send word when I have settled on a day for the move," Megis said, her eyes searching his. "Zack, it will all work out. Trust me." She folded the rest of her clothes into the suitcase, and Zack closed it shut, snapping the latch into place. "All done! We will be starting our futures together soon, babe."

"Yes, we will be," Zack said. His mind floated to the future of marriage, children and most of all, hope for a brighter tomorrow.

Megis had left the next day. Zack had hugged her tight and waved goodbye. His heart hurt knowing that he'd be separated from her for two whole weeks. But something else had crept into his heart, an insidious uncertainty that filled him with dread.

He believed that she loved him with all her heart. Megis would move to Gimli as soon as she could.

But the insecurity in his heart kept telling him otherwise. Every other woman had left him. This was all he knew. No one ever stayed. The negative voices in his head grew. He blinked as he stared at the ceiling, trying to sleep and praying for her safe return.

It was day seven. With every passing day, the insidious feeling grew. He tried to keep it at bay and focus on the good memories that surrounded him. Her smell was everywhere in the house. Zack could smell her scent on his pillows, blankets and even on his clothes. She had been gone for one week. He yearned for her so badly. Zack wondered if he would make it to two weeks or if his heart would simply implode on itself.

He fingered the ring he had bought yesterday with the money he had saved. It wasn't a spectacular ring. It was plain with one small diamond, but it was all he could afford. He wanted her to know that he was ready to commit for the long term. He questioned himself why he hadn't told her before she had left. Zack reasoned that he wanted her to come back because she loved him and not because he had a ring waiting for her. He wanted it to be a solid choice of hers to spend the rest of her life with him.

He missed her dearly. Zack hoped she came sooner rather than later. He had not checked the post office today, Zack remembered. He pulled his pants on and wound his arms into a white buttoned shirt. Zack grabbed his keys and left the house, walking to his truck.

He climbed in and started the vehicle. He would go see if Megis had mailed him any word of the move date yet.

He smiled, but his heart was worried. Zack had opened his heart and his life to this woman. She had the power to crush him.

When Megis had arrived back home last week, she had begun writing the letter to Zack. She thought of him every day and every night. The memories of his scent were still fresh in her mind. She would begin packing today.

Megis hung her summer coat on the overloaded rack at the front door. The entire coat rack teetered then suddenly tipped. She scrambled to save the rack to no avail. It crashed mightily to the floor. She cursed and struggled to pick up the coat hanger, steadying it with many of the coats still on it. Strange, Megis thought, it never did that before.

A harsh cough broke the silence.

"Dad," Megis hollered into the living room as she picked some errand coats up from the floor. "That cough is worsening. We should get it looked at by a doctor."

"I'm fine," Joseph said. "It's just a cold."

Megis shook her head. Her dad was so stubborn.

"Let me get you some tea," Megis said, hanging the last coat up.

"I'm fine," Joseph said. Before he could finish his words, he broke into a severe coughing fit. Joseph's body curled into a tight ball as he coughed harshly.

Megis ran to the kitchen and grabbed him a glass of water, rushing to his side. "Here," she said. "Drink this."

Joseph grabbed the water and drank it all in one gulp.

"You were thirsty!" she exclaimed.

"It feels good on my throat," he said hoarsely, his voice disappearing slightly.

"Please, dad," Megis pleaded. "Let us call a doctor."

"No," Joseph said stubbornly. "I'm fine."

Megis shook her head and looked at her father worriedly. She gazed out of the window briefly then hugged her father. Megis didn't want anything to happen to him. She loved her parents dearly.

CHAPTER 15

The morning rays of sun filtered beautifully into the cottage through the curtains. Zack awoke abruptly, thinking that Megis was in his bed. He turned his head and gazed at the empty cold spot beside him. He rubbed his face disappointedly and sat on the edge of the bed, his forehead in his hands. Zack's head hurt. He had been drinking again. It was the only way he knew to numb the pain in his heart.

Zack stumbled from the bedroom and walked to the calendar. He marked another x on today's date and counted backwards to the day she had left. It had been 29 days since he last heard from Megis. Every day his heart sank further and further.

He questioned his sanity. He didn't understand. Why? Was it all just a lie? Did she never even love him? Did she only want to have fun on her vacation?

Megis said that she would be back in two weeks, and he hadn't heard from her at all. No message sent and no letter at the post office. The engagement ring sat on his dresser, waiting for her.

Zack became obsessed with going to the post office. He thought if he missed a day, then surely that would be the exact date that a letter would arrive from Regina. But every day, there was no letter from Megis and every day, he grew more and more disappointed.

The silence in his life was grim, and the depression was closing in on him. Zack poured a glass of whiskey and drank it in one shot. His heart was breaking, and the pain was too much to bear.

What had he done wrong? What had he said that made her not want to come back? Should he go to Regina to find her? He didn't even know if she lived at the same house near the Square.

The questions flooded his mind and threatened his sanity. All the emotions he had shared with her, all the plans of living together as a family and the proposal of marriage were all lost. It felt like everything had disintegrated into sand that sifted through his fingers. The quietness taunted him with madness as if nothing had happened, and it was all just a dream.

He poured another whiskey and added some water to sip it. Zack sat down heavily on the sofa. Whiskey was a common drink here in Gimli, and Zack saw no reason to stay sober anymore. The love of his life had left him after all. There was nothing more to do. Zack was only a summer fling for Megis and nothing more.

He doubted that he was worth anything to a woman, especially after his actions of the past. The proof of his messed-up life added up like a stack of precarious cards. Zack had an illegitimate child, a woman that hated him and his brother's wife was his wicked secret. Maybe the universe was ricocheting all his evils back onto him.

But Megis was the one. Zack knew it in the depths of his soul. She was the love of his life. No woman could ever compare to her. He couldn't replace her.

Zack drank half the whiskey and gazed out the window at the sunny morning. It was as if the beautiful morning was mocking him. Nothing would ever be the same again, he thought. How could he ever go out fishing again without thinking of her? How could he gaze at the stars without her?

Zack was numb and felt comfortable staying this way because he knew that he could not recover from losing this woman. He loved her too much.

Megis tried to open her eyes, but she was so dreadfully tired. She felt her sweat soaking the sheets and her pillow. Megis was confused. Why was it so hot in the house? Megis kept her eyes closed and tried going back to sleep. She was having a fine dream that she didn't want to end.

She rolled to the side and continued dreaming of Zack hugging her on the boat with beautiful Lake Winnipeg surrounding them on all sides. The waves lapped gently at the sides of the boat as they floated on the open waters. He leaned over to kiss her, his beard wet.

A voice mumbled through the fog.

Someone was calling her name.

She wondered briefly what was going on. Confusion assaulted her on every level. She'd much rather be sleeping. Megis curled onto her side and coughed harshly, clutching her abdomen. The voice grew more urgent. Why was everyone bothering her? Megis tried to ignore the insistent voice and fell back asleep. She had a wonderful dream to finish.

Zack awoke suddenly and felt his skin tingle. It was the middle of the night. He looked at Megis's side of the bed. She wasn't there. Zack curled into a ball and started weeping.

Zack grabbed the pillow on her side of the bed and hugged it fiercely like a small child. It hurt so much, he thought.

He would never have a wife. He would never have a family. She was gone.

Anita rolled over and cuddled Adam, spooning him with her naked body. They had just finished having sex, and it was so wonderful afterwards. It felt so good to have him in her arms, but the nagging truth wouldn't leave her consciousness. She had to tell him somehow.

Anita curled over top of him and gazed into his eyes. Her face dropped and looked more serious than she cared to show. "Have you ever had any secrets from your brother?" she asked.

Adam narrowed his eyes. "No, I don't believe so," he said. "I don't keep a lot of secrets, but I don't tell him everything either." Adam shifted in his chair. "Why would you ask that?"

"Nothing really. I was just curious," Anita said. "I just want us to be open and completely honest with each other." Anita tried to curtail the need to writhe her fingers together nervously.

"I am completely honest to you all the time," Adam replied. "Is there something you need to tell me, Anita?"

"No, no," she replied rather quickly. "Nothing like that. I just want us to have a good solid foundation for the future. I want to be sure that we have no cracks in our marriage. And if we do find one, we need to fill it with love and understanding."

"Anita, look if there's something you need to tell me," Adam stated. "Please just come out with it."

"Oh, of course," Anita said. "I meant you. Do you have anything you wanted me to know?"

"No, not really," Adam replied. "I believe I've told you everything. I am delighted that you're my wife, and we have a child together."

"Good," she replied. So, Zack had never told him, she thought. How many more years can she go on keeping it a secret? One day, she'll have to tell him that she had sex with his twin brother.

The radio was playing, and Zack's head hurt from weeks of drinking. It had been almost two months since he last spoke to Megis. The radio static sounded as another siren blared. It was an emergency news broadcast. Zack felt his heart grow colder every day, and he somehow knew that the announcement would not be good.

"Today is the day that will change history forever." The announcer said in a stoic voice. "Today, Canada has made the decision to join World War 2."

Zack felt a shiver run down his arms, up to his back and over his neck. War is upon us. The world had just progressed from bleak to bleaker, he thought.

"Adam," Anita said softly as she cradled Bjorn in her arms. The baby had fallen asleep breastfeeding, and she was feeling a surge of hormones.

"What is it?" Adam responded tiredly. "Are you okay?"

"Yes," Anita replied. "I just wanted you to know that I love you."

"I love you too, sweetheart," Adam answered back. "Are you sure you're okay?" He rolled over and started rubbing her arm.

Anita blinked and gazed at her wonderful husband. She loved him with every piece of her soul. She couldn't keep any secrets from him any longer. "I have something to tell you, Adam," she said slowly. Her heart thumped crazily in her chest. Adam deserved better than this. He deserved to know the truth. Her throat felt constricted, and Anita prayed that he would understand and realize that it was a tragic mistake.

Silence filled the darkening room.

Adam lifted himself up on one elbow, concern washing over him. It wasn't like Anita to talk like this. She always told him everything. They made decisions together in everything they did. His mind was confused. What could she possibly tell him that he didn't already know?

"Babe, what is it?" Adam said, his voice filled with concern.

Anita hugged Bjorn and rocked him as if somehow her baby would save them all. "There's something I've been keeping from you," she said, her voice shaking. "I didn't say anything before because I didn't want to lose you. I loved you from the day I met you at the Christmas party. I haven't found anyone attractive since. The only face that I ever loved was yours."

"What are you saying?" Adam asked.

"I have something to tell you that might make you mad," Anita said quickly. "But please don't be angry, please reserve judgement and see it for what it was; a mistake."

Adam sat straight up in the bed. He didn't know what to say. He felt bewildered and blindsided. Adam could not fathom what she was talking about. "Tell me," he said stonily.

"Promise me you won't get mad," she said quickly, hugging Bjorn tighter.

"I can't promise you that before I even know what you're going to tell me," he responded. "We are married, Anita, and we have a son. What do you think I'm going to do? I'm not going anywhere. I'm here for you no matter what."

"Promise?" she asked, her voice squeaking in a cracked whisper.

"What is it?" Adam exclaimed, his temper rising. "Tell me now, Anita or don't tell me at all."

Anita opened her mouth, and nothing came out. How does a wife tell her husband that she slept with his brother? "Remember when I told you that I met Zack before?" she said cautiously.

"Yes," Adam said, the suspicion in his voice evident.

"Well, I thought he was you when we met," she said slowly.

"You told me that before," Adam said, clearly annoyed now. "Is that all you want to tell me? Everyone mistakes us. We are identical twins, Anita!"

"No, there's more to the story," Anita said hastily.

"Like what?"

"I was so in love with you, Adam, you have to understand," she said, the words rushing out. "You were the only man that I wanted, and you were unavailable for so long. I thought it was my only chance to be with you, and we were all drunk. Nobody called him Zack at the party, so I didn't know it wasn't you, and I didn't even know that you had a twin brother at the time." She breathed in sharply. Time stood still for a microsecond. "I had sex with Zack that night."

Adam felt the blood rush into his brain, and the room began to spin. What was happening? How could this be kept from him for so long? He didn't know what to say. His entire body froze, and his brain went numb. No words came out of his mouth, no intelligent thoughts came to his mind, except a blinding rage towards his brother.

"Babe, I'm so sorry," Anita said quickly. "Please forgive me. Once I said your name the next morning, he immediately told me that he was your twin brother."

"You waited until morning to say my name?" Adam shouted.

"Please don't be mad," Anita pleaded. "Once we realized the mistake, I left and never talked to him again."

Adam took a deep breath in and then exhaled it out sharply. His blood was pumping in his ears. Nothing she said made any sense to him anymore. He trusted her. He married her. They had a baby together, and now she tells him, a year later. "Why did you wait so long to tell me?" Adam asked, trying to stem the rising anger in his voice. "How can I trust that you haven't buried other secrets?"

"I was so afraid of losing you, Adam!" she cried, her voice reaching a panicky pitch.

Adam stood up quietly and pulled on a pair of pants. He had to leave and think. His mind was clouded and angry; questions and possible answers swirled in his head, making rational thought impossible. He watched his son awaken from the shouting and begin to fuss. Adam grabbed a coat and roughly put his arms into it. Something suddenly made sense, like he had finally connected the dots, and a puzzle piece that was missing for so long was finally found. "Is Bjorn mine?" he asked crazily. "He was born one month prematurely."

Anita closed her eyes and exhaled heavily.

"Oh my Lord, Anita!" Adam shouted angrily. "Answer my question!"

"Bjorn most likely is Zack's," she said, exhaling nervously. "I didn't know until much later or even thought about it. You must believe me, Adam. It was just an honest mistake. Forgive me."

Adam felt the testosterone pump crazily through his arms, and his hands coiled into fists. He was a danger to himself and others. He needed to leave. "Does Zack know?"

"No," she said quickly. "I have never talked to him privately since. He has no idea that Bjorn might be his."

"So is Zack the father or just maybe?" Adam shouted. "Or likely? Which one is it, Anita!"

Anita curled into a ball, hugging Bjorn and started to cry. "I wanted to tell you because I don't want to keep secrets from you any longer," she said. "I want another child with you. I want us to have a big family and trust that there are no secrets."

Adam watched his wife cry, and his heart softened slightly, but his testosterone rage still had the upper hand. "I'm leaving," he said. "I need to walk and clear my head." He stomped out of the bedroom and rummaged in the closet for his rubber boots. It had been raining for many nights, and the fields were full of mud.

Anita stood and rocked Bjorn. She walked to the living room as Adam prepared to leave. "Are you going to tell Zack?"

"Hell, yes," he said angrily. "And then I'm going to break his nose."

Chapter 16

The rain hammered on the roof steadily. Zack felt the rainfall blending perfectly with the misery in his soul. Megis had opened up his heart, filled his life with hope and then filled him with tears of loss. He had cried for months in private, hiding from his family in fear of appearing weak. Every time he stood, his chest physically felt pain like a knife was somehow wedged in it.

There was still no word from Megis or her family. With the absence of communication, Zack's mind came up with an entire catalogue of negative conclusions.

She had simply wanted nothing other than a vacation buddy to take her on boat rides and show her all the sights of the beautiful town of Gimli. She was looking for someone to bring an end to her virginity and teach her all she needed to know about sex. Megis had lied and said she would move to Gimli just to ease the pain of leaving. She had no intention of moving here. Why would she? Megis had a family and a life in Regina. Why would she give all that up to be with him?

He was a fool.

Zack poured another shot of whiskey and stared at the yellowish liquid. He had quit drinking entirely for eight months. Then Megis came into his life, broke his heart and ruined any chance he had at staying sober. Why was life like this? Why can't life be joyful and every day another morning to look forward to? Why was it always something to overcome or drown in alcohol?

He pulled the chair out and stumbled to the bathroom. Mike had helped him transform part of the kitchen into a small lavatory. They had built a wall and moved in a small shower stall, toilet and a sink. The kitchen was much smaller now, but he had a bathroom with running water. He urinated and washed his hands quickly, an idea forming in his inebriated brain.

He was going to write Megis a letter, find her address and mail it. If he couldn't find her address, he would drive to Regina.

He couldn't just accept sitting here waiting like a stupid romantic fool. Zack needed to know the truth. Part of his mind rationally told him that he should wait until he was sober to write a letter, but there was no stopping him now. He was on a mission of enlightenment. This was the answer to his woes. If she rejected him, then Zack would have a conclusion. At least he could be content knowing that he had faced his problems like a man.

Zack stumbled back towards the living room, looking for a pen and paper. He shuffled in the drawer of a small cabinet, knocking over a lamp. It smashed to the ground in a loud bang, glass fragments scattering all over the floor.

Zack cursed. He wasn't sure if that lamp was one of his mom's favourites. He would have to find a replacement lamp that was similar. Maybe she would never notice. Zack searched for the broom to clean up and couldn't find it anywhere. He swore at himself for his alcohol-induced confusion. Where was the stupid broom?

It didn't matter. He'd clean it in the morning. Zack looked around the house. Clothes were strewn on the sofa, some hung on chairs, and several towels were thrown haphazardly on the floor. Cups and plates were left everywhere. The house was a mess, Zack reflected. He resolved to clean the entire house tomorrow.

But tonight, he had a letter to write. His footsteps crunched across the broken lamp as he pulled the chair out and sat down to write. The ink well was full, and Zack was afraid he'd knock that over too, so he switched to a lead pencil instead. He wrote:

Dear Megis,

Where have you been? Why did you say that you would send word and not do anything?

I need answers. I fell in love with you, Megis. My heart opened up for the first time in my life, and it feels like you stuck a knife inside of it. I feel wounded, and my heart needs to know if you love me too or if it was all just a fallacy, some cruel lie.

He looked down at the words he wrote and scribbled out most of them. It was just a bunch of rambling words that revealed his broken heart. Maybe she doesn't care anymore, and he should just walk away and forget her.

A noise sounded outside. Zack looked up, confused. He turned his head to the wall clock; it was midnight. There shouldn't be anyone outside at this time. The gravel on the road kicked up as a vehicle was driving towards the cottage. Then the brakes squealed to a stop, and an ignition turned off, followed by a door slamming harshly.

The urgency of the noises rattled Zack's nerves. He could feel something was about to happen, and he should prepare. Zack's mind ran crazily. How could he prepare when he was drunk? He looked around the messy house and shook his head. Whoever it was outside will see his pathetic state of being for the past month.

Heavy footsteps clomped onto the deck. Zack straightened, and a sudden rush of fight or flight response filled his brain, clearing the cobwebs of alcohol influence. He felt an eerie calm descend upon him. It was his twin brother. He knew those footsteps.

A heavy banging shook the wood door. Adam's knuckles rapped hard on the door. "Open up, Zack!" he shouted angrily.

Zack shouted back, "What do you want?" He took four long strides towards the door and yanked it open.

Adam's fist shot out with fury. But Zack was quicker. He had learned. Zack ducked and swiftly punched Adam in the gut, the impact throwing his twin brother a few steps backwards.

Zack straightened, shouting at Adam. "What are you doing here?"

Adam held his stomach in pain, then scowled angrily at Zack. "You know exactly why!" Adam shouted hysterically. "You had sex with Anita, you useless pig!"

Zack stood shocked by his words. Anita had told him the truth finally. His brother was here for revenge.

Adam charged Zack into the house, ramming his shoulder into Zack's chest. In the same movement, Adam struck out, punching Zack in the stomach. Zack stumbled back and slipped on the broken glass, sliding across the floor as Adam lost his balance, too, his feet flying up from underneath him and landing hard on his buttocks.

Zack looked up from the floor, raising his hands up in exasperation. "It was before you were dating her!" Zack growled angrily back. "I never touched her afterwards. She didn't want anything to do with me once she found out I wasn't you, you ungrateful hog!" He pulled himself up to a standing position, blood trickling from the back of his arm from the glass.

Adam released a roar of fury from the insulting words. He rushed Zack and missed, slamming into the sofa, pushing it against the wall. Zack pulled the back of Adam's collar and yanked his body backwards, knocking Adam off balance and started dragging him to the door. "You always have everything, the best girls, the best jobs, and you're always whining that it's not perfect!" Zack felt the bottled-up anger erupt from his body like a volcano. A year of suppressing his feelings exploded in fiery madness. "I would've given up the world for Anita! I loved her, you stupid shit!"

Adam curled his body sideways and lashed out violently at Zack's words, his legs and arms flailing like a mad man. Zack lost his grip, and Adam came at him like a freight train. He punched out in the air and his fist connected with Zack's jaw, throwing Zack off balance and stumbling a few feet back.

The wall saved Zack from hitting the floor, but Adam rushed him again, trying to pin him. Zack kneed him hard in the hip. They grappled for an eternity, clawing at each other like rabid animals. Adam's fists pounded, but they were too close, his strikes glancing off of Zack's shoulders. They grunted and clutched at anything they could get a hold of on each other. Zack ripped Adam's collar, trying to pull his hysterical brother off of him. Everything he grabbed was of no use; they were too close. He kneed him again and finally got a hold of Adam's ear and twisted.

"Ow, fuck," Adam screamed in a long vowel screech. "Let go!"

"No!" Zack screamed in his ear. "You're the one that barged into my house!"

"You're the one that kept it a fucking secret!" Adam shouted back.

"Your wife did that," Zack answered. "I just followed along because I didn't want to ruin it for you both. I was being respectful. But you don't fucking appreciate that, do you?"

Adam curled out of his brother's grasp and headbutted Zack square on the forehead.

"Fuck!" Zack yelled as dizziness swirled in his head.

Adam curled his right fist, ready to go for the knock-out blow.

"You're a loser!" Adam yelled. "You always were! A drunk and good for nothing."

Zack ducked, and Adam's fist cracked sickeningly into the wall. Adam howled in pain as his knuckle broke. Zack balled his fists into dangerous weapons and hailed a fury of right hooks to his brother's chin and face. Blood squirted from his face, and Adam fell to the floor, clutching his nose. Zack slipped on the glass, and blood ran down his arms. Both brothers splayed onto the floor spread eagle, exhausted from the exertion. Zack held his throbbing forehead, and Adam clutched his bleeding face. They both groaned in agony and panted heavily. Sweat dripped off Zack's face. The insults burned through his soul.

Several minutes passed before either brother spoke.

"Anita didn't want me once she found out I wasn't you, Adam," Zack said quietly. "She said that she was in love with you for a long time and that it was a horrible mistake."

Adam stared up at the ceiling, his right eye throbbing. "Anita told me that Bjorn is most likely yours."

Zack turned his face towards his brother. "What?" He couldn't believe what he had just heard.

"That's what she said," Adam replied. "Bjorn was born one month early. We thought he was premature, but he wasn't. Bjorn is your son."

Zack exhaled heavily and stared up at the ceiling, inspecting the knotted plywood. His mind wandered from the stress of the last two months. Bjorn was his son? "I don't know what to say," Zack responded slowly. "I'm sorry. I didn't know."

"It seems you are good at having illegitimate children," Adam sneered.

The words burned into Zack's heart. His brother was right. He was a mess. His house was destroyed, his girlfriend left him, and he was the worst kind of man there ever was. "Get out," Zack said calmly.

Adam pulled himself up slowly, wiping his sleeve over his bloodied face. No more words were needed. He had said all that he needed to say. Adam stumbled to the door, holding the frame for a few seconds to clear the dizziness from his head. He looked back into the house and watched his brother lying in the middle of a floor full of glass. He deserved everything coming to him, Adam thought.

Adam walked gingerly out to the car and left.

Zack awoke with blood crusted on his pillow. His left jaw was swollen, and his forehead had a large swelled egg-shaped protrusion on it. Zack groaned heavily. The pain was so much that his teeth hurt. His stomach curled in revolt. Zack felt the bile rise in his throat. He sat up gingerly on the bed with his head in his hands. What had he done with his life?

He carefully stood up and swayed. The floor was twirling. Zack stumbled across the living room, taking care not to fall on the broken glass again. He grasped the door frame leading to the kitchen to steady himself. Sunlight streamed in through the curtains, but the room still closed in on his thoughts. He wasn't the man that he always wanted to be. The bile rose in his throat again, threateningly. Zack stumbled to the bathroom quickly and fell to the toilet, grasping the bowl. He vomited, hurling all the liquor and disappointments into the sewer. Zack gasped, trying to breathe. His body was attacked by all means, physically, mentally and emotionally. This was the bottom, he thought.

He began to cry, holding onto the toilet bowl.

His brother's words rang in his head. He was good at having illegitimate children. He was a loser.

It was the cold hard truth.

He didn't deserve someone like Megis or Anita.

He cried heavily, the sobs racking his body with emotional pain. Zack had to do something to fix this, something drastic. He had to quit drinking; he knew that. But there was something more Zack had to do, a calling, a place he needed to go to absolve himself of the evils of his own actions.

Zack leaned back against the shower, his head up, staring towards the ceiling. His entire body felt pain, everything, his jaw, his head, his weak stomach, his mind and his heart. He felt like a car that had been towed to the automobile scrap yard.

Should he join a monastery? What else could he do? There must be something, he thought. Zack stared at the ceiling for some time until he saw a large spider crawl along the wall. It was making its way determinedly from the corner up the wall to a new spider web. It was making a new home, a new life.

That's it, Zack thought.

He needed to start over, a new place, a new city, a new life. He'd quit drinking and never have another drop of liquor, but he was also going to move away. He needed to reinvent himself, and there was a perfect opportunity brewing in the world.

Zack nodded and straightened himself, looking in the mirror. He splashed warm water on his face, rubbing soap on his cheeks and chin, washing his brother's blood off of him. He rinsed his bloodied arms and then dried everything off with a rough towel.

He stared at the image in the mirror. His left chin was disfigured, swelling out like the mumps. His forehead was grossly enlarged with a contusion protruding. His hair was sticky with blood.

"You are going to be a hero," he said to himself. "You are joining the war, my friend. It's about time. Now you can be the man you always wanted to be."

Zack leaned on the sink and stared at the deep blue eyes gazing back at him for several moments. Finally, he straightened and disrobed, discarding the thin robe onto the floor and stepping into the shower. Today was the day that he'd start going in the right direction.

"Momma," Megis cried as she bolted up in bed.

Silence. The room was deathly quiet.

What was going on? Megis opened her eyes and saw her mother sleeping on the sofa in their home. Her father was not in the room. She strained to remember the details of the past few weeks, and a chill of grief poured over her. Tears cascaded down her face, flooding from her eyes uncontrollably.

This cannot be happening. No, she thought. It's unbearable. She fell back asleep quickly, hoping that it was all just a dream and she would wake up with Zack beside her.

CHAPTER 17

The tires crunched over the dirt road as Mike's truck made one last stop on the way to Winnipeg. Zack jumped out at Annabella's house. His mom, dad, sister and all his cousins were saying their goodbyes. Zack felt overwhelmed by emotion at the family support he was receiving. He pushed the diamond ring deep into his pants pocket. Zack didn't know what else to do with it. His brain wanted to sell it, but his heart refused to let go. So he just shoved it deeper into his pocket.

Nath stepped forward first and hugged Zack warmly, his eyes moist.

"I am upset that another war is taking another loved one," Nath said. "First, it was Mike, and I thank God that he came back in one piece. Now, it's my beloved son." Nath hugged Zack tight and tried to stop the tears from flowing out. "You can always change your mind right now, Zack. You don't have to go. Drafting hasn't started yet. This is voluntary what you're doing."

"I know, Pabbi," Zack replied, hugging his father tightly. "It is something I need to do. I've spent too many years making a mess of my life, and now I'm giving back. The Navy needs someone with my boating experience and my wild nature. I will be back, Pabbi. You don't have to worry about me." Zack released his father and looked him in the eyes. "You need to do me a favour while I'm gone, Dad."

Nathan looked into his son's eyes, knowing what he would say next. "I will take care of your daughter and mother."

Zack nodded. "Yes. My daughter and momma mean the world to me, but so do you, Dad. I need you to take care of yourself too. I want to come back and have my father still fighting. Promise me."

Nath blinked and wondered if he could live another few years. His body was quickly deteriorating, and he felt weak most days. He was 81. It was incredible that he had lived to this age so far. He could make it a little while longer. "I've lived this long, Zack," Nathan said. "I'm not going anywhere until I see you again. Trust me."

Zack embraced Nath again and then turned to his mother, hugging her and Josie tight. "Take care of Dad," he whispered in her ear. "And my daughter."

Maria smiled and kissed him on the cheek. "I will always be your dad's angel, don't worry." She released him and looked into his blue eyes. "Your daughter will thrive with us. Don't fret about your family. Be brave, my son, but don't be reckless. Stay strong and come back to us, Zack. I love you. We all love you."

"I'm going to come back, Mom. I promise," Zack said. "And I'm going to come back a better man."

Zack hugged his sister, Annabella, and all his cousins, waving to everyone as he stepped back into the truck with Mike.

"Are you ready?" Mike asked.

"Yes, I'm ready," Zack replied.

Mike and Zack waved to everyone as the truck pulled out onto the highway to Winnipeg. Zack glanced one last time back towards his family and waved again. "I will miss everyone," he said.

Mike looked in the rear-view mirror and noticed something strange. He glanced curiously at Zack, a question nagging at him. "I didn't see Adam at the family farewell," Mike said. "Are you guys on good terms?"

"We're fine," Zack lied. "I heard he got into a fight and got some black eyes." He smiled inwardly, knowing that he had faired much better than Adam had. The swelling on Zack's chin had gone down within two days, and nobody even knew that he had gotten into a major fight several days ago. "He probably doesn't want anybody to see him in that state."

"Strange, do you know who he got into a fight with?" Mike asked.

"Not sure," Zack lied again. "Probably somebody he shouldn't have picked a fight with!" He chuckled cruelly and gazed out the window at the countryside rushing by.

Mike shook his head slightly. "I never understood the rivalry between you two brothers."

Zack smiled and rubbed his sore chin. "Everyone has their moments," he said. "I love my brother, and I wish him the best."

The truck pulled up to the Royal Canadian Navy Volunteer Reserve recruiting office. The Winnipeg Division, as it was called then, was established in April 1923 to provide a training base for the RCNVR. Similar country-wide Navy divisions existed in almost every other Canadian city, including

Vancouver, Calgary, Ottawa, Toronto, Montreal, and many other cities. The Winnipeg Division was run by Commander Eustace Brock. The recruiting office was quite busy. Zack had heard that many seamen were needed to serve in the war.

Mike stopped the truck and stepped out as Zack straightened. "This is the day when your life is going to change drastically, Zack," Mike said seriously. "They'll shave all your hair off, and you'll be exhausted every night of training until your body becomes accustomed to the rigorous demands. Are you one hundred percent sure that you want this?"

Zack closed the truck door gently. "I have never been so sure of something in my life," he replied.

"Okay," Mike said, hugging him warmly. "You'll be fine then. I thought the same way back in 1915, and I made it." Mike leaned on his good leg. "But I almost didn't."

"I know," Zack said. "I heard all the stories of your time serving as a sniper at Vimy Ridge. You were a hero."

"Nobody's born a hero, Zack," Mike said. "You are trained that way. Sometimes you have a gift like I did with sharpshooting or like you do with boats, but it is the training that'll keep you alive. Listen and learn everything you can. Then maybe you can come back home one day when this is all over."

Zack hugged him once more. "Wise words," he said. "I have the deepest respect for you, Mike. I always have. I'll learn and listen like you said."

Mike hugged him tight. He loved Zack as if they were brothers. Mike began to get emotional. He decided to make this a short farewell. He couldn't bear the thought of Zack not returning from war. "Okay," Mike said. "Get out of here and go join the Navy."

Zack smiled and let go of Mike. He walked bravely towards the doors and looked back, waving to Mike. "I'll write!" Zack yelled back as he opened up the door.

Mike waved and whispered to himself as he walked back to the truck. "Stay alive, Zack. Just stay alive."

Zack was quickly accepted as a seaman in the RCNVR. He had undergone a complete medical examination and was tested for his level of physical fitness. The standards of joining the Navy were high, and each sailor needed to be fit and able. They cut his hair down to almost nothing, and Zack now wore a sailor's hat over his short hair.

The Barracks were overflowing with new recruits and only a few experienced seamen. Winnipeg's Naval Reserve Division was an important Canadian recruiting and training base for the war effort.

Zack gazed around, astonished. The Barracks and all the connected areas seemed to be very similar to a ship. There was a deck for drills and classes for man afloat. The Unit held approximately 200 men and conducted parades once a week. Zack had already been thrown into intense training of gunnery, torpedo and seamanship skills. Most of the seaman skills he had already known, but the torpedoes and guns were fascinating. Tomorrow, he would be learning the basics of wireless telegraphy and nautical instrumentation. Zack had never before known anything about telegraphy, so he was looking forward to learning something new. The complex array of navigational instrumentation was something he knew well, but Zack was sure that a large war ship had many instruments he had probably never seen before.

Zack was in a group of new recruits called the Ordinary Seamen. They were having lunch. He sat down at a nearby empty table and fingered the diamond ring in his pocket aimlessly. It had become a nervous habit of his. Zack looked around. Several other junior rank designations sat at separate tables. Their arm bands showed they were the Able and Leading Seamen. The Petty Officers ate farther away in their own section. For now, Zack was at the bottom of the ranks. Not for long, he thought. Zack would prove his expertise and rise in the ranks. He slurped up the soup and bit into the delicious bun.

Another Ordinary Seaman bumped his shoulder. "Sorry," the man apologized, placing his tray down and seating himself beside Zack. "What brought you here to Winnipeg?"

Zack chewed and swallowed the piece of bun in his mouth. "Just needed a change in my life," Zack answered. "I have been a fisherman all my life, so I'm used to living on boats." Zack chuckled. "What's your name, Seaman?"

"My name is Petro Kovalchyk," the man said. "What's yours?"

"Zack Olason," he said, putting his hand out for a handshake.

Petro shook his hand, nodding. "You are Icelandic?" he asked.

"Yes," Zack replied, chuckling. "The last name is a giveaway. And you are Ukrainian?"

"I sure am," Petro said, dipping his bun into the hot soup. "I came here with my cousin Anton as refugees during the famine; barely made it to Canada alive."

Zack stopped chewing and swallowed. "You don't mean Anton Kozak?" Zack said incredulously.

"You know him?" Petro replied, wiping the soup from his clean-shaven chin.

"Anton is my nephew's second cousin!" Zack replied excitedly.

"Oh my, isn't that a coincidence?" Petro said. "Did Anton join the Navy as well? I heard he had moved up to the Gimli area while most of us refugees stayed in Winnipeg."

"I worked with him!" Zack said, laughing. "Mike Kozak owns the fishery in Gimli now. Anton works for him, and I used to help out."

"Small world!" Petro said. "So they didn't join the Navy with you?"

"No," Zack said. "Not yet. Anton never mentioned joining the war, and he's quite busy with the fishery. Mike was injured serving with the infantry during World War One. I'm the only man in my family that voluntarily joined the Navy."

"Ah, I see," Petro said. "Well, hopefully, it is a good choice for all of us."

Zack nodded. He was pretty sure that it was a good decision. It had felt like home since Zack had first stepped foot onto the Barracks. This was his future now, and he was thrilled about the possibilities.

"It is a good choice," Zack said. "I can feel it."

The training was brutal and intense. Zack's muscles had finally started to become accustomed to the daily rigorous demands. It had only been two weeks, but Zack was happy he had made the decision to join the Navy. His new life purpose kept his mind busy. He rarely thought of Megis and his women troubles. He was changing into a better man. Zack didn't have a woman, nor did he care. The sailors had some free evenings when they would prowl the streets in search of women and liquor. Most women had a strange attraction to a man in a uniform, and most of the seamen took advantage of this, having sex in alleyways and taverns during their nights off.

Zack was not attracted to any of the women. He wasn't sure why, but for some reason, nobody captured his attention. It was most likely because his heart still belonged to Megis. It would take time to forget her, he thought. Zack never really knew how it felt to be truly in love with someone until now. His heart still hurt, but it no longer felt empty. Zack was slowly learning how to fill his heart with purpose.

He had made good friends with Petro, and they often prowled the streets smoking cigarettes and talking about life during their breaks. Zack was happy with his new life. Except he didn't have a woman anymore. He fingered the ring in his pocket aimlessly. Zack was content without a woman, he told himself.

CHAPTER 18

Megis lifted the blanket onto her knees and fought the shiver that threatened to overtake her entire body. The weather was quickly growing colder and colder. October had brought a new snow storm, and they had waited until it passed before making plans.

She had started feeling much better in the past few weeks. Her energy had returned, and then she realized with a shock that she needed to see Zack. Just like that, the cloud of grief had lifted.

She loved Zack with a fury like none other, but nothing could have prepared her for the whirlwind of loss that followed. Her father's cough that started in Regina had worsened. After a week, he began coughing so severely that it took his breath away. He had eventually relented, and they took him to the hospital. There was an increasing shortage of doctors because many had enlisted with the war, so it created a chaotic atmosphere in the emergency department. Finally, they were brought in, and the doctor said that it was a simple cold virus. They prescribed a chest rub ointment and lots of rest, sending them all home in a rush.

Both Megis and her mother caught the same virus immediately. They fell dangerously ill too. The virus had invaded their chests. The coughing was terrible; her father had suffered the worst. After many years of smoking, the virus had severely weakened his lungs. The throat infection that developed afterwards was fast and deadly.

Megis and her mom tried everything to help him, but they were also very sick. They gave him warm baths, tea and lots of water. Everything they did was useless; it was as if they were running in circles.

Soon after, a frightening red rash appeared on his face and spread to his neck. They were upset with his refusal to go back to the hospital. The next day, his temperature spiked so badly that they called a doctor for a house visit. The doctor arrived that afternoon and was alarmed at the state of everyone in the house. He looked in their throats and was shocked to find that they all had contracted scarlet fever.

Health officials arrived that day with a quarantine sign for the door. Everyone was prevented from leaving the house. It was a horrible ordeal with Megis and her mom also growing sicker and sicker every day. The fever that Megis had awakened with for three days straight was frightening. Megis's body fought the scarlet fever valiantly. Her fever had improved, but then the fatigue took over. She had slept for an entire week! It took a long time to recover, but she did it. Her mother was able to fight the virus successfully, too, but sadly Joseph had not. Megis's father died in his bed as she and her mother slept.

Her mother was so distraught that it was all Megis could do to keep her small family together. Her aunts and uncles came by after health officials had declared it safe. They helped with the funeral arrangements. They were grateful, although the loss of her father was still a huge blow to their small family.

Megis hadn't even had time to think of Zack until the end of September. She remembered that she was supposed to send word! Megis felt embarrassed that she had forgotten entirely. She had often been sleeping, dreaming of Zack throughout the illness. When Megis awoke, her mind was in a fog. The funeral was emotionally exhausting and left them both in a terrible state of grief.

Finally, in early October, after the emotional haze began to lift, Megis asked her mother if she would like to come with her to Manitoba. They loved it there so much, and they could make a new start in life.

The train rattled as they neared Gimli. She watched her mother sleeping silently beside her in the coach seat. They had been on the train for two long days, and Megis squirmed uncomfortably in her seat. They would be arriving in the next hour.

She felt a sombre hope in seeing Zack again. Had it really been more than three months? Megis wrapped the blanket tighter around her torso. She worried that he would hate her for not sending word. Once he realized what had happened in her family, he would understand. She would make it up to him. Her life had been turned upside down since those glorious two weeks in Gimli with Zack. The memories still made her smile and blush. She loved him more than ever.

The train slowed into Gimli and pulled to a complete stop. Megis and her mother grabbed their luggage and disembarked.

They would send for the rest of their belongings once they finalized everything with Zack.

The ground was already covered with snow, and the cold wind blew harshly in Megis's face. Her heart felt like it was in her throat. She felt so apprehensive and upset like everything was going wrong. Megis helped her mother out of the train car, and they walked to Zack's parents' place first. It was a long walk to Willow Beach, and hopefully, Mike or Ivan would drive them out to the cottage. Megis realized that she had not planned this move very well and tried to hide her fears from her mother. She braced herself for the unknown.

Megis knocked on the door of the large white house on the beach. She heard a baby cry. That must be Josie, she smiled. Several seconds later, the door opened.

It was Maria with the baby in her arms. She looked stunned and quite shocked. "Megis!" she said, startled. "You're here!"

Megis intuitively knew something was wrong. "I'm so sorry," she said, stumbling over her words. "So much has happened since I left back in July. My father caught a bad virus, and we were all quarantined. My mother and I have recovered, but sadly my father did not."

"Oh my Lord," Maria said. "Come in, my sweetheart. I'm so sorry to hear about your father. I am glad you are both okay."

"I would have sent word," Megis said nervously. "But we couldn't leave the house, and then we were preparing for my father's funeral. I brought my mother with me. We decided because of the circumstances that she would also move here." Megis peered into the quiet house. "Is Zack here? I thought we'd come here first because it is such a long walk from the train station."

"You arrived by train?" Maria asked incredulously.

"Yes," Megis answered. "Neither my mother nor I drive." Megis introduced her mother, Janet, to Maria. They chatted amicably until finally, Megis asked the same question again. "Is Zack here? Or is he at work?"

Maria's face fell sadly, the smile erasing from her face.

Megis's skin tingled. Something was terribly wrong.

"I'm so sorry, Megis," Maria said softly. "Zack left for Winnipeg a few weeks ago. He thought you were never coming."

Megis felt her knees wobble, and she grasped the sofa weakly.

"Sit down, sweetheart," Maria said, gesturing to the sofa.

Megis sat down heavily. What a mess her life was, she thought. What was she to do? She didn't want to marry anyone else but Zack. She had no attraction for anyone else. Megis instantly felt remorse for not sending word. Her heart sank for the pain she had put him through. "He must have thought I had left him," Megis said aloud.

Maria sat down beside her and rubbed her back. "Zack was very heartbroken, yes," she said. "If only he could have stayed in town just a few more weeks. He didn't hear any word from you and assumed the worst. I'm so sorry. If there's anything I can do to help, please let me know. You can stay with us."

Megis began to sob. She looked up at Maria as the tears blurred her eyes. "We will go to Winnipeg then," she said through her pain, wiping her eyes. "Do you know his address? I must explain and apologize to him."

Maria swallowed. "He joined the Navy, Megis," she said. "He is living at the Naval Barracks in Winnipeg. I'm not sure if they allow visitors."

Megis felt the weight of the past few months crash down on her, and she cried heavily. Maria hugged her, and Janet came to her side as well, rubbing her daughter's back.

"We will find a solution, Megis," Maria said. "It's obvious that you both love each other very much. There must be a way."

Megis felt the tsunami of grief pour over her. She had lost her father, gotten sick herself, then recovered, buried her father, took care of her grieving mother and now she had lost the love of her life as well. Life was so unfair, and she couldn't make sense of anything anymore. Her life felt directionless and hollow. What would she do? The option of turning back was not even in her mind. She was here to spend the rest of her life with the man that she loved.

Megis sniffled as her mom rubbed her shoulders. "What if we moved to Winnipeg?" her mother asked. "Sailors have evenings off. We can find a place to settle near the base."

Megis's eyes glinted hopefully. "Do you think so?" she asked.

Maria smiled. "Your mother's right," she said cheerfully. "Zack has some cousins in Winnipeg. I can ask them if you can stay for a while until you find housing. Aunt Anita's children had installed a telephone at their house in Winnipeg. Annabella also has a new telephone; we can walk over to her place in Gimli and call the family in Winnipeg."

Megis wiped her eyes and straightened. Maybe there was hope. She just had to believe, Megis thought. She had come this far. Megis had moved to an entirely different province! She could not turn back now. "Okay," Megis said. "I would greatly appreciate anything you could do for us."

Maria pulled Josie onto her shoulder as the baby began to squirm. "Let me feed her, and then we'll go," she said, turning to Janet. "I will introduce you to Nath, and if you can stay with the baby, I will take Megis to Annabella's, and we will get this sorted out."

"That would be lovely," Janet said.

"Thank you, Maria," Megis said gratefully.

"Don't thank me," Maria said, nodding knowingly. "I know how it feels to be helplessly in love. I married Nath twenty-two years ago. He was the love of my life back then, and he still is now. I would travel anywhere in the world for him. My son deserves the same kind of woman, and you're that woman, Megis. You will meet with Zack again, and I'll help you find him."

CHAPTER 19

Z ack learned of the details regarding the passenger liner named SS Athenia. During the evening on the exact same day that Britain declared war on Germany, Athenia was sunk by the German U-boat U-30 on September 3, 1939. Travelling from Glasgow to Montreal, the liner had approximately 1100 passengers and 300 crew members, mostly Canadians, Americans and European refugees escaping the war.

As night fell across the Atlantic, Captain Fritz-Julius Lemp of U-30 spotted Athenia travelling without lights and in a defensive anti-submarine pattern. He quickly concluded that it was indeed an armed enemy ship. Spurred into action, he ordered torpedoes to be fired at the ship.

One of those torpedoes hit Athenia on the port side, striking a fatal blow. The crew members on that side of the boat died instantly as well as many passengers who were flooded in the nearby cabins. Captain Lemp rose the submarine and peered out at the hit, and realized his mistake. It was a grave error. He had struck the passenger liner SS Athenia. Lemp knew that

Germany was under treaty not to sink civilian passenger ships, only merchant and enemy ships. The captain immediately swore secrecy upon his crew, erased his entries in the logbook and attempted to continue on as if nothing had happened.

A lifesaving emergency response on the SS Athenia commenced, releasing 26 lifeboats and sending distress signals. The Norwegian freighter, MS Knute Nelson, and the Swedish steam yacht, Southern Cross, arrived on the scene after midnight, rescuing survivors and offering aid. HMS Electra and two other Royal Navy destroyers also reached the sinking ship during the night, rescuing the remaining survivors. Athenia sunk fully before noon, her stern sinking first and then heeling over into the ocean, claiming over 100 lives.

The German government had denied involvement and implied that the British had sunk the ship to force the USA into the war. Public opinion in Canada, Britain and the USA was much different. Germany had deliberately sunk a passenger liner. This judgement was confirmed with the sinking of several naval and merchant ships following the attack.

The war on the Atlantic had begun.

Canada, Britain and the USA needed sailors, ships and training. Convoys were immediately introduced. The first such convoy set sail from Halifax, HX-1, with the escort of HMC Ships Saguenay and St. Laurent on September 16. The destroyers' duties were to protect the convoy from submarines. The role of the convoy system was to support the safe arrival of ships and avoidance of German submarines. Special intelligence was being formulated to break the German operational codes for the North Atlantic, and Zack was learning this in training as well. But sometimes, the commanders said, the U-boats could not be avoided, and the role of RCNVR could quickly change to an intense fight on the Atlantic Ocean.

Zack had finished his weapons training by the first week in October. The Vickers guns were mainly used on the ships, and he was quickly becoming well-trained at shooting the large guns. But even more valuable was his seamanship. He knew direction and boats better than anyone. Coupled with his mechanical skills, he was the perfect navigational seaman for the RCNVR.

Some special ships were being proposed to amass a stronger presence around the convoys. Zack and his shipmates would most likely be on these vessels. It would take time for the government to build boats, and Canada was scrambling for ways to increase the Navy's presence on the open seas. They would know more very soon. The war on the Atlantic was in their sights.

"I'm sorry, Miss," the sailor said. "Seaman Zack Olason is not available at this time. He is in the middle of nautical training right now."

"But," Megis objected. "I need to see him. We were separated when my father passed away. He doesn't know that I finally came back to be with him. Please, I need to speak to him."

The sailor tilted his white hat down over his forehead, as was required by the Navy. He looked thoughtfully down at the ledger book. "I am sorry, Miss," he said solemnly. "I wish I could help, but I can't interrupt him right now." He rubbed his smoothly shaven chin. "You can return later this evening after dinner for a quick 30-minute visit. But wait, I think his crew has an evening off tomorrow." The sailor checked the schedule. "Yes, they have tomorrow off. The men mostly go to the taverns down the street. You will be able to see him there all night tomorrow evening. They are not due back until 7 am. Your choice, Miss."

"Thank you, Sailor," Megis said. She turned and left the base, walking out into the blistering wind. It was a cold autumn day, and the winter loomed ahead. She was disappointed and elated at the same time. Megis had moved all the way to Winnipeg for him, and she could not see him today. However, her heart lifted with joy at the chance to see him tomorrow for an entire evening!

Mike had driven Megis and her mother to the relative's house in Winnipeg. The relatives were more than happy to supply them with accommodations in exchange for childcare. It was wartime, there was so much to be done, and many women had to work the jobs left vacant by the men. The household was delighted to have live-in childcare.

Megis slumped her shoulders and walked back home. It was a far walk, more than five miles away from the Winnipeg Division. She looked at her watch; it was 10 am. Megis had to walk all the way back home and then return to the tavern tomorrow night.

But it would be worth it if it meant she would be looking into his handsome face again, Megis thought.

She straightened her shoulders and told herself that the strong persevere. Megis would do anything to hold him in her arms again. Hopefully, he is there tomorrow night, she thought.

His body hurt. His muscles ached, and his brain was overloaded with training, procedures and methods. Zack felt his weary body crave whiskey intensely. His sailor mates invited him to the tavern tonight. At first, he was going to decline, but lastly, he accepted at the final moment. He needed to get out and just have an evening off. He handed in his duty card at the door and left with the group.

They arrived at the tavern in a rambunctious mood. Petro, Zack and five other young sailors sauntered into the saloon, their hats tilted up in the usual defiance of Navy regulations. If caught, they would be reprimanded, but it was common for the sailors to tilt their hats, so Zack joined in.

Petro walked up to the bar, smashing his hand down. "Two whiskeys!" he said to the bartender.

The bartender nodded and poured the golden liquid.

Zack watched as the other five men ordered their drinks. Petro handed one glass of whiskey to Zack. He accepted it, looking down into the liquid as if something magical was in it.

"Are you alright?" Petro asked.

"I'm fine," Zack said. "I actually quit drinking before joining the Navy. So I'm not sure whether I will be drinking at all tonight."

"Give it to me then," Petro said, laughing. "I will have your drinks for you."

Zack hesitated briefly, then handed over the drink. Petro tilted it up and downed the entire glass in one swoop, wiping his chin with his sleeve. "Let's get closer to those girls over there," Petro said, nodding in the direction of the back wall partition separating the men from the women.

Several girls giggled on the other side of the wall, but they couldn't hear what was said. Petro tried peering around the partition. "You'll get caught!" Zack said as they sat down at the table.

"No one is looking," Petro said bravely. He leaned back in the chair, feigning stretching, and smiled as he caught a fleeting glance of the women. Petro leaned forward. "They are all pretty," he whispered. "I want them all, every single one of them."

Zack laughed heartily, "Too much time in the barracks, Petro?"

"Ha!" Petro chuckled. "Most likely true!" He drank the second drink and stood to get another. "Are you sure you don't want a whiskey or rum?"

"I'm sure," Zack said, smiling and enjoying the night. "Grab me a water on the rocks!"

"Will do!" Petro shouted back as the remaining men in their group crowded to the small table, seating themselves loudly.

Zack strained to hear the women on the other side of the partition. He could only catch a few phrases. Sailor, war and handsome, were some of the words Zack had picked up. He was curious what the women looked like. Zack was a single man, after all.

One of the sailors chuckled drunkenly. "We should go meet up with these girls outside after our drinks!"

Petro joined in, slamming Zack's glass of water on the table. Zack eyed the whiskey in Petro's hand. The temptation was strong. He could have only one or two drinks, Zack thought. He stood and deliberated silently in his head.

Suddenly Petro slapped his shoulder hard. "Let's go outside and meet these beautiful women," He yelled deliberately at the partition, hoping the women would overhear.

It worked! The women were quiet. One chair scratched over the floor.

"Come, Zack!" Petro said joyfully. "You and I are the most handsome here! We will get the women to notice us!" Petro pulled Zack by the arm out the door and into the street.

Zack laughed and followed along. Petro stumbled over the uneven pavement and almost lost his balance as three young women stepped out onto the street, covering heavy shawls over their shoulders to stay warm.

Petro straightened and approached the women. "Beautiful ladies tonight," he said, tipping his hat off. "Do you ladies live around here?"

All of the women giggled. One woman responded, "Yes, we are all from Winnipeg, Sailor."

"Name is Petro," he said gallantly, bowing. "Pleased to meet your acquaintance."

One of the women eyed Zack. "And what's your name, Sailor?"

Zack smiled shyly. "My name is Zack."

"Nice to meet you," she said smoothly.

Petro moved into the group of women with amazing speed, his arm around two of the women already. The third woman moved beside Zack. She was pretty, her hair long and light brown, although she didn't have the alluring brown eyes like Megis. He grinned and chastised himself. Megis was gone. He should just accept it and move on.

But something held him back. He wasn't attracted to this woman. Zack couldn't force himself to be attracted to someone that he was not. The woman pulled slightly away from him, sensing his discomfort.

Suddenly, a familiar voice lilted behind him. "Zachary Olason," another woman said, her voice ladled with a sultry hint of intimacy. "That's his full name, right, Zack?"

Zack felt a shiver run up his entire spine. Were his ears playing tricks on him? He swung around and came face to face with the love of his life.

Megis stood confidently, one hand on her hip and her other hand curling the hair around her ear.

"Megis!" Zack shouted.

"Zack," Megis replied smoothly, even though her heart was hammering in her chest at seeing him again. His handsome blue eyes bore into hers.

"You're here!" Zack said in shock. "How is this possible? You never came back from Regina!"

The girl faded away and joined Petro and her friends, obviously excluded from the reunited couple.

"I did come back, Zack," Megis said. "Last week. My father was very sick after we returned. Sadly, he passed away. We all caught Scarlet Fever and were forced to quarantine. I was very sick too." Her brown eyes glowed in the night. "I'm sorry, Zack. I should have sent word." She touched his arm.

Electricity from her touch shot through his forearm. He instinctively reached out for her hand and held her tiny palm in his. "You moved to Gimli?" Zack asked, still astonished that he was talking to Megis on a random street in Winnipeg.

"Yes, I moved with my mother," she said simply. Her entire body wanted to hug him fiercely. It was as if a large magnet was pulling her to him. "We spoke to your mother, Maria, and she told us that you joined the Navy. She arranged for Mike to move us to Winnipeg."

"You're living in Winnipeg?" Zack said incredulously.

"Yes," Megis said softly, feeling a bit embarrassed. "We are living temporarily with your relatives in Winnipeg. We will find a place of our own when I start working in one of the factories."

Zack leaned towards her, the magnetic pull too much for him to resist. His arms slid around her waist, and he pulled her in close, hugging her. She melted in his arms. "You must feel so uncertain and out of sorts in a new city," Zack said calmly.

"Yes, I do," she mumbled into his shirt.

"Let's go for a walk," Zack said, pulling her away from the group and slipping his hand into hers.

They walked along for several blocks as Megis told him all the details of her arrival in Gimli, Winnipeg, her father's death and the sailor at the base telling her to go to the tavern. Zack filled her in on the past two months and his decision to join the Navy and quit drinking.

"Oh! You quit drinking?" Megis asked curiously. "Why?"

"Megis," he said, stopping on the street. "I have a problem with alcohol."

"What kind of problem?" she asked innocently.

"I think I am addicted," he confessed. "It's a real struggle for me."

"You didn't drink that much when we were together in Gimli," Megis pointed out.

"True," he said. "I had quit because of my daughter." Zack looked down at his shoes as they continued walking. "I started again after I thought you had left."

"I'm sorry," she said sincerely.

"No," Zack interrupted softly. "It's not your fault. Alcohol is just my way of dealing with life's problems. I know it's not right, and it's not healthy, but I get addicted to the pain."

"Oh," she said quietly.

"You shouldn't be with me," Zack said. "I'm not a good man."

Megis stopped abruptly and faced him, her head almost an entire foot shorter than him. "Listen to me, Zack," she said softly. "I fell in love with you in Gimli. The moments we spent together were beyond special. You are still that wonderful man." She grabbed both of his hands, and their eyes glinted together in the dark. "I know you're not perfect, but neither am I."

"So you still want me?" Zack asked.

"Yes," Megis replied. "More than ever." She looked down, tears welling in her eyes. "You must have been so hurt," Megis said, thoughtfully. "You must have thought I decided not to return to you. I'm so sorry, Zack, for putting you through that."

Zack swallowed and looked up at the moon. Several seconds passed before he said anything. "You were sick?" he said simply.

"Yes," she replied. "We were all very sick. Our home was under quarantine."

"Oh, my," he said, his emotions fighting with the pain of heartbreak.

She stopped and hugged him hard. "Please forgive me, Zack," she said, her voice muffling into his chest. "I should have sent a note for someone to send to you. I was very sick. I dreamt of you every night."

Zack looked at her with concern. "I'm sorry I wasn't there for you," he said.

"There was nothing you could have done," Megis said. "The health officials refused to allow us to leave our own home."

"That must have been horrible," Zack said sincerely.

"It was," she said softly, burying her head in his chest.

His heart broke wide open, and tears threatened to escape his eyes. He couldn't believe he was actually holding Megis in his arms again. Was she really here to stay?

"You came here to Winnipeg for me?" Zack asked.

"Yes," Megis said. "I want to be with you, just like we had planned. But I guess it'll be a bit different now since you live at the Navy base."

"I love the Navy, Megis," Zack blurted out. "It gives me purpose. More than I ever thought it would."

"I can see that in your eyes," Megis said proudly.

"So," Zack said slowly. "Would you still be with me even though I will be away serving with the Navy?"

"Yes, of course," Megis said reassuringly. "I will stand by you. I didn't come this far for just anyone. I came here for you, and I won't ever leave you again."

Zack hugged her tight and laid his chin on top of her head, kissing the crown of her hair. He felt a single tear escape his eyes as he fought to maintain his composure. His heart lifted, and his hopes soared. They hugged underneath the moonlight for several moments, just swaying in each other's embrace, enjoying the scent of each other and the physical warmth of their bodies.

After several minutes, Zack leaned down and kissed her lips. She reached her neck up and stood on her tiptoes. He crouched down to reach her smaller body, and his hands grasped her small waist as they kissed again, the chemistry building between them. His tongue explored her mouth and tasted her honey sweetness. It felt like he was floating on a cloud of impossible happiness.

Finally, he broke the kiss and looked into her large brown eyes. He aimlessly put his hand in his pocket and fiddled with the ring, just like he had been doing for the past month. Then as if a light bulb had been suddenly switched on in his head, Zack clutched the ring in his fist. He swallowed, his heart full of hope.

Zack smiled broadly. "I bought you a ring a long while ago," he said nervously. "I didn't know what to do with it, so I just put it in my pocket."

"You bought me a ring?" she asked incredulously.

"Yes," Zack replied. "It was supposed to be a surprise when you moved to Gimli."

Her large brown eyes moistened with emotions. "You walked around with it in your pocket?" Megis asked.

"Yes," Zack answered. "I never wanted to let it go. I couldn't."

Megis smiled with tears streaming down her cheeks as he removed his fist from his pocket. "What?" she asked in surprise.

Zack grasped her hand and bent down on one knee. "I think I need to do this the right way," he said. Zack opened his fist and in his palm was the small, simple gold ring with a tiny diamond. It twinkled back at her. "Megis, would you marry me?" he asked, his voice cracking with emotion.

Her face broke into the biggest smile he had ever seen. "Oh my Lord!" she said passionately. "Yes, Zack! Yes!" Tears streamed freely down her cheeks as she half cried and laughed at the same time.

Zack's heart soared. He smiled broadly and slipped the ring onto her finger. "My wife," he said sweetly.

He kissed her again, his tongue probing her mouth, eager to claim her as his wife. He felt compelled to fill her with his manly urgency. She met his desire back with an intensity that spiralled both of them out of control. Zack peered down the street and noticed it was deserted. They were standing beside an alterations shop with a closed sign hanging over the inside of the door. The red brick exterior walls were clean, and the canopy over top of the entrance shielded them from prying eyes. Zack grasped her hand and ran with her to the darker alcove entrance, as they both giggled like teenagers.

They kissed feverishly, unable to contain their passion.

"It's been so long," she said breathlessly. "I missed you so much."

"I missed you too," Zack said as he kissed her lips and ran his hands along her cheeks. "I love you, Mrs. Olason."

She kissed him back passionately. "I love you, Zachary Olason," she said breathlessly. "Please. I want you inside of me. I want a family with you."

Zack rode the waves of passion and lifted her legs up over his arms. She was so light that he held her suspended against the brick wall. Megis panted and started lifting her dress up hastily.

"Yes," she breathed. The passion burned like a hot fire between them, hastening them to reunite intimately.

Zack fumbled with his pants and zipper. He balanced himself and held her up while she brought her slender legs high around his waist, suspended in the air. Zack dropped his pants and entered her vagina smoothly and quickly. There was no holding back tonight. She breathed heavily into his shoulder, panting from the urgency. Zack was overcome with testosterone, driven by an instinctive urge to reproduce. He thrust into her like an animal, pushing her slightly higher up the wall. She groaned, clutching onto him, mumbling words of love.

Zack thrust several more times until his control completely vanished, and his orgasm threatened to rob him of his sanity. He groaned heavily, releasing all the passion and love of the past two months into her vagina. His legs shook with intensity as he ground his hips deep inside her.

Megis moaned in his ear as his seed filled her impossibly full. "Baby, I love you so much," she cried softly, tears falling from her eyes.

Zack's legs continued to vibrate from the intensity. His legs suddenly felt weak, so he propped himself against her and exhaled heavily into her shoulder. "Babe," he said, his voice shaky and emotional. "I missed you so much. You mean everything to me."

Chapter 20

They were married at the base the following week in a brief group ceremony. The Naval padre performed the marriage ceremony for two other couples as well. This was common, it seemed, for the men were all very young and eager, some in their teens, some in their twenties like Zack.

Megis had found a job in an ammunition factory. She began working five days a week while her mother took care of the house full of nieces, nephews and cousins. Zack and Megis only saw each other twice a week on his evenings off. He always came home to see her every chance he had.

The tides of war were changing, and there was a sudden urgency for more ships. Canada had six destroyers and desperately needed more to fight in WWII. RCN procured a collection of 60 assorted boats to serve as warships. They were mostly from the Royal Canadian Mounted Police or Transport and Fishery government vessels, but others were civilian yachts, trawlers and whaling craft converted to carry out naval operations. In addition, three modern 6000-ton liners were taken over by the RCN from Canadian National Steamships to act as armed auxiliary cruisers for the time being. The only issue that remained now was the RCN had to man these ships. A rush to train and recruit as many men as possible for the Navy began in earnest.

Canada and Britain signed an agreement to build 169 corvette ships. RCN's plan was to increase the convoys and protect the merchant ships from the threat of U-boats, armed German ships and the Luftwaffe air force. The convoy passage stretched from Halifax harbour to St. John's, Newfoundland, all the way across the Atlantic Ocean, north to Ireland and Scotland. They desperately needed the merchant ships to reach the British Empire for livelihood supplies.

But there was one problem; the highly maneuverable corvette ships would take a year or more to build. In the meantime, they were stuck trying to man these temporary vessels hastily converted into warship escorts.

The convoys were in an organized pattern amongst the merchant ships. The senior RCN destroyer ship sailed in the front and a rescue vessel in the rear of the convoy. Along the sides were the Navy escort ships, providing support and protection. The convoys numbered between 50-150 merchant ships, the most vulnerable tankers in the middle of the convoy.

In mid-ocean, the RCN would hand over the convoy of merchant ships to the British Royal Navy. The RCN would then sail back to Halifax or St. John's with a return convoy. Most convoys were successful, but there was always the constant fear of U-boat or air attacks.

It was the spring of 1940, and Zack expected to be drafted to Halifax in the next few months. He felt torn between his wife and the Navy. Zack was very passionate about being a seaman. It felt that he had finally achieved his purpose. It was as if all the disastrous pieces of Zack's life had fluttered like scattered leaves falling down precisely, forming this special path to Naval Operations.

But one thing churned in his gut.

Megis was five months pregnant with his first legitimate child.

"I will move to Halifax!" Megis said passionately, curling her hair nervously behind her ear. She could only spend two glorious days with Zack every week, and she didn't want to spend it arguing.

"No," Zack said adamantly. "I most likely won't be drafted to Halifax until June or July. You will be eight months pregnant by then!"

"I can find a way!" she said, her heart bursting from her chest.

"No, Megis," he said calmly. "Please don't endanger our child or yourself. Stay here in Winnipeg with our relatives. They will help you with the baby."

"You may not even meet your own baby then!" Megis shouted, her hands shaking. She started sobbing and held her head in her hands. "Maybe it was wrong to get pregnant so soon."

"No, sweetheart," Zack said calmly. "I wanted a baby with you as much as you did." He pulled his chair closer to her and wrapped his arm around her shoulder. "Look at me, babe."

Megis looked up at him, her eyes swollen.

"I love you more than any woman I have ever met in my life," he said slowly. "I know this is not easy. I know marrying me was not easy either. None of this is." He paused and kissed her shoulder. "But this is what we have, and I can't change it. I love the Navy. It is in my blood. But I love you too, and I need you to be safe. I cannot lose you again."

Megis hugged him, burying her face in his neck. She sniffled. "I love you too," she said. "I don't want to lose you again either. I'm scared if you leave, I'll never see you again."

"You will see me again, babe," Zack said confidently.

"You don't know that," Megis said. "You might die."

"I won't die," Zack replied. "I have lots to live for now."

Megis smiled and kissed him on the lips. Zack kissed her back and smoothed her hair, holding her in the most loving type of way. He could not imagine losing her and his unborn child. It was unfathomable.

"Promise me, Megis, that you won't come to Halifax until the baby is at least four months old."

Megis gazed into his sensitive eyes and knew that she had to honour his wishes. He was the father of the baby in her belly. "I promise," Megis said softly.

"Thank you," Zack said quietly.

"It's terrible timing," Megis said thoughtfully.

"I agree," Zack replied. "In November, we can reunite."

"I won't see you for four months," she mumbled, almost to herself.

"I know," he said. Something warned him that it might get a lot worse than that. "Megis, we are a country at war. Even in Halifax, I could be drafted to the convoys for months without shore leave. It may not matter whether you live in Halifax or here in Winnipeg."

His words sank into her heart like an anchor. She looked up at him, her eyes wet with emotion. She loved him more than anyone in her life. There was no other option. If she wanted to stay with the love of her life, she needed to accept this.

"You need to be strong for me, babe," Zack said. "We will be alright. Our love is strong."

Megis smiled, her cheeks wet with tears. "Yes," she agreed. "Our love is powerful. Nothing can stop us now."

Adam hugged his baby girl. She was born only two weeks ago. He was so happy. Anita and Adam had resolved everything back in September after the fight. She found out that she was pregnant with his baby shortly after Zack had joined the Navy. Adam didn't feel bad about Zack joining the Navy at all. It served him right. He was a wild, uncontrollable buffoon; a rigid Naval career was probably what Zack needed to bring him to his senses.

He had forgiven Anita but still felt bitter over his fight with Zack. He suffered a broken nose, two black eyes and a swollen jaw. He couldn't work for two weeks. The reeve's office wouldn't allow him into the town hall looking so frightful.

Everything had settled down once Zack had left, it seemed. It was a good thing he was gone, Adam thought.

He briefly wondered what the war held for them all. Hopefully, the Canadian government will uphold the pledge of no conscription. He hoped his brother lived through the war. He loved his brother Zack once. They were even very close when they were younger.

Adam wasn't sure what had happened to make them drift so far apart. He mused over it briefly as he held his baby daughter. Maybe Zack and Adam just grew into different people. Zack was more interested in alcohol and destroying his life, and Adam was a responsible family man.

Maybe one day, they'd meet again.

CHAPTER 21

Her belly was huge. Zack ran his hands along her round tummy proudly. His baby was inside of her, he thought incredulously. Zack was finally going to be a father with his wife. He almost hoped she would have the baby a month early. Then he could meet his child before leaving for Halifax.

They were told that they would be boarding a train to Halifax in early July. It was a hard pill to swallow. His baby was due in mid-July. It was so unfair.

They both lay naked in bed, cuddling and enjoying their last days together for a long while. Megis murmured and shuffled backwards into his embrace, moving her buttocks closer to his abdomen. She was too large to hug any other way, he mused happily.

"Have your commanders told you when you'll be leaving for Halifax yet?" Megis asked.

"Yes," he said solemnly. "Early July."

"The worst possible time," Megis said softly. She had accepted their distance love more and more. She loved seeing him for that one or two days per week. It thrilled her and excited her beyond words. When they were separated, she dreamt of him and yearned for him.

"I know," he said softly. "Our baby will be due a week after I arrive in Halifax."

"Maybe," she said. "Or right before you leave."

"I could only hope," Zack said.

"Please ensure that you provide us with the telephone number of the barracks in Halifax, so I can call you when our baby is born."

"I will make sure everything is as secure as possible for you," Zack said. "I will continue paying for the rent here in our Winnipeg home. It would be best if you didn't work for a while. You don't need to worry about such things; just worry about our baby's health."

"I will, my sweetheart," Megis said.

Adam was in shock. He stood at the doorway of his house with the documents in his hand. Anita looked up and smiled, then her face dropped. "What is it?" she said, alarmingly. Adam's face was ashen and pale.

He threw the call-up papers on the table.

"What are those?" Anita asked.

"I'm being drafted," Adam said, his voice shaking. "I will try to fight it. I can't believe this."

"Oh my God," Anita exclaimed, her voice high and panicky. "No, Adam, no."

Megis felt her husband's arms around her, hugging her belly tightly. It was the middle of the night, and the darkness enveloped them. Zack was asleep, and she could hear his steady breathing.

He was leaving tomorrow, and she was still pregnant. They weren't lucky enough to give birth to the baby before his departure to Halifax. Megis had prayed and prayed, but the universe was not going to make this easy.

She felt herself get emotional. A tear escaped down her cheek. She couldn't fathom not seeing her husband for four months, although she tried to stay strong for both of them and the baby.

Zack stirred and hugged her tighter, intuitively knowing her anguish somehow. Megis took his hand and wound her fingers through his.

He stirred again.

"Babe," he asked sleepily. "Are you alright?"

Megis choked back her tears. "I'm going to miss you," she said softly.

Zack ran his hands over her hair, kissing her gently and began to hum the native song. Megis cried freely as her husband soothed her. The melody warmed her soul and brought back memories of the cottage in Gimli when things were so simple. Her heart felt like it was wide open on the bed for anyone to harm. But her husband was petting it affectionately instead. It made her happy and emotional at the same time.

When Zack finished the song, he kissed her hair again. "You are the most important person in my life, Megis," Zack mumbled into her hair. "I'm going to miss you like the desert misses the rain. We both have to be strong, my sweetheart. Trust me; we will be together again soon."

Zack held Megis's hand amongst a crowd of well-wishers and family. It was a huge send-off from the Winnipeggers at the Naval base. Zack held her close for as long as he was allowed. Her huge belly stuck straight out in front of her, but she carried it well. Her small legs had become thicker, and her butt was lusciously fuller. Zack loved the way her body had changed to fulfill their baby's needs. He loved her any way she looked. She could be just waking up in the morning, and he still thought she looked beautiful.

Zack was proud of himself, his wife and his family. He reflected back on the last year and how much he had changed since he had lived in Gimli. Zack liked the man he had grown into.

The sailors were told that a train would take them across Canada to Halifax. He inhaled deeply and kissed her hair again.

She turned and looked up at Zack, kissing him softly on the lips. He kissed her back passionately. His tongue danced in her mouth as he clutched her waist for dear life. He wouldn't be seeing her for many months. Zack's heart thumped crazily in his chest, knowing that the separation was imminent.

They kissed like this for an eternity, it seemed, oblivious to the crowd around them. It was like this moment existed just for them. The entire world was blocked out, and this was their last kiss for a very long time.

Finally, Megis pulled back, her lips swollen and red from kissing. "I love you, Zachary Olason," she said, her voice thick with desire. "I will see you in Halifax."

Zack openly cried as he pulled her into his arms, hugging her tight. "You mean the world to me, babe," he mumbled into her shoulder. "I don't want to let you go. Take good care of our baby, my sweetheart." He straightened and bent down to look into her eyes. "You are the love of my life. I need you." Zack kissed her one last time before she left with her mother. The crowd was immediately instructed to disperse so the sailors could prepare to leave.

He watched her backside in the crowd of people. Then she turned to wave goodbye. Zack waved back, his hand floating in the air wistfully.

It would be a long four months.

It was only July 5th, and Zack already missed her painfully. They had been travelling by train for three days. Zack shuffled uncomfortably on the wooden seat. Every morning, he awoke wondering where his bed and his wife were. Then he stretched, trying to ease the pain in his back and legs. His body ached terribly from sitting on the hard wood seat for three days. He wondered if his decision was right for Megis to stay in Winnipeg until the baby was old enough to travel. Zack felt sad and conflicted. He didn't want any harm to come to either his wife or his baby. Zack tried valiantly to keep them both in a bubble so nothing could hurt them. He knew it was impossible. No amount of sheltering could stop bad things from happening. The rational solution would be to keep them both with family for the first crucial few months of his baby's life.

Zack had prayed that the baby would be born before he left, but the baby was in charge of his own birth, it seemed. He was anxious to know when the baby was born. Megis had said that she might even give birth while he was travelling to Halifax. Zack briefly wondered why life always never seemed to go his way. Maybe the universe was testing his resolve. Or perhaps it was simply circumstance and nothing else.

He yearned to get to Halifax quickly. He was anxious to learn whether he was a daddy yet. Zack shuffled onto his side, curling up in the evening car as the sunset shined through the windows. The countryside was beautiful and reminded him that a new life would be born soon.

"Momma!" Megis shouted.

Janet ran over and held her hand. "Breathe, sweetie!" she said excitedly. "We will be at the hospital soon!"

The truck raced crazily to the hospital as both Megis and Janet held on. A neighbour had volunteered to take them, and his driving was rapid but frightening.

"Hold on, Megis!" Janet shouted.

"I can't, Momma!" Megis yelled. "The baby's coming!"

"Pull over!" Janet yelled at the driver. "The baby's coming!"

"Oh my God!" he yelled. "Hold on! We're almost there!" He pressed the gas pedal harder and raced down the street, speeding for blocks. Finally, the truck jumped onto the sidewalk and careened into the hospital parking lot, slamming on the brakes. "We're here; we're here!"

A baby cried.

Janet held the baby in her hands and screamed at the neighbour. "Go run inside and get a nurse. The baby is here!"

"Momma," Megis breathed. "Is it a boy?"

"It is a boy, yes," Janet replied, smiling. "You have a baby boy!"

"Nathan is his name, Momma," Megis said. "His name is Nathan Joseph Olason. Named after both of his grandad's."

Janet smiled as tears of joy streamed down her face.

Several seconds passed, then finally, a rush of medical personnel came to the truck, cut the umbilical cord and whisked mother, baby and grandmother into the hospital safely.

It was July 6th, 1940.

Zack awoke suddenly on the wooden bunk in the middle of the night. The train must have jostled him awake. He peered into the blackness of the train car. Zack felt a wave of love rush over him. Megis was the most wonderful woman he could ever have hoped for. He felt so blessed to have her in his life. Zack began to cry softly, the emotions spilling out of him unexpectedly. She was going to have his baby! It was incredible, and his heart felt like it had split open, laying on the floor of the train car.

He loved her so much.

Zack stared into the darkness for several minutes before finally drifting off to sleep again.

When he awoke, the train was stopped in Halifax. Zack bounded out of the train car and rushed to the base with the crowd, his heart in his throat.

His commander at the base had found Zack and delivered the news immediately.

Zack's baby boy, Nathan Joseph Olason, was born at 23:45 hours the previous night. Zack smiled, tears welling in his eyes. He must have known on the train, Zack mused happily. He felt like someone had just placed him on a cloud in heaven. Zack was thrilled beyond comprehension. He couldn't wait to see his son. A long few months awaited him.

CHAPTER 22

Zack trained at HMCS Stadacona, located west of the waterfront at the north end of the Halifax peninsula. The Stadacona Barracks was an expansive training base initially built by the British Army. After the British forces left in 1906, the site changed to a fishery, then soon after was appropriated into the current Barracks.

The nature of the war was changing. On June 23, 1940, France surrendered to Germany. On that very same day, Germany began inspecting French Atlantic ports to serve as possible submarine bases. A couple of weeks later, U-30 was the first submarine to operate from Lorient, and the Germans now had improved westward movement of the submarine fleet. Southern Britain waters were unsafe now. Transatlantic convoys began to sail from New York and Halifax to the northwestern ports in Ireland, Scotland and northern Britain.

By the end of August 1940, a new terror began for the RCN. The Germans had enough boats in the Atlantic now that submarines began mounting group attacks, dubbed the ominous term "wolfpacks". Submarines stealthily spread throughout the high traffic convoy routes, often with one sub radioing headquarters near Lorient with a confirmed convoy sighting. Headquarters would then guide other subs to the target. The U-boats attacked in formidable numbers. Five submarines could seriously damage half of a convoy, attacking at night when they were nearly invisible.

The U-boats converged at high speeds within torpedo range, firing at the highest number of ships possible and disappearing into the waters before the RCN escorts could react.

From July to September 1940, the losses were tremendous. U-boats had sunk 350 ships. In October, 63 ships were lost to submarines, almost decimating some convoys. Convoy HX79 suffered grave losses. Twelve out of twenty-four merchant ships were sunk by only five U-boats.

The German air force also sent out Condor bombers from French airstrips onto the Atlantic Ocean along with German warships to join the melange, forcing the British to react. The British appealed to the USA. In September 1940, fifty old American destroyers were sent to Britain and Canada in exchange for leases at eight British bases in the Caribbean and Newfoundland. RCN commissioned six of the old destroyers, including the HMCS St. Croix. All six ships were dispatched to Canada in the autumn of 1940.

The first Canadian-built flower class corvette, HMCS Windflower, was also commissioned on October 26. Nine more corvettes were due to be commissioned soon as well. To man all these ships, the RCN needed to train 7,000 men before the spring of 1941. The training establishments were short of instructional staff, and the RCNVR was quickly becoming the navy of raw recruits.

During this time, Zack had already been drafted onto the C Class destroyer HMCS Ottawa, working his way up to navigational Leading Seaman. HMCS Ottawa formed part of the hard-pressed Halifax Escort Force, carrying out the onerous burden of convoy escort work in the Canadian Atlantic. Four of RCN's destroyers had been hastened overseas to Britain to brace for a German invasion. That left only three ships HMCS Saguenay, Assiniboine and Ottawa, to perform the Halifax escort.

HMCS Ottawa saw heavy action in the Atlantic, rescuing survivors of torpedoed vessels, hunting U-boats and firing at enemies.

Zack was wholly consumed with his duties in the RCNVR. He rarely had time to call his wife, but when the ship reached shore, he called her immediately. When he heard her voice, it felt like he was in heaven again. Megis said that they were preparing to move to Halifax on November 5. Zack loved her so much and couldn't believe his luck. He was certain that being married to a Navy Seaman must be akin to torture. Zack wouldn't marry himself, he thought. He hadn't been there for the birth of his son, nor was he able to help with the move and wasn't even sure if he would be there in Halifax for her arrival. Zack felt frustrated, although he knew this was a crucial time during the war. He could only try his best.

He had picked out a home for her and his mother-in-law with the aid of the local commanders. Zack put down rent money on a small house in Halifax for them to move into in November. He was excited and thrilled to finally see his baby and his wife. Zack was granted leave for a short day to meet his baby boy whenever the ship returned to shore.

~

On November 2, Zack was aboard HMCS Ottawa sailing from Clyde River in Scotland with another convoy. They were to escort the convoy to a mid-ocean point off the southeast coast of Ireland. Then HMCS Ottawa was to pick up a slow southbound convoy from Canada.

In the evening on November 4th, as she was approaching her rendezvous point, an urgent signal came in ordering Ottawa to join a British destroyer in attacking a U-boat shadowing Convoy OG-45 bound for Gibraltar.

Zack navigated the destroyer towards their target and searched for the submarines, communicating with HMS Harvester. Clark Anderson Rutherford was a young 26-year-old lieutenant commander of the HMCS Ottawa. He was a good commander, great with the sailors, creating a harmonious crew. He worked hard, and it was infectious. The signalmen took shifts, and sometimes they'd see something, only to be disappointed with open seas. It was frustrating and eerie, looking for an unseen enemy in the Atlantic. Nobody admitted it, but the U-boats scared everyone. They were stealthy machines that could pop up from nowhere. The crew aboard HMCS Ottawa were an inexperienced group, never actually hitting a U-boat. After two days, the crew's nerves were raw.

Suddenly, a signalman shouted. They had sighted the submarine on the surface.

"Attack!" Rutherford shouted at the gunnery ratings.

The gunnery seaman fired from the two forward guns while closing in on the U-boat at high speed. The submarine immediately dived.

HMCS Ottawa and Harvester searched for another frustrating hour. They heard another echo on the radar and raced to the new point, attacking again.

Zack's pulse raced, and his head was entirely focused on navigating the ship into position. Both ships pursued the phantom submarine relentlessly, performing another seven attacks throughout the night. By morning they saw a large oil slick. They searched but couldn't find the remains of the U-boat. Uncertain, they turned back.

"Did we hit the U-boat?" Zack asked.

"I think we accomplished what we came here to do," Rutherford stated confidently.

It wasn't confirmed, but they were sure they had hit something. Little did they know that HMCS Ottawa and HMS Harvester had just sunk the Italian submarine Faà di Bruno, the RCN's first submarine kill of the war.

Zack returned to Halifax a week later, missing the arrival of his wife and child. His training base commanders had welcomed her home and settled his family in while he was gone. He was grateful for the Navy's support. He rushed to the base, showered and changed into a clean uniform, racing out to his new home. He had only 24 hours to reunite with his family. They needed his mechanical aid with several repairs to the ship while it was in harbour. Ottawa needed to sail out in less than two days on another convoy.

Zack adjusted his sailor's hat and walked briskly down the street with his heart in his throat. He would finally meet his baby boy today and see his wife! Zack couldn't stand the adrenaline anymore and just started running. He ran for ten blocks straight before slowing to a jog! The white house was just around the corner; Zack could see it. He broke into a full-speed run until he was at the front door, fumbling with the keys.

Someone was turning the lock inside.

His heart jumped.

The door swung open wildly.

It was Megis!

He grabbed her and picked her right up into the air, hugging her, then pinned Megis against the wall, kissing his wife unabashedly in front of her mother. Janet sat in the rocking chair, smiling shyly and holding the baby while they kissed.

Finally, as if a light bulb went off in Zack's head, he turned his head and broke the kiss. "My son!" he exclaimed and ran to Janet.

She smiled and handed him the baby.

"We have been calling him Nate," Megis said. "So we don't confuse him with your dad."

Zack felt his heart gush wide open as the baby boy smiled at him and gurgled a cute laugh. Zack felt tears of joy escape his eyes. The emotions bubbled up, and he struggled to maintain his composure. Nate had dark brown hair and dark eyes, just like Megis, although he had Zack's nose and chin.

"Hey, Nate," Zack cooed. "I'm your dadda. I've been waiting so long to meet you."

The baby giggled and smiled again.

"He knows it's me," Zack said, smiling broadly.

"Yes," Megis said, hugging his waist. "He's been waiting a long time to meet you as well. And so have I."

Pepper, his old dog from Willow Island, came bounding out of the back bedroom. The dog crashed into his legs and leapt up onto Zack's leg, yipping excitedly. "Pepper! You brought Pepper!"

"Of course," Megis said. "We couldn't leave him there." She shooed the dog to the back bedroom as Zack held the baby.

Zack laughed heartily. He had his family back, he mused happily.

Megis awoke in the middle of the night, the blackness surrounding her. She curled into the sheets, the familiar loss creeping into her heart. Her husband was busy at war, her sleepy mind knew. She felt her heart jump into her throat every time she woke up alone.

Then she heard his steady breathing.

She bolted, sitting up in bed.

He was sleeping beside her!

She was astonished! He was actually in bed with her! She had not seen him for four long months, all the while she had given birth to his baby and became a mother. The longing, the yearning, the tough nights awake with the baby and only her momma there to comfort her came rushing back to her. But now, he was actually here with her! Relief flooded her body. Megis began to sob softly, releasing all the pent-up emotions of the last four months. It had been difficult raising the baby herself without her husband. She loved Zack so much. Megis knew it was a temporary setback, an obstacle to overcome. Things would be better once the war was over. Megis worried that it would be many years before the war ended. She knew he was battling something in the ocean today; she could see it on the expression of anxiety he wore on his face.

Megis laid down and curled into his warm body, hugging him warmly. They had urgent sex several times earlier in the night. She could feel Zack absorbing every moment of his family life before being sent out to sea again. The tension in his body was evident. At first, he looked exhausted, but as he laid in bed, his body was physically on fire. Megis had melted to his touches and spread her legs around him easily, loving him back with each thrust. She loved the scent of their sex on the sheets. It filled her nostrils with a heady aroma of love and urgent passion.

Megis murmured satisfyingly and buried her nose into his back as she hugged him in his sleep. She worried about him, about herself and about the world. Her sobs wet his back while he slept.

After several minutes, she wiped her eyes and cuddled closer into his warmth. "Come back alive, babe," she murmured. "I can't lose you."

PART FOUR

THE BATTLE OF THE ATLANTIC

1941-1943

CHAPTER 23

Winston Churchill called it The Battle of the Atlantic in 1941. The convoys became essential to the preservation of Britain's lifeline for supplies. Convoys were split into slow and fast groups. Slow convoys usually consisted of older ships that were more vulnerable to attack from U-boats. These convoys were guarded by escorts on four sides, one destroyer in the front, one in the back as the rescue ship and two corvettes on each side. Several more of the corvette fleet ships were being commissioned every month, although the majority of them wouldn't be ready for service until the second half of 1941.

Each corvette commissioned was being manned hastily with crews of young inexperienced seamen and already obsolete equipment. The RCN was under extreme pressure to dominate the sea with as many boats as possible but lacked the training personnel and necessary updates to the rapidly-changing radar equipment. This conundrum resulted with corvettes of sometimes only ten experienced seamen to eighty crew members. The experienced seamen were also sometimes only capable fishermen and engineers quickly trained as RCN volunteer reservists. These ten men barely slept and were grossly overworked. The tasks at hand were more than any single human being could accomplish, and the amount of on-the-ship training was incredibly high. Sailors were worn out from lack of sleep and lack of quality shore leave.

To make matters worse, the U-boats were moving into the mid-Atlantic, where there was no air cover from the Royal Canadian Air Force.

RCN agreed to provide escorts for trans-Atlantic convoys throughout the entire duration of their passage. A newly formed Newfoundland Escort Force was created. The plan was that each escort group would have twelve days after each convoy for rest, maintenance and training.

"We're going to Newfoundland, men," Rutherford announced. "We will return to Halifax one more time; then we will join the newly created Newfoundland Escort Force."

Petro and Zack stood on HMCS Ottawa in the cold winter, both chipping ice off the rails when they heard the news.

"Another adventure," Petro said worriedly.

Zack nodded and immediately thought of Megis. He didn't know what this meant, although he was certain that it would result in even less time with his family. He grunted sadly and chipped until another ice block fell into the ocean. Zack watched the ice-wedge splash into the rough seas.

He hoped she wouldn't leave him. Zack prayed that Megis would hold on for a little while longer.

"I will move to Newfoundland then," Megis insisted as they sat on the sofa talking.

"Megis," Zack said uncertainly. "I don't know how long I will be there. I don't know how much longer this war is going to last. They said we would get more shore leave, but this I cannot be certain about either. The U-boats are getting more aggressive. There are so many raw recruits, and it seems I am one of the few with honed navigational skills. I don't have any answers, Megis." Zack shook his head dishearteningly. "What if I don't get shore leave for two months because I am near Iceland or Britain? And you are waiting for me in Newfoundland?"

"Zack," she said softly. "I lived four long lonely months without you. I don't ever want to do that again. I'll take one day every month just to lay with you in our bed, kiss you and feel your skin against mine." Megis sniffled back a tear. "You can't keep me away this time. I won't. I can't." Her voice cracked at the last word, and the dam of emotions breached. She succumbed and started weeping.

Zack wrapped his arms around her and rested his chin on top of her head. She sobbed into his chest, and he felt all the tough, lonely nights he had forced upon her spill onto him. He didn't know what to do. Zack was helplessly in love with her. He couldn't even imagine living without her in his life. She was part of his soul, part of the air he breathed. Whether he was on the Atlantic or on a brief shore leave, Zack always carried Megis around in his heart. She was a part of him, and his heart pounded strongly for her. He would agree to what she needed.

Zack rubbed her back as her sobs subsided. "It will be alright, babe," Zack said, reassuring her with words he wasn't entirely sure of himself. "You are right; let's find a place in St. John's. You can pay for it from our bank account. Don't worry, baby." Zack felt his own tears slip silently down his cheek. "I will be the best father and husband that I can be."

Megis sniffled into his chest. "Okay, I will look," she said. "We will prepare to move again."

Zack kissed her head gently and rocked her body within his. Where the future was heading, he didn't know, but his heart filled with fear for his family and his own life.

Megis pulled away slowly and looked into his eyes. "I have some news," she said softly, her eyes swollen and red.

"What?" Zack said, confused.

"I am pregnant again," she replied softly.

CHAPTER 24

The move to Newfoundland happened without any problems. Megis had begun to make some close friends with the wives of the commanders. She felt comforted knowing that many others were going through the same thing. Her mother moved with her, along with Pepper and little Nate. She had a swollen tummy and chased after her rambunctious toddler all the time, it seemed. Life was hard without a husband, but it was a lot harder on the open seas, she knew.

The Battle of the Atlantic was reaching into the mid-Atlantic open waters, and the Canadian Navy was using all the ships they had. The flower class corvettes were originally built for shoreline service, with the boats being short and stubby riding the waves rather than cutting through them. The destroyers were the longer ships that cut through the waves. Seamen had to make the best of the situation.

On the open Atlantic waters, the corvettes pitch and rolled, riding each wave and crashing down as the ship plunged the bow downward into each trough. A critical design flaw was the low open deck which was often washed out with seawater. Only in the calmest waters would the deck stay dry, which was never possible in the open ocean. It was so perilous, in fact, that the cooks often lost their meals while crossing this open area attempting to deliver the dishes to the seamen's mess deck. The ocean claimed many of these dinners, or they were delivered very wet and well-salted.

The convoys had anywhere from 30 to 170 merchant ships at one time. In the front was the merchant commander, responsible for organizing the convoy. Most ships were armed, and the vulnerable tankers were located in the middle of the convoy. If these ships were torpedoed, the resulting explosions could result in mass casualties.

Despite all these precautions, the convoys were still attacked. The U-boat wolfpacks grew in size, and German intelligence was able to crack the British encryption code, effectively attacking convoys at will.

Another problem for the RCN was the radar and communication. The British had upgraded their communications system and radar, but the RCN fell behind, only installing the obsolete systems. So not only was radar inferior, but communication between ships was also hampered. To further hamper the peril, every depth charge that was released from the back of the corvette resulted in temporary loss of radar, sometimes for long periods of time.

These issues were an extreme source of frustration for the sailors, including Zack. He had become accustomed to being the Leading Seaman on HMCS Ottawa. He would soon find out the difficulties of living on a corvette boat. HMCS Arvida had arrived in September 1941. Zack was being promoted to First Class Petty Officer Navigation to man the new flower class corvette. Life aboard HMCS Ottawa was difficult, especially being at sea for months at a time and lacking proper communication. But he would soon find out how much more difficult it can be aboard a corvette. Despite anticipating all the problems, Zack felt passionate about defending the North Atlantic waters from the enemy, regardless of the setbacks.

He had good reason to be excited about leaving HMCS Ottawa. A personal issue arose in the late summer that prickled his temper so badly it left most people failing to understand the complexities of his inner ego. A man was aboard Ottawa that he didn't want to be near. It would feel so much better to be on his own ship. He would be transferred to the new ship when they returned to shore.

"I'm going to miss you," Petro said, slapping Zack's shoulder. "They should have made you the engineer with all your mechanical experience."

"Ah," Zack answered. "I still help out when needed. Ottawa was desperate for an experienced navigational seaman. I am comfortable in that role now." Zack half hugged Petro. "It's for the best."

"I understand," Petro nodded. "I will be lost without you."

"No, you won't," Zack replied. "You've learned so much since the early days."

"Yes," Petro agreed. "I certainly have."

Zack smiled. "I don't feel that Ottawa is a good placement for me anymore. My commanders were right to transfer me to another boat."

Petro patted Zack on the shoulder knowingly. "I sympathize," he said. "It's tough living on a ship when you don't get along with another seaman."

"I don't understand why they drafted him here," Zack said, shoving his fists in his pockets stubbornly.

"Probably because this ship needs all the help we can get," Petro replied calmly.

"Yes, I suppose," Zack said. "I'm going to miss you the most, my friend."

Megis knitted her husband some new mitts. She was incredibly proud of her husband. Zack was a strong, experienced seaman. Megis was fearful every day that he would be injured, or worse, but she knew there were things in life that a person had no power to control.

One of the things she had influence over was the baby in her tummy. Their new baby would be born soon. Her abdomen had grown quite large, and she waddled more than walked these days. She did not hold any hope that he would be able to see their new baby on the day of birth. Megis only saw Zack once every two months if she was lucky. Then he was gone on the open seas again.

She sat on the sofa and cried, for her country, for her husband and their unborn child.

Adam was not pleased with the course of events his life had taken. He had little influence over the wave of public opinion on conscription. His work at the town hall was reduced to only a one-person office, and the remaining people were enlisted in the war. It was popular opinion to be brave and join the many men risking their lives for the freedom of the country. Adam didn't want to join the war, but he also didn't want to become a staunch objector.

He arrived in Halifax on July 24, 1941. After training as a cook, he had been drafted to HMCS Ottawa. It was tough being at sea all the time, without his wife and his children. Anita had chosen to stay in Gimli and, to make matters worse, his brother was on this ship. Zack had risen to a commanding position that infuriated Adam. The physical argument in the late summer of 1939 was still festering in both of their minds.

It infuriated Adam that Zack had proved him wrong and risen as a very capable seaman. It was a hard pill for Adam to swallow. It was Adam that needed to prove himself capable now, not his loser brother.

Adam was inexperienced in almost everything with ships and gunnery. He learned what everyone else did but never really could grasp it all. He became a cook because it was one of the things he actually enjoyed doing. His father, Nathan, had been a strong influence with his deer soups and fruit teas since Adam was a small boy. It came naturally for Adam, although he somehow still felt trivial compared to his brother, an experienced Leading Seaman.

The entire month of August was a constant struggle with avoiding Zack as much as possible. The drift between them seemed to widen, not lessen. The attitude of the other seaman did not help. Once they found out that they were brothers, they snickered behind his back, comparing the Leading Seaman to a lowly cook.

Adam made up for it with his delicious dishes, though. Food was limited on the ships, but he made the best of what he had. The bread would stale within days, although the cans of food were extensive, and Adam made wonderful chilis and stews that the men loved. The worst food was hardtack, a bread substitute that literally needed to be sawed into quarters. This he could not change, so he just added the hard square pieces onto the plates and delivered them dutifully.

When his brother took a meal, Adam didn't even make eye contact. He had no desire to cause another fight aboard the ship and endanger his tenable position. His ego was damaged, and he knew that it would only take a pinprick before he would fly into a rage. His nose was permanently crooked from the fight at Willow Island. His brow had an ugly permanent scar too. Adam didn't think it was fair that he had suffered such injuries, and his brother was perfectly fine.

Adam sighed and sat down for a cup of watered rum as the ship steamed ahead on the open waters. He would make the best of an unfortunate situation.

"Hey, Adam," the head cook said.

"What is it?" Adam responded. "I'm taking my twenty-minute break."

"No, it's not that," the cook said. "I just heard the news that your brother is being transferred to HMCS Arvida."

"Good," Adam said sharply. "This boat is too small for the both of us."

HMCS Ottawa slid into the dock, and Zack excitedly cleaned up and headed to their house in St. John's, Newfoundland. He was happy to see his wife again. It had been 46 days since he last saw her. The sailor's last shore leave was in Iceland. Even though Zack was Icelandic, he had not learned much of the language. He could get by and be able to ask questions in butchered Icelandic, but that was the extent of his language abilities. The Icelandic community was resentful of the Allied occupation of their island and the streets being filled with drunken sailors while the ships had scheduled maintenance. The Icelandic people were more friendly with him than the other sailors during their shore leave. Once they knew he was Icelandic, their demeanour changed.

St. John's was the friendliest and liveliest stop in their voyages. There was plenty to do, and most sailors would drink at the local taverns and look for women. Luckily, Zack had a wonderful woman, and he didn't partake in the alcoholism that was so rampant within the sailor crews. It wasn't as easy onboard the ship, though. The non-commissioned officers had neat rum, and they would draw tots of rum for the sailors during special occasions. He succumbed to the temptation several times and felt terrible at his lack of control, drinking until he was sick, hurling vomit overboard. A few men were reprimanded for drunkenness, and he wanted to avoid that at all costs. Zack resisted the temptation of alcohol as much as possible, but he realized now that it was a constant struggle for him and that it may always be this way for his entire life.

Zack had talked to Megis more about his fight to overcome alcoholism, and she supported him unwaveringly. But the days he drank on the ship, he didn't tell her about them. He was weak on the ship from the constant threat of attack. Zack swore never to drink at home with his wife and family. So far, he had been successful.

Zack walked quickly to their small home in St. John's. It was a thirty-minute walk from the harbour, and he quickened his steps to close the distance sooner. The sun was shining. It was a beautiful morning. He had seen the Arvida in the harbour preparing for the next convoy. Zack needed to report to the ship tomorrow morning at 7 am. He would have one day with his wife.

He reached the quiet street and ran the rest of the way, bounding the steps and removing his key and opening the front door. Strange, he thought. Usually, Megis opens the door when she hears the key in the knob.

The door creaked open, and the house was deserted.

Zack's mind went on high alarm. Where was everyone? He searched the rooms, and the bedroom drawers were hastily opened with clothes hanging out. That was not like Megis, Zack thought. He looked in his mother-in-law's room, and her drawers were open too. Some clothes were strewn on the floor!

Zack told himself to think rationally and not overreact. Where could they possibly go in such a hurry? Did she go into labour? Zack hurriedly checked the closet in their bedroom. The baby sling was gone.

Zack's hair stood up on end. She's having my baby!

He rushed out of the house and hailed a cab. "To the hospital!" Zack shouted at the driver. "Hurry! My wife is having my baby!"

Zack's heart pumped wildly as he watched the street, buildings and people rush by his car window. He fidgeted in the cab, willing it to travel faster and hopefully magically appear at the hospital in ten seconds. Zack tapped his foot urgently in the back seat. It felt like an eternity before the cab finally pulled up at the hospital doors. Zack threw money on the front seat for the ride and opened the vehicle door before it even rolled to a complete stop.

His long legs strode to the front door, and he rushed to the front office in a panic. "My wife!" Zack yelled. "She's having my baby right now! Her name is Megis Olason! Where is she? I need to be there!"

"Calm down, Mr. Olason!" the front attendant replied. "We will find her." The woman consulted a large ledger book with entries. Finally, she looked up. "She's in room 42B! On the fourth floor."

"Thank you!" Zack fled to the stairs before the attendant could stop him.

"Mister!" she shouted at his back. "You can't go in the delivery room!"

Zack didn't hear. He was bounding the steps two at a time. Zack reached the fourth floor in less than a minute. He opened the door and searched all the numbers for her room when he suddenly heard her scream. Zack knew her voice better than anyone! That was his wife!

He rushed to the door where he heard her screaming. Zack put his hand on the knob and opened the door. A nurse immediately rushed at the door. "Sir!" she yelled. "You can't come in here! An active birth is happening!"

Zack wasn't listening. "That's my wife!" he yelled.

Time slowed down in a brief three seconds. He saw his wife squatting on the floor with a nurse behind her and a midwife in front, both talking to her. For a brief instant, she looked up and saw her husband. At first, her mind didn't quite register that it was him, then she shouted. "Zack!"

The door slammed in his face. "Megis!" he hollered, banging on the door like a gorilla.

The nurse yelled from the other side of the door. "Mister! Husbands are not allowed in the birthing room!"

"For Christ's sake! Why not?" Zack screamed in a fury, beating his fists on the wooden door. "Open this door!"

Then just as suddenly as the commotion started, it turned abruptly quiet. Zack listened.

A small baby's cry lilted into the air. He felt the hair on his arms stand up. Then the cry turned into a loud wail.

"It's a girl!" the nurse shouted happily.

"Let my husband in!" Megis yelled.

"We cannot!" the midwife replied. "It's against the rules."

"Then get my baby and me back to my room immediately!" Megis shouted angrily.

The nurses worked quickly, washing the baby and cleaning up the afterbirth. Zack stood rooted to the spot in suspense, his ear to the door. A few minutes later, a nurse came out and escorted Zack back to the room. "Your wife and baby will be in the room soon. Please, sir, wait in the room. I promise we are getting her cleaned up for you."

Zack entered the hospital room, and Janet was there with Nate in her arms. "Zack!" she shouted in surprise. "You're here! How? Oh my Lord, this is wonderful!"

"I'm on a brief shore leave to change ships," he said. "I went to the house, and everyone was gone. I rushed here as soon as I could!" Zack smiled and held Nate briefly, then handed him back to Janet, pacing back and forth like a caged animal. "I have a daughter!" He announced.

"It's a girl?" Janet asked. "How do you know?"

"I tried to get into the birthing room," Zack replied nonchalantly.

"What!" Janet exclaimed. "Oh my, Zack. No husbands are allowed in there."

"For heaven's sake, why not?" Zack asked, removing his sailor's hat and running his hand over his closely cropped hair.

At that moment, Megis appeared in a wheelchair with the baby in her arms. She beamed happily as the nurse wheeled her next to the bed. "Zack, sweetheart," Megis said wearily. "I'm so glad you made it."

Zack smiled broadly. "Our daughter has better timing than our son!" he joked.

Everyone in the room erupted into joyful laughter. The nurse bent down, taking the bundled baby to the glass bassinet.

Zack interrupted her. "I would like to hold my daughter," he demanded.

"Okay, Mr. Olason," the nurse replied. "First, please wash your hands."

Zack kissed his wife on the forehead, then obediently went to the wash basin and soaped his hands thoroughly. When he turned around, the nurse was holding the baby out for him.

"She is a newborn. She has no neck muscles, so make sure that you hold her head with one hand and her body with the other," the nurse instructed. "Like this." The nurse demonstrated with the baby gently and passed the little girl into his arms.

She was so light, Zack thought. He cradled the tiny newborn and cooed at her as she snuggled into his arms. "Daanis," he whispered loudly. "You are the cutest baby in the entire world."

"Are you sure you want to name her an Ojibwe name?" Megis asked, watching her husband hold their new baby daughter.

"Of course, my sweetheart," Zack said soothingly. "We can call her Dana as a nickname, but we will list her birth name as Daanis Olason."

He fell asleep on the chair in her hospital room. Zack awoke when the baby cried. He watched his wife breastfeed and then took the baby gently, changing his daughter's diaper and pinning the clean cloth garment into place. Zack wanted to do as much as he could to help with the short time allotted to him. It wasn't much, he barely had twenty hours to spend with them, but he thought it was important. Zack could ask for a longer leave, but the ship would have to wait in the harbour for him or find a replacement. He was needed on that ship.

Zack laid Daanis down in her bassinet and covered her up with the cotton baby blanket. He turned, and Megis was already asleep. Zack curled into the bed with her, cuddling her petite body and smoothing her matted hair. She moaned lightly as her dreams overtook her tired body.

Zack felt a wave of gratitude wash over him. It was sudden and unexpected; he was ill-prepared for it. Tears welled in his eyes, and he grasped her even tighter, hoping for the emotions to dissipate. They bubbled up to the surface like a quiet volcano, erupting with intensity but with little sound. Zack sobbed into her hair and felt the dangers of the past year on the ocean melt away, leaving just the intense love he felt for his wife and children.

He looked up to the ceiling, wondering how he had become so lucky to have such a devoted wife. She was there for him no matter what befell them. Megis had moved four times in two years just to be near him. Was it really four times?

The tears spilled out of his eyes with a renewed intensity. He wept for the loneliness she must be imprisoned by on a daily basis. He wept for the incredible strength she had for raising their children with an absent father, and he cried for the helplessness he felt to change their situation. It was all too much, and the sobs racked his body as he held onto his sleeping wife.

She turned sleepily as if noticing something in her dreams and snuggled into the pillow contently with her husband's arms around her.

Zack felt a new emotion creep into his heart. It was fear, an all-encompassing fear for his own safety. The Battle of the

Atlantic was getting more and more dangerous every day. It was strange because he was never one to be afraid for his own life. He had been through riots, alcoholic debauchery, car accidents and war, but now something sneaked into his heart, making him fear the very basic of things, and he realized why. He was terrified of losing his life now because it meant something to the people that he loved with all his heart. He must stay alive for his wife, for Nate and for Daanis. His survival was paramount to their security.

He dried his eyes and wondered where the war would take him from here.

All he could do now was to be strong enough for everyone. The war would not take him down. Never. If he had to tough it out for another five years, he would. Zack will be her rock, and he will stay alive no matter what befell them.

Any other outcome was too grim to comprehend.

CHAPTER 25

Zack stood aboard HMCS Arvida in the wheelhouse during the early morning shift. It was 4 am, and the skies were still dark. He had been a First-Class Petty Officer for over a year now. As he had suspected, things had not improved. The RCN's good intentions of more shore leave for sailors never materialized. The Newfoundland Escort Force was just as busy as he was in Halifax. The U-boat attacks had intensified. The radar and communication upgrades to the ships never happened. There was little they could do but ram the subs and roll off depth charges hoping for a blind hit. Once in a while, the escorts succeeded with a hit on a submarine, but more often than not, the U-boats won. It was frustrating. Zack and all the crew members were becoming weary and upset. The one saving grace was that many convoys still made it safely across the Atlantic without one incident, but the fearful waiting for an attack was out of this world.

The fog on the Atlantic floated up in waves, landing alongside the ships, then just as quickly disappearing. The last year had been challenging. From January to August 1942, there were many wolfpack attacks resulting in massive casualties and huge ship losses. It made Zack angry and fearful at the same time. The U-boats were growing in numbers as well. Some attacks had eight to fifteen submarines, all converging on the same convoy. The sea would light up in flames and explosions, many men dying from the impact, drowning or barely surviving. In only extreme attacks was air cover from the RCAF Catalinas called upon to end the attack. This frustrated the entire crew on the ships, and the morale was getting to an all-time low.

Zack watched the fog settle on the convoy beside him. It was a gift in disguise. It made the ships more difficult for the German submarines to spot.

He mused about his two children and his lovely wife as he steered the boat. He missed them so much. He hadn't seen them in over thirty days. He was hoping the next convoy back would allow them for a Newfoundland shore leave. His nerves were raw, his sleep constantly disturbed by the rolling corvette ship, and his stomach growled for a better meal than hardtack and beans. He felt like he was languishing on the open seas, waiting for a break in the war so he could see his family again. He never forgot that night he slept with his wife in the hospital bed with their newborn daughter beside him. He kept a baby picture of them together in his pocket as a lucky charm. The war would not take him. It simply could not.

He watched the ship rise on the next wave and felt the ship tilt up and up, giving his stomach a weird sensation. When he had first sailed on the HMCS Arvida, he had instantly felt the ship's equilibrium much different than the Ottawa's long destroyer ride. The corvette rode like a corkscrew, turning and twisting with every wave and then crashing down into the bellows of the waves. Zack had earned his sea legs many years ago as a young fisherman, so it didn't bother him as much as the other crew members. During rough seas, there were sometimes sixteen or more men holding onto the ropes, hurling the contents of their stomachs into the Atlantic.

Living on the Arvida was tough. Zack was wet all the time. The open area of the deck immediately aft of the fo'c'sle was always wet, the ocean washing over onto the deck. The water seeped into the sleeping quarters beneath. No one washed themselves or changed their clothing anymore. It was futile; they just became wet again. The lower mess deck smelled like everyone's sweat, and it was a disorganized mass of coats and hats.

He looked at his hands on the large wheel. Zack wore cotton gloves with leather pads that Megis had handknitted for him. He also wore a wool hat that she had made for him too. These two articles of clothing were the most precious items in his possession. They were like his guardian angels, keeping him warm on the cold open seas.

The Arvida had a large 4-inch gun at the bow, one 2-pound gun at the stern, two 20 mm guns on each side and depth charges at the back. The crew consisted of 85 men, including cooks and a Sick Berth Attendant. The smaller vessels did not have a doctor like the larger warships. The SBA was a young fellow by the name of George, whom Zack felt great sympathy for. The young sailor had rudimentary medical training and had an onslaught of 84 crew members to deal with, from everything like constipation to open wounds. George was learning fast, and he kept mostly to himself, although Zack often went down to the mess deck to share a Coke with him on breaks. Zack's best friend Petro stayed on HMCS Ottawa in the boiler room as one of the engineers, and Adam was still one of the cooks.

Zack missed his friend Petro and often looked for him in the taverns during shore leave. It was uncommon to have HMCS Ottawa in the same convoy as Arvida; those times were few and scarce. But this time, they were finally sailing together on convoy ON-127. Zack was looking forward to seeing his best friend once they arrived in St. John's.

The convoy ON-127 was picked up mid-ocean from Liverpool by the Mid Ocean Escort Force C-4 Group, which combined Newfoundland Escort Forces, American warships and British warships. Arvida was sailing on the front left of the convoy with the destroyer St. Croix in the lead, Ottawa in the back and the other corvettes, Sherbrooke, Amherst and the British corvette Celandine surrounding the remainder of the convoy. It was a cold September day on the Atlantic, but Zack felt confident that this particular convoy was well guarded.

It was September 7, 1942.

Adam was content with his duties on HMCS Ottawa. He had been on the ship for over a year now. He had made some friends and was regarded highly for his stews and chili. Adam liked the commander C. A. Rutherford and insisted on delivering the captain's meals himself. Sometimes they would chat, sometimes he was too busy. Today was an uneventful day.

"Good evening, Commander," Adam said formally. "It is an unusually calm day today."

"Yes, it is, Adam," Rutherford replied in a friendly tone. "Hopefully, it is not the calm before the storm."

Adam laughed nervously. "Hopefully not," he said, placing the tray of stew and potatoes on the captain's table. "Do you see the war easing up anytime soon?" Adam asked politely.

Rutherford smiled. He was a tall thin man with a long face and a cheerful smile. Most of the crew admired him, and he had grown into a much-loved commander. He addressed the men as equals, and it was much appreciated because living on a warship was stressful work for everyone, regardless of position or authority. "It's quite the opposite, unfortunately," Rutherford stated sadly. "Rear Admiral Len Murray is fully aware of the problems facing the escorts, especially the MOEF. The Canadian policy of building and manning as many ships as possible and shoving them out to the mid-Atlantic without the necessary training, maintenance, experienced personnel and add to that the lack in updated equipment, well, one day it will backfire. Murray has been warning our superiors of this recipe for disaster for some time, but it continually falls on deaf ears." Rutherford paused to open his mouth for a spoonful of stew. "Oh my God, Adam, your stew is the best." He chewed thoughtfully. "To make matters worse, Donitz's submarines are multiplying and forming two patrol lines on the main shipping lanes. At the very least, we need to be able to hone in on the enemy's positions with HF/DF and avoid surprise U-boat attacks. If that can't be done, they need to supply us with constant air cover, leaving no mid-ocean gaps like the one we are approaching soon." He chewed another morsel thoughtfully. "Let's just pray that the RCN does something to solve these issues before disaster forces them to."

Adam stood listening intently. "It does seem like a perilous situation for us to be in," he replied.

"It is, Adam," Rutherford said, in between bites of potatoes. "We can only do what we have been doing, our best."

"Yes, we are, Captain," Adam said strongly, then scurried out back to the kitchen to retrieve the next plateful of food for delivery. As he crossed the open deck, he saw the aircraft still flying overhead. It was a comforting feeling knowing they were protected, although they would soon be out of range. Adam shivered involuntarily as a sense of doom crawled up his spine. He ran to the kitchen in a mad rush to make sure everyone was fed. He thought of his brother aboard the Arvida. Adam wished that he and his brother had made amends. Adam told himself that once they arrived in St. John's, he would talk to Zack and make things better between them, even if that meant just to put the past behind them. He would love to visit his niece and nephew.

It was the evening of September 9, 1942.

Zack awoke suddenly from a loud underwater clanging noise and then a guttural explosion. He swung out of his hammock with his clothes and boots still on and rushed to the wheel-house, his heart pounding in his chest. Zack feared they had been hit!

When he arrived at the wheelhouse, there were already two men inside. The entire crew was rushing to deal with the emergency.

"The convoy has been hit!" a navigator exclaimed, searching for the vessel that was hit. "Torpedoed by Donitz's damn U-boats! I don't know how many subs are out there, but it seems like a lot!"

Zack felt an evil shiver run up the back of his neck. "Can't Celandine tell us where they are? They have the Type 271!" Zack shouted, mentioning the newest radar the British had for detecting subs in close proximity.

"We've lost contact with Celandine!"

"What ship was hit?" Zack asked.

"It looks like merchant ship Elizabeth van Belgie No. 12, the second ship in the first column. Deep in the water, she's sinking."

Zack peered out. They were eerily close. The ship was sinking, a large oil stain spread in the water, and a small column of smoke rose.

Just as they were all observing this startling observation, another explosion hit. A ship adjacent to van Belgie, the tanker FJ Wolfe was struck port side by a torpedo. Immediately after, a third eruption rocked the ocean, hitting the tanker Svene.

Ottawa and Celandine were immediately sent to hunt the U-boats. Sherbrooke was rescuing FJ Wolfe.

Arvida rolled off a depth charge hoping for a hit.

Nothing.

The convoy trip had just gone from good to terrible. Zack sailed the corvette around towards the survivors. He watched in the distance as Ottawa sailed full speed to the outer reaches of the group. His brother was on that ship.

HMCS Ottawa and Celandine performed a coordinated attack, searching for the U-boats. Several depth charges and the four-inch guns were blazing, opening up the seas with explosions on the sunny afternoon.

Adam was chilled to the bone. He felt an impending sense of doom that he just couldn't shake. A man on the ship had just recovered from an appendicitis operation. He was still in the sick bay. Adam was on the mess deck with several others, grabbing coats and hats, as the loud four-inch guns opened fire.

Ottawa and Celandine spent the afternoon patrolling astern of the convoy to drive the subs down.

At 17:00 hours, St. Croix was in the lead of the convoy and had obtained asdic sonar contact. The commanding warship turned to investigate. In a terrible turn of events, at 17:15, the heavily armed Empire Oil was torpedoed by U-659 on the engine room side. A large underwater thud sounded, then debris and smoke filled the air.

The master of Empire Oil reported, "We seen nothing of the track of the torpedo! We had seven lookouts, and all gunners were at action stations!"

Four minutes later, Empire was hit again on the port side.

"Abandon ship!" the master shouted.

Ottawa changed course and sailed full speed to rescue the survivors. Rutherford smashed his open palm on the navigation table. It was maddening to see one ship after another being torpedoed and not even given a chance to grapple with the villains responsible!

Four ships lost in one day!

"Dammit!" Rutherford cursed as his fist connected with the door frame.

Zack barely slept. Convoy ON 127 continued valiantly battling thirteen U-boats throughout the no air cover zone. It was infuriating. Zack felt the ship ride the waves as the explosions brought up the waters, sometimes so close that the debris landed on the deck. Smoke filled the air in heavy clouds from the tankers, and oil spread sickeningly over the water. Ottawa had picked up the oil-soaked survivors from Empire, and the crew was busy attending to all the casualties.

Meanwhile, Arvida spent the next three days hunting the U-boats, releasing depth charges from the stern and firing heavily from the four-inch, two-inch and 20 mm guns.

A sailor came running up to the wheelhouse. "I think we got a U-boat! I don't know which ship scored the hit, but we at least got one! St. Croix says it was U-659."

"At least we're keeping the wolfpack at bay!" Zack shouted, running his hand along the back of his neck. He was exhausted and running on very little sleep. How much more of this could he take?

At the end of the long three days of battle, the six Naval escorts struggled valiantly to protect their charges, but the German subs still managed to sink seven merchant ships with four more heavily damaged, in exchange for only one submarine hit.

Adam delivered breakfast to his commander early on September 13, 1942. He brought the tray of pickled eggs and fried potatoes to the bow of the ship. Food supplies were dwindling with all the rescued survivors of the sunken tankers aboard.

Adam found his commander in the front by the wheelhouse. Rutherford was rarely found in his quarters these days. Adam couldn't understand how the commanders managed to survive with no sleep. He left the food and didn't engage in conversation. The commander was obviously too busy.

He overheard a shout from Rutherford. "Thank God we are finally getting air support! Two more destroyers are steaming towards us. We are running out of fuel! Contact HMS Witch. We have to conserve fuel and slow down!" Rutherford shouted.

HMCS Ottawa was approaching 500 miles from Newfoundland.

Miraculously, the fight was over, Adam thought.

But something told him that it wasn't.

Adam returned to the mess deck to shift with the other cooks for a quick 20-minute break. He slept as soon as his head hit the pillow.

When he awoke, there were shouts of relief that HMCS Annapolis and HMS Witch were approaching and would be the relief destroyers. Ottawa was running out of fuel and slowed to ten knots. A dangerous but necessary precaution. ON 127 was considered a fast convoy, but they were slowing considerably. Adam scratched his head. He didn't understand why the German's decided to attack the fast convoy; usually, they focused on the slow convoys. He didn't have much knowledge of the U-boat strategies, but he did know that the fight they had endured for three long hectic days was unusual and unanticipated. He felt terrible for the commander. Rutherford looked like he hadn't slept in three days. Adam thought of Zack and wondered how Arvida was doing.

"Does anyone know how Arvida is doing?" Adam asked as he tied up his hammock and sat down at the mess table underneath in the cramped quarters.

A young seaman, not much older than 17 years old, responded. "Arvida is joining the hunt for the subs. A submarine hit was reported! We are winning this one finally. A hard win, though."

Adam smiled. He was glad that his experienced brother was part of the coordinated attack.

"Isn't your brother the First Petty Officer on Arvida?" the young sailor asked.

"Yes, he is," Adam said, smiling.

"You must be so proud!"

"Yes," Adam said. "I am proud of him. We've had our personal struggles, but once we get to shore, I'm going to make amends."

"That's wonderful!" the young man responded. "Sometimes family is all we've got."

Adam smiled. If only Zack accepts his apology. He had called him a loser many years ago. He would need to apologize for that. Zack was no loser. If anything, Adam was the one that had to take a good look in the mirror at his own self.

The seas were calm, and the night was slowly falling. Zack watched the battered convoy sailing to Newfoundland. He felt relieved. They had fought hard and won. The lack of communication and mass confusion was infuriating, though. He wished the RCN would do something soon about the obsolete equipment and at least provide them with HF/DF. It felt like they were out in the open seas battling an unseen enemy with nothing more than guns and ramming subs. It was like a fistfight on the Atlantic Ocean.

Zack remembered the fistfight so long ago with his brother. Ever since he had heard those insulting words from his brother, he had made the biggest decision in his life to change the course he was heading on, and it had worked. He was happily married with two children and had a promising career as an RCNVR Officer now.

The stars in the falling night sky lit up as if one by one, somehow fooling everyone that a brutal attack had just happened. Zack mused on his life so far and wondered if one day he would make amends with his brother if it was at all possible.

A cook came into the wheelhouse handing him his evening meal. Zack immediately thought of Adam.

Then just as the thought crossed his mind, an explosion rocked the calmness with a menacing turn of events that he would never forget in a million years.

Petro was in the boiler room onboard HMCS Ottawa standing his engineering watch and was explaining to Rutherford about the fuel situation.

"We have enough to get to shore if we keep sailing at ten knots," Petro said nervously. "There's nothing else we can do."

Rutherford nodded. "Thanks, Petro. We just confirmed HMS Witch is only 1000 yards away. Radar showed two contacts; we immediately closed in and radioed Witch. We are close to the end of this mess. RCAF should be here soon as well. You did an amazing job, Petro. Keep doing what you do best, keeping us afloat."

It was eerily quiet with just the sounds of the boiler chugging. Petro acknowledged the kind captain. "Thank you, sir."

Rutherford nodded, climbed to the deck and walked back to the wheelhouse. He heard the gentle swishing sounds of the waves falling against the shoulders of the ship. The night stars were appearing slowly, one by one, and he thanked God for his crew.

Before he was able to reach the wheelhouse, a massive explosion rocked the destroyer. A brilliant flash of orange light lit up the port bow, just forward of A gun. Rutherford ran, his heart in his throat.

The ship's forward structure, funnel and bridge were all momentarily silhouetted by an orange glow. A geyser of water cascaded down onto the gunners of B gun, just behind the explosion. The fore-castle deck opened up like a sardine can, and the barrel of the gun bent crazily down.

The silence that followed was deafening. The debris of his stricken ship was falling into the sea and clattering onto the upper deck. Several dan buoys were flung into the sea from the blast and floated beckoningly with their attached calcium flares burning brightly. Rutherford ran to the wheelhouse in the ensuing silence.

"Ottawa has been hit!" Rutherford yelled into the mouthpiece. "Repeat, Ottawa has been hit. Everyone on deck!"

He turned just in time to a startled young cook with his meal.

"Adam!" he shouted. "We've been hit!"

Adam looked nervously at the chaos erupting from all directions and laid down the food tray in the wheelhouse. He rushed to the forward mess, his home for the past month. It was carnage with men trapped in compartments by twisted metal. He could see the ocean waters where Ottawa's bow used to be. His senses were disorientated at the sight. The stoker's living quarters were transformed into a waist-high jumble of bent lockers, hammocks, mess tables and torn steel. Several bodies were smashed in their hammocks into the ceiling, blood seeping into the cloth hanging beds. Adam couldn't even quite understand what he was looking at. He grabbed a knife and flashlight from the carnage and ran to the deck.

Two young sailors were entombed in the ASDIC compartment in the bowels of the ship. They were pleading with the captain through the voice pipe.

"Save us!" they pleaded. "Tell my wife I love her. Please, we're trapped! Help!"

Rutherford's heart fell to the floor. There was nothing he could do to save these men right now. His only hope was to limp back to shore. He gently mouthed the voice pipe and said whatever he could to ease the distress. "It will be okay, men. We will send help when we can. Ottawa has been hit. We're still afloat. Hold tight!"

Rutherford felt the blood drain from his face and his hands grow cold. He needed to do what he could to save his crew. "We need to make it to shore in reverse!" Rutherford shouted. "We have 400 miles to go. It's possible! The bulkhead is holding! We're only slightly down on the bow!" He turned to yell at gunner L.I. Jones. "Set those depth charges to safe immediately in case we fail, so we're not all blown to pieces!" Jones rushed to the stern in a panic.

Rutherford looked up and saw St. Croix arriving on the scene. He didn't give the order to abandon ship. There was still a chance.

Rutherford communicated to St. Croix. "We are hit port bow, but we're still afloat! We are going in reverse to shore! We have a chance!"

St. Croix turned to speed away. Ottawa would make it; they didn't need to be rescued.

At that exact same moment, lurking in the ocean waters, the German captain of U-91 was peering through the lens viewer at the confirmed hit on HMCS Ottawa. Then as he pulled away, he noticed St. Croix returning to help the stricken destroyer.

Heinz Walkerling pressed his eyes harder through the viewer to confirm it was St. Croix. The U-boat captain thought briefly and made a split decision. "Circle back, turn back immediately!" he ordered excitedly.

St. Croix was a floating duck. An amazing feat, Walkerling thought, to hit two destroyers in one fight!

"Fire!" he ordered.

The second torpedo whizzed through the water with the eeriest sound Rutherford had ever heard. He was managing the crisis and preparing to return to shore in reverse when things went from bad to worse.

St. Croix sped away just in time, narrowly missing the strike, but as the large destroyer edged away, the torpedo slammed into the ship behind it, the HMCS Ottawa.

Rutherford's body flew forward from the explosion. Ottawa rocked hard from the impact. They were hit twice! The starboard side of Ottawa was struck fatally, right in the number two boiler room Rutherford had just come from. He clambered to hold on. Huge columns of water rose from the Atlantic, raining down on the stunned crew. Rutherford swung his head around in alarm.

He could see the explosion had broken Ottawa's back. The ship began to roll, and a loud twisting metal sound began to warp the ship.

"Abandon ship!" Rutherford shouted over the debris, bodies and water falling everywhere.

Everyone was clambering to hold on; some sailors started jumping into the ocean.

"Abandon ship!" Rutherford shouted again, frantically. "Abandon! Repeat, abandon ship immediately!"

Rutherford and another commander quickly pushed a buoy that had been flung onto the deck by the second explosion. It landed with a splash in the sea. In all the confusion, the two commanders rushed to release as many Carley floats into the sea as possible. Two floats were inextricably jammed under the whaler, and they were quickly running out of time. His ship was sinking fast. Several RCAF Catalinas flew overhead, chasing the submarines responsible at extreme range.

The brave destroyer, HMCS Ottawa, began to tilt crazily and then, with a loud grind, completely split into two. Everyone scrambled to jump off the sinking ship.

Adam grabbed another Carley float with a sailor and flung it overboard. Then he ran across the tilting bow, grabbed the ropes and hurled himself over the side, falling into the cold Atlantic waters with a splash.

Rutherford remained on the tilting half of the ship, urging everyone to jump. Then finally, he secured his lifejacket and jumped into the cold waters himself.

CHAPTER 26

Adam submerged into the cold shock of the open sea, his uniform clinging to his body. The din of the muffled noises underwater was terrifying. He swam crazily to the surface, the bubbles of water following him up. He breached the surface and gulped the moist Atlantic air. Adam heaved himself up with his strong arms and swam hard amongst hundreds of other swimming sailors in the chaotic open seas.

Several Carley floats bobbed up and down on the ocean. Adam swam towards them with panic rising in his throat. He swam mightily in a front crawl, closing the distance. Hundreds of sailors' hats floated ominously on the waves. There were flares, life rafts and oil spreading everywhere. People were shouting and screaming.

Adam reached the Carley float, but it was already full, and several others were holding onto the side, threatening to capsize it.

At that moment, it capsized and rolled over, releasing all the inhabitants and then a rush of sailors re-entered the float, stabilizing it.

Adam waded in the open waters, watching HMCS Ottawa sink before his eyes. He was going to die, Adam thought.

The ship groaned loudly behind him. Everyone turned their heads to watch the sinking of the majestic broken destroyer with heavy hearts. Then suddenly, in a swift motion, the torn bow tilted and disappeared into the depths of the Gulf Stream, the ocean swallowing it up. HMCS Ottawa was gone forever. It felt anti-climatic somehow, like everything that had just happened was swiftly taken from them, leaving a hundred survivors bobbing on the open ocean in shock.

The large swells lifted the Carley floats and splashed them down repeatedly, throwing many survivors overboard again. Even if he reached another Carley float, Adam thought, the chances of surviving this disaster looked slim.

The darkness of the open ocean settled on him like a heavy cloud. He tried to calm the panic in his heart and analyze his chances of survival. The water surrounding him was colder than he thought. Adam wasn't sure if he should keep treading swiftly to keep warm or stay afloat with less energy to keep himself from wearing out. It seemed either option would still result in his imminent death.

A splash sounded nearby, interrupting his thoughts. Adam turned around in shock, and his heart lifted to find Rutherford beside him!

"Captain!" Adam shouted.

"You have to get to a Carley float!" Rutherford shouted. "You can't tread water forever."

"They are full, sir!"

Rutherford struggled and twisted himself awkwardly in the chaotic ocean swells. Adam didn't know what he was doing. Then just as suddenly as he had appeared, the captain was swimming away.

Rutherford's lifejacket floated beside Adam.

"Take it!" Rutherford shouted in the waves. "I will get to a Carley float! Don't worry about me! Find a dan buoy! They are less crowded!"

Adam clutched onto the lifejacket and struggled to put it on in the chaotic waters. He managed to get his arms through but couldn't clasp it together, although it was enough. The lifejacket bobbed him onto the waves. He turned and kicked his legs to see which float Rutherford had climbed onto, but the commander was gone from sight into the dark seas.

Adam kicked his legs to get closer to a group of men and grabbed an injured man's arm. "Put your arm around me!" Adam yelled. "Let's get to that dan buoy!"

The man laid his bloody arm around Adam's shoulders, his weight sinking both of them a little, but they still managed to barely stay on the surface. He watched another Carley float topple from the weight and sent several more men into the sea. It bobbed back up, and fewer men were on it now.

Adam and the injured man arrived at the dan buoy and grasped onto the rope, then clutched onto the bright floating arm. He held the injured man's arm onto the buoy as two other sailors grasped the other end. They all floated, clenching onto the life preserver with hope.

Suddenly, a ship passed by them very close.

Adam turned his head in panic. It was St. Croix!

The floating sailors all hollered in unison, "Saint Croix! Saint Croix!"

Their hopes rose then crashed mightily. The old four-stacker destroyer raced past them, intent on its hunt for surfaced U-boat U-411. It seemed that St. Croix was allotting the rescue to another ship.

Adam watched with hope as yet another ship sailed through the wreckage of Ottawa. It was so close that he could see the cavernous hole in her side. Adam saw the words F.J. Wolfe. It was the damaged tanker that was torpedoed on September 10th!

It didn't stop either. Adam's heart sunk. They were being left behind.

Several other convoy ships followed, sailing through the wreckage of floating sailors and twisted ship fragments. Some sailors clung to the torn pieces, hanging on for their lives. Some men just let go, disappearing into the waters randomly.

The SS Athelduchess, a merchant tanker, floated by and threw over some more Carley floats to the survivors. Immediately, twenty or more men clambered into each one.

Someone shouted from the tanker. "Celandine is on its way! Hang tight!"

Adam felt his hopes soar and pitch darkeningly as each ship passed while the survivors bobbed on the open seas. He felt tiny stings on his legs and cursed. Wonderful, he thought despairingly, there were jellyfish in the area too.

As night slowly descended on them and the last ship passed, Adam tried to stay floating with the others, except his mind was exhausted and sleep threatened to overtake him. His grip lessened. He shook himself awake and noticed the injured man was gone, swallowed up by the sea. There were only two others left on the dan buoy, including Adam. The seas had become calm again, lulling them all into a dangerous exhaustive sleep.

As the eerie silence of the night descended fully, a few sailors started singing:

Nights are growing very lonely
Days are very long
I'm a growing weary only
There's a long, long trail awinding to the land of my dreams!
There's a long, long night of waiting
Til the day that I'll be going down that long, long trail with
you!

Adam joined in the chorus of the old war song, singly passionately:

There's a long, long trail awinding to the land of my dreams!
There's a long, long night of waiting
Til the day that I'll be going down that long, long trail with
you! [1]

The waves of the dark ocean lapped against the men as their voices filled the heavens. The eerie chants of men waiting to be rescued lifted into the clouds on deaf ears. Adam tried to hold on and sang mightily to keep himself awake, watching as many men disappeared around him. His legs were numb from the cold, and jellyfish stings.

He cried softly to himself, "Someone, please rescue us."

At that moment, the wind picked up speed and churned the ocean into swells, drowning out the war songs as the survivors of HMCS Ottawa succumbed one by one to the Atlantic depths.

"My brother was on that ship!" Zack yelled. "Tell Celandine we are going to search for survivors right now!"

The captain of Arvida nodded. "Zack, you just got your wish. Saint Croix just radioed for us to rescue the survivors."

---

1   There's a Long, Long Trail (King, Stoddard 1915)

Zack turned the boat in the direction of the sinking. The convoy ships that passed through the wreckage had sent word of the location. Zack's heart was in his throat, and his stomach curled in evil twists as he imagined losing his brother to the sea.

Zack was so close to the rescue. He whispered softly to himself, "Hold on, Adam. Don't give up."

Zack felt his heart hammering in his chest as he mentally urged the ship to travel faster. His eyes were glued to the darkening ocean, hoping to see his brother materialize from nowhere.

"Try to focus on the task at hand, Zack," the commander said softly, standing beside him. "I know it's your brother, but we need to stay calm and keep our focus." He laid his arm around Zack's shoulders. "We don't know how many survivors there are, but the merchant ships said they saw hundreds of sailors, so there's hope."

The night descended with a frustrating blackness that obscured the seas. A slight wind picked up, and the Arvida sailed to the approximate sinking wreckage of HMCS Ottawa.

There was nothing. They couldn't see anything.

"Fuck!" Zack cursed as he navigated the boat, then peered out at the blackness. "Where are you, Adam?" he hollered into the dark seas.

The commander gently nudged Zack. "You've been awake for almost 36 hours, Zack," he said. "You need to take a break."

"Pardon my insistence, captain," Zack said. "But I cannot sleep when my brother is bobbing in the ocean somewhere."

"We cannot afford to lose you either, Zack," the commander ordered. "It's after midnight. You need to take at least a twenty-minute nap. We will wake you up when we find them."

Zack slammed his open palm down and stood. He stormed out of the navigation deck and walked towards the stern. The sea was eerily calm, and he leaned over the side, scanning the black sea. At first, he saw nothing, but then his eyes adjusted. He noticed small strange colours. He thought he was seeing things at first, but then his eyes adapted further to the darkness. He was certain that he saw something. A strange colour bobbed.

He rushed back to the wheelhouse.

"I ordered you to the mess deck, Zack!" the commander shouted.

"Captain!" Zack shouted back. "I spotted the survivors! Port side stern! Turn this ship around!"

The Arvida turned sluggishly, as if in slow motion and reduced almost to a float as Zack peered over the side. Many sailors joined him. They could barely see the survivors, but there was definitely something in the water.

Suddenly Zack saw a man holding onto a small piece of wreckage right beside the boat! "Cut the engines!" Zack hollered. "We are right on top of them!"

Several crew members rushed wildly about the Arvida, cutting the engines, and Zack threw a lifesaver overboard. "Grab the ring!" He shouted at the blackness. "Turn the ship's lights on, dammit!" Zack yelled at a young group of seamen.

The men scurried about, and immediately the ship's searchlight shone brightly down into the waters. Suddenly there were thirty or so men visible, floating on various buoys and wreckage.

"Grab the Kisbee!" several crew members shouted. A few survivors tried but failed to get a good grip on the lifesaving ring and slipped off from the oil slicking the waters.

"For fuck's sake!" Zack hollered, the adrenaline shooting in his veins. He threw his coat towards the wheelhouse, stripped down to his undershirt and pants, grabbed a lifejacket and jumped overboard.

"Zack!" the commander shouted after him.

Zack landed in the seas with a splash and gestured the crewmen to throw him the lifesavers. He swam to a man clutching a dan buoy. He pulled the dan buoy to the Kisbee ring and tied it secured, motioning the crew to pull it up. They pulled the first survivor up successfully as Zack swam to the others with another lifesaver in his other hand.

He approached a Carley float with eight men in it and did the same, instructing them to hold on.

A chorus of men's voices were awakened from the slumber of floating on the sea. "It's Arvida! We are saved! Wake up, everyone!"

Several other crew members jumped into the sea to help Zack recover the survivors.

Zack was running on pure adrenaline, and his body fired him onward to the next victim and the next.

He noticed a dan buoy that had drifted from the group, and he swam mightily towards it, letting go of the Kisbee ring. His heart pumped wildly in his chest amidst shouts from the men on Arvida. It took him ten minutes to swim that far out, but when he finally arrived, he found two lone men clutching a dan buoy.

One of the men slicked with oil looked up lazily, one more second from letting sleep overtake him. "Oh my God, Zack?" Adam mumbled. "Is that you?"

"Adam!" Zack hollered, his heart lifting into his chest. The fear of losing his brother was more than he could accept. He kissed his brother on the cheek. "I found you, you damn asshole!"

Adam laughed lazily. "Am I ever happy to be called an asshole today!"

"I thought I lost you!" Zack shouted. "Okay, I'm bringing you both in. Hold onto this damn buoy with every little thread of strength you have left. I'm going to swim it to the Arvida."

Zack swam with one strong arm while his other arm clutched the long arm of the dan buoy. His strength was incredible, and he kept pumping his arm through the waves until he neared the hull of the Arvida. Zack grabbed the Kisbee ring and motioned to Adam, throwing it right over his head and flipping one arm over. "Don't let go of the dan buoy until they've got you. It's slippery with oil. Listen to me for once, bro!"

Adam clutched the dan buoy as they all were pulled closer, then finally he let go and was hauled aboard with the lifesaver around him as the dan buoy flung back out.

Zack pulled the dan buoy in and waited for another lifesaver. A few minutes passed then another Kisbee ring sailed through the air. Zack helped the other man into the ring and let go, watching as the crew of Arvida pulled him up.

Zack and the crew continued rescuing 27 survivors in total until HMS Celandine showed up.

Finally, Zack climbed aboard, exhausted but relieved that he'll have another chance at having a brother.

Arvida sailed solemnly into the Newfoundland harbour with the weary survivors. HMS Celandine had rescued the remaining 49 sailors of the Ottawa disaster.

Adam hugged Zack as he was led to the sickbay, suffering from multiple jellyfish stings and nearing exhaustion. "I want to apologize," Adam said wearily. "You never were a loser. You were just lost, and now you've found yourself. You are a better man than me."

Zack fought back the tears welling in his eyes and hugged his brother tightly. "If you wouldn't have said the things you had said," Zack replied, his voice cracking. "I wouldn't be where I am now." He pulled away briefly and mussed Adam's hair. "I'm sorry for breaking your nose."

Adam chuckled wearily. "I probably deserved it," he said.

"Yeah, you did," Zack chuckled in jest. "Come on, let's get you taken care of."

A sailor motioned to Zack. "You left your jacket," he said, handing him the warm coat. "Keep yourself warm. You're all wet."

"Thank you, sailor," Zack replied.

Zack grabbed the heavy garment from the sailor, opened it and wrapped the warm coat around his brother. "Here, you need this more than I," Zack said to Adam. "You're alive, and I am so grateful. Next time we have a fight, let's try not to kill each other."

Adam laughed, "That's a deal."

Zack supported his brother by wrapping his arm under Adam's shoulders and led him to the sick bay as the night enclosed on the battle-worn ships.

The crew was granted a few day's shore leave to recuperate. It was sorely needed to restore their hopes and strength. Zack had barely slept for four days throughout the battle of convoy ON 127. He took Adam into his home and gave him the spare bedroom. Zack and Adam were physically and emotionally depleted. After disembarking, he looked for Petro and couldn't find him anywhere. Adam told him that he was most likely in the boiler room when Ottawa was torpedoed.

Zack felt numb. He had almost lost his brother, and most likely, his best friend was claimed by the U-boats. Zack came home and ate, then immediately went to his bedroom and removed all his clothing. Megis crawled into bed with him, her emotions worn and battered. They lay for over an hour in silence, just wrapped within each other's naked bodies. Zack absorbed his wife's intimacy like a prisoner needing freedom. They barely spoke, just relishing in the moment and thankful for their lives.

Finally, after a long while, Zack spoke. "How are you dealing with all this?" he asked. "You must have been distraught."

"I thought I had lost you," Megis said, her eyes swollen from days of crying. "Every single time that you walk out of that door, I'm afraid that I'll never see you again. When the commanders told the families of the battle, I thought that was it. I had lost you." She sobbed in his arms, the heaves racking her body.

"I'm sorry, babe," Zack replied, kissing her hair. "You don't have to worry." He smoothed her back and hugged her tightly. "Heaven or hell will never stop me from coming back home to you and my children. You're special. You are the life in my blood and the heart in my soul. My life simply isn't complete without you."

Megis smiled, wiping her eyes and kissed his hand. She snuggled into his naked body, wrapping her legs around his.

Zack treasured these moments. They were so rare. He hugged her tightly and inhaled her womanly scent, relishing in the present.

After several minutes, Megis looked up at him, her eyes moist with tears. "One day when this war is all over," she asked, her voice rough from emotion. "Can we just lie down and stare at the stars again, just like we did on our first date?"

"I would love that," Zack replied sleepily. "Look at me, sweetheart." He grabbed her chin and looked into her eyes. She blinked, swallowing back her tears. "I promise you, Mrs. Megis Olason, that one day soon, we will be gazing at the stars again."

Sleep overtook him quickly, and he melted into her embrace as they slept soundly in each other's arms for days.

CHAPTER 27

After the disaster of ON 127, the British, American and Canadian Navy organized a coordinated attack on Donitz's U-boats with US aircraft carriers and constant air cover. They immediately began strengthening the training and equipment aboard the warships. It took a disaster to make things happen, but they finally got it right. The US aircraft carriers made it possible to have constant aircraft coverage, and the combined efforts led to a massive change in the course of the war on the Atlantic. The Allied besiege lasted until May 1943.

Faced with the losses of too many submarines, with some entire wolfpacks being wiped out, Karl Donitz began withdrawing his submarines from the North Atlantic.

Not every battle was won by the Allies during this time, but the losses began tipping in their favour. For one wolfpack attack, Donitz would sometimes lose four subs to only one merchant ship. It was unacceptable for the Germans. The RCAF Catalinas picked off the submarines with such great accuracy it was becoming impossible to continue with such losses.

After losing 33 submarines and approximately 1500 of his highly trained men, the German commander made a decision. On May 19, 1943, his own son, Peter Donitz, became one of the casualties. U-954 was sunk in the North Atlantic with heavy losses, the entire crew going down with the submarine, including Peter. On May 24, 1943, only five days later, Karl Donitz pulled his submarines out of the mid-ocean to redeploy in areas less endangered by aircraft.

The Canadians were jubilant. Suddenly, the Atlantic was free of the iron grip of U-boat terror.

The RCN could relax now. The convoys proceeded uneventfully for a few peaceful months. The sailors were granted more leave, and life seemed to go back to a bit more normal, or whatever normal meant during wartime.

Zack put down his empty glass, kissed his wife and patted her shoulder as he stood from the table to grab the water pitcher. Zack had managed to completely quit drinking for the past two years. He felt good about that decision. He laid his hand on Megis's knee under the table as she held Daanis on her lap. Megis was pregnant again with their third child, and he was thrilled. The Navy had granted him some well-deserved shore leave. They had decided to vacation back home in Gimli together to connect with family again.

"I can't believe they granted you three weeks," Mike said incredulously, reaching his hand out. "Pass the potatoes, please, Annabella."

Annabella lifted the large bowl over to Maria, who then passed it to her husband, Nath. Nathan passed it across Josie's lap to Nina, then Vira took the bowl and finally handed it to Mike. Nina was surprised and happy to see Zack and his children. Life changes so quickly, she thought, giggling to herself. Nina had started working last month at the same mechanic shop where Zack used to work. She had just recently met a younger man just three weeks ago. Nina would keep her new love a secret for a little while longer.

Josie pulled Nina's hand. She was a bright four-year-old girl and was quite enthralled with her young cousin Nina.

Nath leaned over and cleaned his daughter's mouth. "You are always such a messy eater!" he said sweetly.

Josie squirmed and smiled at her dad, then looked shockingly at Zack. "So is Zack!" she pointed at Zack's shirt.

Zack looked down, and everyone laughed. He wiped at the gravy on his shirt. "You are a keen little girl!" he chuckled.

"Yes, she is!" Nath exclaimed proudly. "Just like her brother." Nath winked; the secret of her adoption would remain a secret for a little while longer. They would tell Josie within the next few years that Zack was her real father, but for now, Nath rejoiced with his new daughter. She had given him reason to live just a little bit longer.

Zack smiled at them both and was thrilled to see his father healthier than before. Nath was taking care of Josie as only a caring parent would. He was elderly now, and it was evident in the way he walked gingerly and sat down. Nath had a walker that he used now to move around more safely. Zack was happy that his father was still miraculously alive. The entire family treasured any time they had left with Nath. Every extra day with Nath was another day to be thankful for. After all, he had been the settler who had created this wonderful family from nothing more than a wood boat and some nails.

"Thank you, sweetheart," Mike said, kissing his wife's cheek and grabbing the bowl of potatoes from her. He spooned them onto his plate as he glanced up at Nath across the table. "Afi," Mike said, his voice full of pride. "Look at the large family you made!" He laughed. "I still remember when you told us all those stories about you and the settlers banging together the wood huts with nails in the middle of winter."

"Those nails were too short!" Nath exclaimed, his aged voice cracking but still full of joy.

"You did a good job with what you had!" Mike said proudly. "You even used the boats to build the huts!"

Everyone laughed.

"Yes, we did what we could with what we had," Nath said. "But so did all of you, the many hardships, the depression and wars. Mike, we were all so scared that you were never going to walk again, but you did. You overcame your war nightmares and had your own large family. You even took over my fishing business like you said you would!"

"Yes, I did," Mike replied. "Zack went through a lot with the war as well. He's changed so much."

"Yes, I'm so proud of you, Zack," Nath said smiling, his wrinkles creasing at his eyes and mouth. "The man you were and the man you've become are one now. I always knew you were a strong wild spirit. Now you're helping to win this war. Who knows, maybe the combined Navy forces are the ones who will be winning this war for us all."

"We're not done yet," Zack said as he squeezed Megis's leg under the table. "Donitz has withdrawn his subs for now. Hopefully, he doesn't come back."

Little Nate struggled in his seat, pulling on Zack's arm. "Dad," the three-year-old boy said sweetly. "I'm full."

"Okay, you can go play," Zack pulled out the chair for his son as Daanis bounced away towards the boys.

Adam smiled across the table as Nate and Daanis rushed towards Bjorn. They all shared the toy cars Bjorn was playing with. The two boys looked quite different, astonishingly opposite. Bjorn was light-haired, and Nate was dark-haired.

Adam had long accepted that no matter the biological circumstances, Bjorn was still his own son. He was Bjorn's father in all the important ways, and he even looked like him. The brothers never spoke of it again, not even telling the rest of the family. They would take the secret of Bjorn's real father to their graves. Anita smiled and kissed him, sliding her chair closer. His wife had committed to returning to Halifax with him in two weeks, and he felt happier than ever. Almost losing his life had changed the way he viewed living.

"Being in the Navy is a humbling job," Adam said softly.

"It sure is," Zack agreed.

"When I heard that Rutherford was missing," Adam said. "I sobbed terribly for the first time since the sinking of Ottawa. It was like all the events of those tense four days had caught up with me."

Zack looked up at his father, Nath. "Rutherford was the commander of the warship Ottawa," Zack said. "He was one of the commanders that died from the sinking that day."

"I used to talk to him every day," Adam said solemnly. "He was the best commander. He gave me the life jacket from his back. Then he swam away. I never saw him again. I still feel guilty some days."

"Don't," Zack said. "Rutherford was just that type of man. It was his ship. He decided to do that, and who knows, maybe he didn't want to be rescued. We will never know."

"True," Adam said. "We will never know."

Zack looked down at his food and swallowed back a tear for his old friend, Petro. They never found him. He most likely died in the boiler room upon impact of the second torpedo on HMCS Ottawa.

"I'm sorry about your cousin, Anton," Adam said, pushing his food around his plate.

Anton chewed and drank some wine. "Petro was a brave man. He fought with me to escape the Terror Famine in Ukraine. So brave, and yet he still met his end with a German torpedo." Anton shook his head in disgust and sorrow.

Zack nodded solemnly. "They say that he most likely died instantaneously when the second torpedo hit the boiler room," Zack said, trying to keep his voice steady. "I lost a close friend that day." Zack salted his roast beef and looked directly at Adam. "But I still have my brother, which I will be eternally grateful for every day."

Adam nodded and raised his glass. "Cheers to that," he exclaimed.

Everyone stood and clinked glasses, happy to be together again, even if it was just for one more joyful week. They were due back in Halifax soon, transferring to yet another corvette, the HMCS Sackville, this time.

"Cheers to family!" Zack said, standing strongly with a glass of water in his hand. "And cheers to being two years sober!"

Nath beamed. "I'm so proud of you, Zack," he said. "You really pulled it together." Nath clinked his glass with Zack and then with Adam. "And you as well, Adam, you've changed into a better man too. I can see it in your eyes."

"Yes, I have, Dad," Adam said thoughtfully, nodding. "I definitely have."

Nath watched as both of his sons sat back down and chatted quietly. Nathan squeezed his wife's hand and thought back to all the parenting struggles they had gone through in the past twenty years. Maria kissed him softly on the cheek.

They had done a good job, somehow. He smiled at Maria and kissed her hand. His sons were fine men, Nath thought, both of them.

~

"What are you doing, you silly man?" Megis chuckled as Zack grabbed her arm and rushed her out of the big white house onto the beach.

"Just follow me," Zack said, holding onto her hand tight. "Don't trip! I want my baby safe."

"The baby is just the size of a walnut right now!" Megis exclaimed, chuckling.

Zack hollered in laughter and hugged her as they reached the beach. "You're hilarious," Zack said. "My baby is not a walnut!"

"No, but he is the size of one!" Megis said, chuckling. "I'm only four months pregnant. I'm not even showing yet."

"You think it's a boy?" Zack said.

"Maybe, I don't know," Megis said. "I just don't want to call our baby an it."

They both roared in laughter as they walked along the shoreline, hugging each other. The night was descending quickly. In the distance, they could see the ruined shadowed remains of the lighthouse.

"Look," Zack said, pointing. "My father said the lighthouse was destroyed a few months ago."

"Yes, I heard," she replied. "He said it was ruined in a spring ice jam."

"I guess Adam was right about his ignored pleas to build an island for the lighthouse," Zack said. "He's a smart politician. I hope he returns to council when this war is over. He makes a difference around here."

"What about us?" she asked. "Will we return after the war?"

"We will do whatever feels right," Zack said. "We can stay out in Halifax, St. John's or move back to Gimli. I'll leave that up to you, beautiful. You deserve that choice for everywhere you've moved for me."

Megis's eyes flooded with tears upon hearing the endearing words from her husband. "I love you," she replied simply, her voice heavy with emotion. Megis kissed his shoulder and laid her head on him as they slowed to a stop, peering into the descending darkness.

Zack abruptly sat down in the sand and pulled her down with him.

"What are you doing, babe?" Megis said, chuckling and wiping the tears from her eyes.

"Come here," Zack said, pulling her buttocks down onto the sand. "I'm fulfilling a promise."

Megis looked at him, confused.

"Lie back, my sweet," Zack said softly.

Megis laid down onto the sand with him and looked up.

A million stars brightly shone back at them. She burst into tears of joy. "You remembered," Megis said, her voice cracking from the rush of sudden emotion.

"Of course I remembered, sweetheart," Zack said, gazing up at the stars with her, holding her hand in the sand. "I looked forward to this moment every day since you mentioned it." He pointed suddenly with his other hand. "Look, there's the Big Dipper! Straight up ahead. Do you see it?"

Megis sniffled as she struggled to keep the joyful tears from overwhelming her. "Yes, I see it," she said softly. Her body flooded with intense love like nothing she had experienced before. She felt so extremely gifted to have Zack with her on this journey of life, and every day she thanked the stars for his love.

"Babe," Zack said. "Are you okay?"

"Yeah," Megis said, nodding with the tears streaming freely down her cheeks. "I'm fine. I've been waiting so long for this."

"I love you," Zack said. "I'd do anything for you, babe. You just tell me, and I'll do absolutely anything in this world for you." Zack leaned over and kissed her lips slowly under the crescent moon. Their lips touched as he tasted her honey mouth. He felt so grateful to the universe that he was married to the love of his life. Zack pulled back briefly and gazed into her dark eyes in the blackness. "I'd give you the moon and the stars, babe."

THE END

DON'T MISS THE FINAL BOOK IN THE OLASON CHRONICLES

Prequel Available in 2022

FINAL NOTE TO READER

The Battle of the Atlantic started on September 3, 1939, with the simultaneous declaration of WWII and the sinking of SS Athenia. During the nightfall on that fateful day on the Atlantic, Captain Fritz-Julius Lemp of U-30 spotted Athenia travelling without lights in a defensive anti-submarine pattern. His decision to torpedo the passenger liner went against the German commitment not to sink any passenger ships. The event threw the Allied Navy into a fevered pitch.

The Royal Canadian Navy immediately joined the British, catapulting Canada into the global war from day one.

With a small fleet and a severe shortage of men, the RCN scrambled to rush to the WWII stage on the Atlantic. Training and recruitment were flawed as the Canadian Navy hastened to man as many ships as possible with scarce resources. Meanwhile, the Germans were sending increasing numbers of U-boats into the Atlantic to sever Britain's supply lines.

A deal was struck between Britain and Canada to build 269 corvette ships. It would take over a year before the first one was commissioned and put into service, but it was a start.

In September 1940, the United States struck a deal with Britain to turn over 50 mothballed destroyers in exchange for long-term leases on eight British bases. One of those destroyers was HMCS St. Croix, the Senior Officer's ship that steamed in front of convoy ON 127.

HMCS Ottawa was the rescue ship in the rear of that convoy. Convoy ON 127 was attacked by 13 U-boats during a sustained attack that lasted three long days, with the sailors barely sleeping. The most senior men slept even less. The convoy was attacked in the air gap, the area in the North Atlantic that was not supported by constant air cover from the RCAF Catalinas. The air force posed a deadly threat to U-boats, bombing the submarines with skilled accuracy, and the enemy knew this. During the three long days of the U-boat attack, convoy ON 127 lost 10 merchant ships while the escorts fought hard to protect their convoy. HMCS Ottawa was hit on the third day just as they entered the air cover zone.

The warship Ottawa was one of the original Canadian destroyers. It was a tough battle-worn vessel that had fought valiantly with the Mid-Ocean Escort Force and the Newfoundland Escort Force. It was a long large destroyer that had seen significant action on the Atlantic, bravely fighting with reduced resources and inexperienced crew.

In the early years of WWII, many of the Canadian ships were manned with poorly trained brave young men, some of whom were only teenagers. An overwhelming amount of these recruits lost their lives to the sea, escorting the merchant ships to and from Britain.

The convoys were organized in formation, with the most vulnerable oil tankers in the middle. The Navy escorts protected the convoys from both sides, front and back. But they were still attacked by the ruthless U-boat wolfpacks, which converged in coordinated torpedo attacks upon the convoys and their escorts.

After three hard-fought years, HMCS Ottawa sunk on September 13, 1942, from two direct torpedo hits, one to its bow and the other to the destroyer's stern, snapping the ship into two. Approximately 140 lives were lost. HMS Celandine, a British ship, rescued approximately 49 survivors, and HMCS Arvida rescued 27 more. The loss of the major destroyer with heavy casualties was a huge hit to the RCN. Suffering from obsolete radar, outdated communications equipment and poor training, HMCS Ottawa was a disaster waiting to happen. Several commanders had expressed their concerns repeatedly, but the British were in their own battle, resisting German occupation of their homeland.

Winston Churchill finally made the decision to focus efforts on the Battle of the Atlantic. The disaster of convoy ON 127 made it clear that Britain needed to take control of the Atlantic. Combining the resources of US carriers, Royal Canadian Air Force Catalinas and the battle-weary RCN ships, the war began to turn in the Allies favour. The British, Canadian and US Navy struggled throughout the remainder of 1942 and the spring of 1943, with many more grievous losses and victories. Until May 1943, when Allies sunk 34 U-boats to the bottom of the Atlantic in only one month.

Karl Donitz made the decision to withdraw from the Battle of the Atlantic on May 24, 1943, only five days after his son, Peter, was killed in another submarine loss.

The RCN was finally free of the U-boats. Black May, as it was later called, had been a success for the Allies. The German submarines had returned to the Atlantic several months later in 1943, but they never reached the same intensity as the first three and a half years of WWII.

I chose deliberately to end my story before the end of WWII to shed knowledge on the importance of these early years of the war and to highlight the chaotic lives of Navy personnel during this time. Many men and their wives were separated for long periods of time. Some men never returned and were lost at sea. Others sometimes returned for only one day every two months.

My research took me to many different warships and battles until I found ON 127, the battle I wanted to write about. I hope you enjoyed The Wars Between Us and the poignant story of a man's brave fight through alcoholism and war. During these times, many sailors drank heavily. It was the only lifeline they sometimes had left.

The corvette flower class ships were eventually all put into service starting in late 1941 to the end of the war in 1945. HMCS Arvida survived WWII right to the end. The vessel was paid off on June 14, 1945, and later sold for commercial use. To this day, only one corvette ship remains in Canada, the HMCS Sackville. It has been maintained lovingly as a floating museum in Halifax, Nova Scotia, through the Canadian Naval Memorial Trust.

The fate of countless other warships didn't have such happy endings. St. Croix, the commanding destroyer, was sunk in a triple torpedo attack from U-305 southwest of Iceland in September 1943. It sunk within six minutes with heavy loss of life. HMCS Windflower, one of the first corvettes to be commissioned, sank in a convoy collision during heavy fog in Dec 1941, losing 23 lives. Countless other warships and corvettes were sunk, torpedoed or damaged in action. In total, during the Second World War on the Atlantic, the Allies lost 50,000 sailors and merchant seamen, 2,603 vessels and 175 warships. In return, the Allies shared in the destruction of 756 U-boats, 28,000 U-boat fatalities and approximately 40 enemy surface ships. The RCN's share of the losses was 24 warships and approximately 2,000 men. The Battle of the Atlantic was the most desperately fought and important battleground of WWII. Without these brave sailors, the outcome of the war could have been starkly different.

A Halifax Memorial stands solemnly in Point Pleasant Park, with the names of 3,257 men and women who died at sea throughout WWI and WWII. The monument is a large granite Cross of Sacrifice that looks out over the Atlantic Ocean. The tip of the cross reaches over 12 metres high and can be clearly seen by the merchant ships approaching Halifax harbour. A poignant reminder of the many Canadians buried at sea.

Researching this book was a very emotional experience for me. I have an immense appreciation for the brave Navy seamen that risked their lives for our freedom. I have many people that I need to thank. I would like to start with the 98-year-old RCNVR veteran that I interviewed over the telephone in April 2021. His name is James Clark Silvester. He was only 16 years old when he joined the RCNVR in Winnipeg. He told me his story in vivid detail over the telephone. He served as Second Class Petty Officer aboard the corvette flower class HMCS Quesnel as well as many other ships until the end of the war in 1945. Without his poignant descriptions of life on the corvette ships, I am not certain that I could have written this book as well as I have. My deepest gratitude goes out to this wonderful man. I have created a scrapbook of pictures he sent for my children and me to remember forever.

I would also like to thank Richard Cummings, a 25+ year RCN veteran, for originally planting the Navy seed in my story. I am grateful for this. The events blossomed beautifully into a story that needed to be told.

My deepest gratitude also goes out to everyone at HMCS Sackville, including William R. Gard Cdr (Retd) CD RCN, Gary Reddy and Douglas Struthers from the HMCS Sackville Canadian Naval Memorial Trust for his wonderful pictures of the last remaining flower class corvette. They were all an immense help in developing a very real portrayal of life at sea, and the connections they extended to me were priceless.

Even though this is a work of fiction, I take historical novel writing very seriously. One hundred years from now, someone will pick up this book and learn something from their past. I have made every attempt to keep the facts and dates as true as possible, but with every fictional story, there will always be circumstances beyond my control. Some events and characters may be used solely to propel the saga. It is a fictional story. This book should be read as such.

Every character in The Wars Between Us is fictional, except for the following historical individuals:

Clark Anderson Rutherford, Lieutenant Commander of HMCS Ottawa (died September 13, 1942, following the sinking of HMCS Ottawa)

K. H. Walkerling, captain of German U-boat U-91, responsible for the sinking of HMCS Ottawa

Karl Donitz, German Admiral naval commander

Peter Donitz, German seaman, Karl Donitz's son

Fritz-Julius Lemp, German Captain of U-30, torpedoed passenger liner SS Athenia

Arthur "Slim" Evans, leader of the On to Ottawa trek, industrial labour union organizer during the Great Depression

Many of the historical events in my story did happen, including the Regina Riot, C. A. Rutherford's death and, of course, the sinking of HMCS Ottawa. I have fictionalized it as best as I could. Writing this book has been an emotional journey for me into the lives of our ancestors and heroes. I hope you loved it as much as I did.

No acknowledgements page would be complete without thanking my two teenaged boys. They are the light in my life and fill me with purpose every single day. Their support is pure and unwavering, something rare in this world. I love them with all my heart and am blessed to have such wonderful sons.

In conclusion, I would like to thank you, my reader. I am nothing without my readers and fans. Some of you have been there since day one and, like Megis, have stood beside me and encouraged me to keep going no matter what obstacles emerged. Without this, I don't know if I would still be writing. Thank you so much from the bottom of my heart.

Lastly, I'll leave you with some original photographs and words of wisdom.

Try to live life without pain in your heart. Be kind always and believe in the impossible. When life gets too much, remember to always stop and gaze at the moon and stars. One day, you might find someone so very special to share it with.

HMCS Sackville is the sole surviving ship of the 269 corvette escort vessels built during the Second World War. Corvettes such as HMCS Sackville fought valiantly during the Battle of the Atlantic, the longest-running battle of the war. Built in Saint John, New Brunswick, and now on display in Halifax, Nova Scotia, HMCS Sackville is operated by the Canadian Naval Memorial Trust. Sackville represents all the ships and personnel who served courageously at sea during the Battle of the Atlantic in World War 2.

The above photograph is the original picture that appears on the front cover. This beautiful photo was taken on a very early summer morning in June 2019 by Douglas Struthers of the Canadian Naval Memorial Trust. It is displayed here and on the cover with his permission.

The wheelhouse of HMCS Sackville. To the right is the steering wheel and in the forefront is the wheelhouse telegraph which sends instructions to the engine room. Photo courtesy of Douglas Struthers and the Canadian Naval Memorial Trust.

Shown above is the forward seaman's mess onboard HMCS Sackville. Only one hammock is shown as hanging. During active service, many hammocks would be hanging alongside each other, with sailors sleeping in each one. Photo courtesy of Douglas Struthers and the Canadian Naval Memorial Trust.

All Photographs of HMCS Sackville are used with permission from Douglas Struthers and the Canadian Naval Memorial trust. Thank you for reading and keep believing!